Switchback

KL Griffiths

Cottonwood Fire LLC

Published by Cottonwood Fire LLC

www.klgriffiths.com

FIRST EDITION

Cover design by Creative Paramita

ISBN: 979-8-9887038-4-6 (pbk)

ISBN: 979-8-9887038-5-3 (eBook)

When the storm comes—when night falls—what's worse:
the danger or the fear of danger?

Vincent van Gogh

Chapter 1

IN THE DEAD OF night, Seth lay in his hammock. Not sleeping. Something clawed at the fabric of his bug net, and after listening long enough to be sure it was a tiny something, Seth poked out his head. The nocturnal visitor scampered away before he could get a look at it, but Seth was rewarded with a gargantuan moon shining like a floodlight. The moon rays shot off in four—he counted—*four* directions, cutting thick bars of light through the woods.

Although technically a trespasser, Seth was more at home in a tent or a hammock than in his old apartment. Definitely more comfortable than when he lived out of his truck. The forest anarchy and the shambles of his insides were close cousins. Owl hoots, buzzing things, even the manic screaming of feral cats were white noise drowning out his thoughts and memories. His hammock was hedged about by tangled grasses, prickly briars, and crowds of trees, upright or dying their way back into the forest floor. The thicket was a buffer between himself and the rest of the world.

It wasn't the whole world Seth wanted to keep out.

Just her.

Seth would be sleeping right now, had he not thought of her, had he not realized what day it was. His bladder reminded him of all the beers he had drunk before switching to whiskey. With a sigh, he peeled his body from the hammock and ambled to his peeing spot behind the oak tree. Seth wanted to believe that time and a rushing river of whiskey had scoured away his past. Tonight's insomnia meant he had not yet reached the critical mass of boozy forgetfulness, but he would be at it again tomorrow. Seth was no quitter.

At thirty-four years old, Seth might have been married, maybe living in a starter home with a wife and kids, beginning each day with a mediocre cup of coffee and a walk around the block with the family dog. Instead, he was camped out in the forested land behind Green Spirit, the manufacturing plant that gave him a paycheck for ten hours of stamping steel brackets—sixteen thousand on a good day.

It was as great a life as he could expect.

His ex would never come knocking on his door because he didn't have a door. Not even a car. Bingo.

Having served a life sentence, Seth's ex could be paroled any day now. Or she was already free. Since Seth made sure he couldn't be found, he would not be notified when Ivy was released from the Bedford Hills Correctional Facility.

At that thought, a sudden, powerful craving for a fresh bottle of whiskey seized his guts, and a blood-splashed memory forced a grunt from him. There'd be no liquid forgetfulness for Seth, not in the middle of the night in the middle of the woods he didn't own and in which he technically shouldn't be pitching his tent. The liquor store within walking distance wouldn't be open for...ever.

Eight hours was an eternity when you had a powerful urge for a Kentucky hug.

He folded himself back into his hammock and stared at the moon and the rays that made an X or a cross, depending on which way he tilted his head. Even the critter who woke him, who resumed noshing on its midnight snack, couldn't distract Seth from his fears once his mind got going about Ivy. What else could he do but lie in his hammock and think about the past?

No one, neither old friends nor enemies, had contacted him for many years (which was how he wanted it), and he almost let the anniversary slide by. He reminded himself that her prison was two states away, and if she found his address, it would lead her to an empty apartment.

Seth had lost his apartment and his car, and it was convenient—no, it was *great*—living in the woods. With no rent or gas bills, he had cash for necessities like whiskey and sometimes extra for scratch-offs. The hammock was a thrift store score (say that ten times fast), lightweight but sturdy, a backpacker's castoff. The tent beside it was from his high school days and was hard to set up, unlike the new models, but it offered protection and—unlike his hammock—he could sit upright and eat or drink in it. Even when it rained, Seth was dry. Rainy days were the *best* days to get lit, to sprawl inside his nylon dome and drink himself to sleep with the sound of drops banging on the fabric, trying to get in and not being able to.

On nice days, he reclined beneath the leafy canopy in a folding lounge chair or in his swinging hammock and watched the birds and squirrels. He had hung feeders made of empty toilet paper rolls slathered with peanut butter, and he set out dry corn cobs when he could, when all his money wasn't spent. Since it was summer, Seth had little reason to drink at the bar. It was cheaper to grab a couple of six-packs and take them to his tent. He could even keep them cool in the nearby creek, which was the place he slaked his thirst, but only when he was hungover and desperate to hydrate an aching skull. He didn't trust creek water. Whether it was the alcohol or creek amoebas that battered his bowels, he couldn't say, but he knew this: his guts let him down sometimes. Enter cat holes. He always had at least two dug out and ready to go with a roll of toilet paper skewered on a branch—pilfered from the bathroom at work.

Be prepared, said the Boy Scouts.

Deep in the woods behind Green Spirit, Seth had a real working system in place, beginning when he woke at 5 o'clock to his phone alarm singing Ludo's "Love Me Dead," a song the bartender suggested after his most recent woman trouble, the trouble being he couldn't hang onto her. Torn from sleep by Ludo, Seth lumbered across the five lanes of Foyton Road to Love's Truck Stop, the twenty-four-hour gas station and convenience store that had everything, including pay showers.

He waved to Nanette the night cashier.

"Morning, Gorgeous," she greeted him as he poured himself a coffee.

"Morning, Nanette," he replied.

He showered while Ludo's album played out and his phone charged. After that simple pleasure, he ordered a maple hotcake griddler and hash browns and ate them at one of the plastic booths while scrolling (and charging) his phone. Love's even had apples, bananas, and hard-boiled eggs if he wanted "something Tarzan would eat." That's what Nanette called healthy stuff. She was flirting with him; he was pretty sure.

On his way to the cash register, he grabbed one of those little tubes filled with sausage and cheesy goodness that warmed on heated rollers...mm-hmm. On a couple of dangerous midnight trips to Love's to satisfy his belly, he had cleaned out the entire stock. Midnight trips happened at the end of a particularly full bottle of whiskey; the danger being crossing the five lanes at night, jaywalking, drunky skunky. He'd take one of the big beers back to wash the snacks down. His tent smelled like sausage and Old Spice deodorant, and he liked it. Liked Nanette, too, because she never asked where he was going or where he had come from. She looked at him starry-eyed, like he was a mystery. And he'd keep it that way. Here, a woman he could keep.

"If you finish it before I ring up your kitchen order, I'll pretend I didn't see that," Nanette winked and nodded to the almost-finished cheese roll.

"I don't mind paying," Seth said. Her comment felt a little too much like charity.

Nanette's face fell.

"Here," he said. "Keep the change."

"Thanks, Gorgeous." She was all smiles again. "Don't forget to top off your coffee."

With the size of his hangover, forgetting the coffee was impossible. Of course, Seth's super (short for superintendent) couldn't know that some mornings Seth arrived at work with last night's whiskey still swirling in his blood.

Today was such a day.

As he crossed the street, he saw the super's car turn into the parking lot. The super got out and eyed Seth as he crossed the road. He waited for Seth to approach the employee door.

"Good morning, Seth." He held the door open.

Even with the shower and still-wet hair, Seth worried the super would smell the booze coming out of his pores. His eye drops were in his work locker, so the eyes that tried not to meet the super's were still bloodshot. Argh. What Seth missed about his apartment, besides electric outlets, were hot baths. Yes, he was a dude, but his job involved constant lifting, pushing, and pulling that made his body both strong and sore. Back in the day when he paid rent, his idea of luxury was two capfuls of eucalyptus bubble bath and three fingers of whiskey while having a long soak. After a scalding hot bath, he stepped out of the tub a new man.

After a night of drinking too much, a morning bath put Seth back together again.

Eviction had put an end to baths.

The expression presently on the super's face said something else might be ending, hopefully not his job.

"Got a minute, Seth?"

Seth had been holding up his end of the job bargain: wearing his safety glasses, not using his phone at his workstation (indeed, he needed to charge it during the days while an outlet was available), returning on time from breaks.

Seth being called to the office at the beginning of the shift? Not good. He pocketed his phone charger and locked steps with the super. Every eye was on them as they made their way across the shop. Thirty-four years old, and it still felt like the walk of shame to the principal's office.

A blast of air conditioning slapped Seth in the face as they entered the super's office. He closed the door and gestured to a chair. "Have a seat, Seth."

His dim smile wouldn't fool anyone. A *coaching*—that's what they called it, "coaching" like they were going into the locker room and Seth was Rocky, and the super was that old dude who helped him win.

The super let out a deep, world-weary sigh.

Seth blinked and feigned ignorance and innocence, the latter of which did not feel right on his face, and his eyelid began to twitch.

After rubbing his cheeks vigorously, the super began, "How are you, Seth?"

"Fine."

"Great, well, it's come to my attention that you've...uh...set up a tent in the woods behind the parking lot. You can't do that, Seth."

"Who told?"

He waved away the question. "Look, we're not pressing charges for the trespass, but you'll need to clear your belongings out as soon as the shift ends." The super wiped his bald head as if it were a lamp and a genie would come out and give an answer to the impossible situation.

"I'm not bothering anybody," Seth said.

The super sighed, "You can't live on company property. It's a liability."

"It's just for the summer. I don't see what's the harm."

"Maybe you don't see any harm in it, but just because you don't see it that way, doesn't mean it's okay for you to be there."

"Can I stay till Friday?"

"Look, I'm doing you a favor letting you work the shift, but when that bell rings at the end of the day, we're going to get your things out of the woods. I'm sorry. I know you've had a rough...situation years ago, but whatever happened, the past is in the past. You need to move on, Seth. You've got a good thing here, a bright future. We have resources, and if you want it, counseling." He interrupted himself and shook his head *no* to someone at the sliver of window in his door. "We can put you in touch with a shelter till you get a place. Kerry in human resources will..." ...*blah blah blah*. Seth knew a shelter was out of the question. They didn't allow Kentucky Deluxe. The food sucked compared to Love's. Lots of people, too. No trees. No way.

The past might be in the past, but Seth's "past" was about to be set free on parole, and having an address was the last thing he wanted right now. All the other woods were too far to walk to Green Spirit. Over and over Seth turned the question in his head: How would he live? When he had asked the super, what if he didn't leave the woods, what then? The super answered that he hoped they wouldn't have to cross that bridge. Seth pressed. The super said other things, including *police, jail,* and *termination.*

For the rest of the morning, Seth's head was in the woods.

But even with his troubles and anxiety brought on by the super's ultimatum, Seth managed to finish the job on his production schedule, and his press was ready for a changeover. Unfortunately, the decoiler on the press for his next job had gone down the week prior and was still not repaired. Bunch of losers. Maybe if they'd spent more time working and less time spying on Seth and tattling, the decoiler would have been fixed.

What to do about that wasn't Seth's problem.

It was the super's problem. The super did his best thinking while rage-eating a bagel and pacing the shop floor. Finally, he gathered Seth and the set-up guys and directed them to move the decoiler from Seth's press to one he could work on. Seth shrugged, not caring one way or the other, busy as he was turning over solutions to his home (*homeless*) problem. He was less than helpful as they maneuvered the awkward and unbalanced decoiler onto a thick strap attached to the forks of the tow motor.

"...Earth to Seth," a co-worker's irritated tone eventually penetrated his mind, still grinding over where he would lay his head that evening. "Steady this, will ya."

It wasn't a question.

He meant for Seth to prevent the machine from swinging on the straps, to walk beside the forklift as it carried the enormous decoiler from one stamping press to another.

They passed the bender station and Tight-dress Sage, the one semi-beautiful woman who worked at the plant. In any other environment, Sage would have been a four. In the plant she was a nine. Seth could still conjure the image of her wearing a red bodycon dress to the company Christmas party.

Seth gave her a tentative wave.

She averted her eyes. Usually, she waved back. The news was out, then.

The forklift rolled by two toolmakers working on yet another press. (*Did anything work in this place?*) The two glanced Seth's way and bent to whisper to each other. Seth overheard his name and *woods* and *weirdo* and *homeless*—

—and the forklift rolled over his foot.

It sounded like popcorn in the microwave but was the steel in his steel-toed boots, cracking. And the bones on the top of his foot, splintering. The agony burned, blooming like a tongue of flame up his calf, melting his knee. He did not realize he had stopped walking while the forklift rolled on. When Seth looked down, there was a flattened boot, a spritz of blood and white splinters, and meat, like for a stew—Seth's foot. Even through his jeans, he could see where the blood and meat squeezed, bulging his leg. With nothing to hold him, the shock took him down sideways. His head met the cement floor before he could tell his hands to stop his fall.

Scarier than the feeling that his foot had become lava, were the looks of horror his co-workers gave him, the way their faces accordioned in disgust before they cupped a hand to their mouths and fled or, in the case of the trained employee responders, fell to their knees at his side while barking orders, a pair of hands shakily unclasped a belt, someone yelled for scissors—scissors appeared—the blade reflected harsh light from overhead, a cut to his jeans, an impatient rip of the seam, and cinching the belt around Seth's leg. Tight. Holy hell, tight. A small puddle of oil darkened the jeans of the beltless co-worker tending to Seth. What was the guy's name? Seth couldn't recall. The overhead lights—Seth had never seen them from this angle before, had never been on his back on the floor—they were big and bright and dizzying. Beltless yelled for a blanket because Seth was going into shock, he said. The oil wasn't oil after all because when Beltless pushed his hair from his eyes, his hairline was painted in blood. Seth's.

The bloody forehead tossed Seth backward in time, back to the ill-fated day with Ivy. Sixteen years ago. A face awash in blood, even some in the mouth, smeared on broken teeth. It was all Seth's fault, she had said. Everything was Seth's fault.

In this moment, what he heard was the bass drum pounding of his blood, the squeak of shoes running on the polished concrete floor, the wheels careening toward him, how they spun crazily, even as they approached in a straight line.

A paramedic dropped to his knees beside Seth, unclasped the belt, and tossed it away.

"What's your name, friend?" he asked.

He swallowed, tried to think. "My...?"

"What's his name?" the paramedic demanded.

Several coworkers answered, causing Seth to feel shame when he finally remembered the thing he shouldn't have forgotten. SETH. Seth was his name.

"Anyone get his vitals?"

Talking, meaningless numbers. The paramedic's finger pressed against Seth's neck.

"Seth, we're going to take a ride, okay?" Medics hoisted Seth onto a gurney and strapped him in.

As they rolled him past the decoiler, he saw a piece of his steel-toed boot stuck in the forklift's tire tread. Unfocused operators like Seth should know better than to walk inches beside a nine-thousand-pound machine, three times as heavy as the average car.

"This is my fault, isn't it?" Seth asked.

For the second time in his life (the first being sixteen years ago), he asked that question before passing out.

Chapter 2

SETH SLIPPED ON A mossy rock and took a brutal hit to his kneecap. In cheap flip-flops, he navigated a craggy path toward the top of a volcano, judging by the smoke belching and the seismic activity threatening to knock him off balance.

He wasn't alone.

Nanette, the cashier from Love's, trekked beside him in a pair of tight khaki shorts, a tighter tank top, and a set of pricey hiking boots.

Wasn't it hot out? She asked casually. And true enough, there were beads of sweat dotting that creamy, unsunned space on her chest.

Seth told her not to worry. They were almost at the top of the volcano, he said, though he didn't know whether it was true. Just as he was about to point out Venus burning brightly in the night sky, he heard Nanette gasp.

"Watch—" was all she got out before Seth stepped into a puddle of molten lava up to his knee. The lava puddle had a hold of his foot so that he couldn't pull it out. And oh, did it burn. Fucking hell, it burned.

Howling in front of the gorgeous Nanette was not cool. Worse, the volcano began erupting, shaking Seth from head to toe. From the night sky came the voice of God, commanding him. God was a woman. God said, "Seth, can you hear me? Seth? You're out of surgery."

Wait.

Harsh lights greeted Seth when he opened his eyes. God and Nanette and the volcano vanished, replaced by a pony-tailed nurse with a ring in her septum, inches from his face.

"Good, you're awake," she said. "I'll call the doctor." And she was off.

"Wait." This time Seth managed to say it.

She didn't wait.

Seth searched his mind for his history. Why was he in the hospital? The answer eluded him, like a word he wanted but couldn't think of. He rummaged around in his addled brain for the recent past and came up empty.

But he found another dream. A nightmare. Someone's belt around his thigh, blood all over somebody's hands and then blood on his forehead when he pushed his bangs out of his eyes. Bright, eye-stinging lights like the sun but long. Fluorescents. Two men wearing blue gloves running toward him. Bloody hands waving them over and calling for them to hurry the stretcher.

The event and all its horrors sprang back into his consciousness like whack-a-moles.

His body confirmed the memory. His left leg was one hundred percent flaming agony. He risked a look, dreading the cast and pins and staples. That's what they used these days, not stitches. He'd be a Frankenstein for sure. He'd owe the hospital a fortune. Augh. He squeezed his eyes shut, steeled himself for a freak show, and peeled his head from the pillow.

Nothing. Just a hospital blanket.

But...

...off. What was the word?

Something was...

asymmetrical.

No.

NO.

NO. NO. NO. NO. NO.

Only one leg-shaped lump went all the way to the end of the bed. The other stopped at the knee.

NOOOOOOOOOOO.

The doctor arrived in time to stop Seth from tearing off the gauze and getting a look at his work. A swarm of hospital staff were on Seth in a blink. Since he was hooked up to an IV, he didn't notice when a nurse sedated him. All he knew were tears, big, unwieldy ones that wracked his whole body even as he fell back into the black, yawning mouth of the volcano.

While Seth recuperated in the hospital, Green Spirit sent a gift basket of nuts, cheeses, and summer sausage along with a card signed by the super and other boss-types. An unopened summer sausage and a handful of nuts from the basket were in the pocket of his hoodie, squirreled away for when he got released. In addition to the gift basket, Green Spirit sent a guy in a suit to Seth's bedside who introduced himself as Connor. Connor handed Seth a bank card he said was pre-loaded with Seth's paycheck and promised there would be further compensation, pending a settlement agreement they'd have to talk about when Seth was feeling better.

"You mean when I'm not doped up."

Connor gave a dim smile.

Besides any other reimbursements Seth and his employer agreed upon, one thing was certain: Green Spirit would pay all Seth's medical bills. Rehabilitation too. Whatever Seth needed.

Hmmm…whatever? Connor didn't know that Kerry in HR regularly did a solid for Seth, cashing his checks "as a courtesy," since Seth didn't have a bank account.

Seth told him, "I want cash."

Connor gave Seth a withering look. "The bank card is safer than cash. Green Spirit's got your back. I've got the okay to do whatever you need to make you comfortable, Mr. Olivern."

"My foot back."

Connor cleared his throat.

After a few beats of silence, Seth continued woozily, "But a bottle of something expensive from the liquor store will do."

What he got instead was coffee from Starbucks. "The Pistachio Frappuccino is to die for." Connor offered the drink, spilling a couple drops on the white hospital blanket.

Seth tried to console himself with the idea that someone who was wearing a suit and tie waited upon him. And the sweet, foamy drink filled his belly and zapped him awake.

For an hour.

Then he felt like a zombie. And he had to take a leak again.

A social worker came by to make sure Seth had someone at home to help him with medicine and rides and whatnot. He gave Ivy's name and her old address and congratulated himself on his ability to bullshit. Several lawyers called, using big, expensive-sounding words that he didn't completely understand. Seth deserved to be compensated, they said. But after enduring Ivy's lawyers on the witness stand, Seth harbored a prickly hate for anyone who made their money in courtrooms. Besides, he wanted to be invisible. Sticking around for court appearances was not (in Seth's mind) what the doctor ordered.

Days later, the social worker returned. "The nursing staff told me they haven't seen your girlfriend yet. You guys in a fight?"

Seth harrumphed. "Something like that. And she's a germophobe. And it's none of your business."

"What's her name again?"

"Ivy."

"And her phone number?"

"I already told you."

"That number's not in service."

Seth shrugged. "Am I my girlfriend's keeper?"

The social worker pursed her lips and made notes. "You have a weekly standing physical therapy appointment paid for by your employer, Mr. Olivern. Not everyone is so lucky. My job is to make sure you don't miss the appointments."

"Your job is to get off my back."

She rolled her eyes and pivoted. "I'll be back."

The social worker huffed out the door. She did not see Seth shiver at her choice of phrase. She couldn't know those were the words Ivy spat in Seth's nightmares.

Chapter 3

AFTER TWO WEEKS, THE hospital released Seth. His refusal to be transported to a halfway house as well as his inability to produce a significant other to act as his caretaker, meant Seth was brought to the curb. Because of liability, a wheelchair transported him there. The phrase *kicked to the curb* rattled around in his head, especially when they wouldn't allow him five minutes to sit on his wheelchair in the sun. Without the extension pad that could hold his stump, he would be in agony. He waited until the nurse was gone and helped himself to one of the wheelchairs the valets used for transporting patients. He felt very Robin Hood in that moment.

"Borrowing from those who can afford it," he said under his breath.

With what remained of his strength, he wheeled himself the three blocks to the liquor store. Entering the store in his wheelchair proved impossible. The clerk saw him through the glass doors, came out from behind the counter, and held the door. It was tight, and Seth's fingers got banged on the doorframe. The whiskey he wanted was too high for Seth to reach from his chair, and the shame of that fact made him ask for a second bottle. His plans were to find a nice place to wheel himself to and have a liquid picnic, but after the hardship, he changed his mind and started drinking in earnest in the shade provided by the storefront. Why not? He looked at the place where a foot should be. He imagined

Nanette, the Love's cashier, looking in disgust at his stump, shaking her head and grimacing.

He imagined all the looks of pity he'd get from women, but he didn't have to imagine for long, because a customer, a middle-aged woman with eggplant-colored hair shellacked into an enormous mane, glanced his way before entering the store. The way her garishly painted face broke into pity made him want to howl and throw things at her. Instead, he pulled on the bottle, and when she disappeared inside the store, he muttered to himself that she should stop trying with the hair and the makeup and the short shorts.

Seth wanted to be mean to someone, and if she said as much as "boo" to him on her way out, she was going to regret it. Was he feeling sorry for himself? Damn straight, he was. What he really missed was a standing pee. He felt like a bitch every time he had to go. Thoughts about peeing made him pull all the harder on his bottle of Kentucky Deluxe, which was going down alarmingly fast. Even in the shade, he was sweating his balls off.

Seth tucked his chin and kept his eyes down when the woman exited. Into his field of vision came an age-spotted hand full of veins and knobs and holding a chocolate bar. "It's not much, but I..." She didn't finish.

Overwhelm and...rage zapped Seth. His eyes stung and he couldn't make his hand move to accept the candy bar. She hesitated before setting it in his lap, then strode away.

That did it. He'd be finishing the bottle here and now. The chocolate bar went in his pocket for later.

He was buzzed to the point of forgetfulness when the cop appeared. Someone probably called when Seth started peeing from his wheelchair. Not like he was rude about it. He'd spun his chair to face away as he took his leak, but...bunch of pansies.

At least the cop was young and pretty and had a lot of tattoos. Too bad she was a cop. Too bad.

"Hi there," she said amicably, but even with half a bottle in him, he noticed her hand resting on her sidearm, so he barely grunted and made sure not to make any sudden moves.

"It's my understanding that Oakcrest Hospital is missing one of its wheelchairs. Have you seen it?"

Oh, she was funny. But Seth didn't trust anything wearing a uniform.

"I know you've fallen on hard times...Mister...." She checked a tiny spiral notebook in her non-firearm hand. "...Olivern, and I want to help you. Do you think you can help me too, and hand over that bottle? Open containers aren't allowed in public spaces."

He took a long pull while giving her the stink eye, then handed it over.

"And the wheelchair."

Seth looked at his chair. "I need this."

"The hospital gave me these, for you." She pulled crutches out of the cruiser's trunk. "They say you can keep them."

"How generous."

"Can I drop you off somewhere?"

Seth told her the jackoffs at Green Spirit took his home in the woods away, that his tent was at Green Spirit, along with everything he owned in the world, including his phone.

She said she wasn't the wizard of Oz, a genie in a bottle, or God that she could solve all Seth's problems. A ride was her offer, and he'd better take it or she would be forced to put on her purple gloves. "You don't want me to put on the gloves, Mr. Olivern."

"Hmph. Just cause you're pretty doesn't mean I don't—" That was as much as he got out before she manhandled him out of the wheelchair and into the back of her cruiser. His chocolate bar had melted into the shape of his chest.

"Warned you," was all she said.

She guided him onto a bench at Doe Pond, leaned the crutches against it, and pointed out the sidewalk corner where a charity food cabinet was located "conveniently beside the library and the police station." Like she was giving him a gift. Bah. Cop stole his open whiskey (but not the other one) and left him to sort things out.

The cop said to check the cabinet several times a day, as people were always dropping things off. She said if Seth ever spotted a bright blue Subaru parked there, he should waste no time in heading over because the blue Subaru gave "the best goodies." She winked as she said this, which made Seth wonder if the blue Subaru would be dropping whiskey, for that was the only goodie he wanted.

A small band of forest framed Doe Pond Park, but it would be ten times harder to set up a tent there. He was down a foot, for starters, and he didn't have his tent. From the city pool came the shrill calls of children and lifeguards' whistles. Like they mocked him personally. As the alcohol abandoned his bloodstream, he became aware of his itchy, painful stump and the hardness of the bench and how the sun was moving the shade away. He believed he now knew what a rotisserie chicken felt like. And hell's bells—he had to pee, again.

With the stupid crutches, Seth made his way into the library and was dazzled and invigorated by the air conditioning. A youngish clerk wearing a sweater asked if he could help him.

Oh, you have no idea. "Bathroom."

"Of course." The cheerful clerk pointed at the door behind Seth.

After taking care of that, Seth approached the reception desk again. "You don't have a phone, do you?"

"We sure do." He pointed behind Seth to the wall next to the bathroom.

"And computers, can I use them?"

Yes, yes, and yes. The library became Seth's instant friend. He wanted to hug the tattooed man with rogue hair who spoke to him with kindness—not pity. Losing his foot had tuned Seth to detect pity in the smallest amounts.

The library guy gestured to the candy wrapper sticking out of Seth's pocket and said he had good taste in candy bars.

"Are you vegan?" Library Guy asked.

"Aw hell, no." Seth saw that his vehemence made the library guy wince. "No offense."

"It's not for everybody." Library Guy waved away Seth's insult.

"Want it?" He offered the vegan candy bar that had melted into the shape of his chest.

The clerk scrunched up his face. "No thanks...I'm good."

Seth shrugged and found he was glad the clerk didn't accept the melty vegan chocolate bar. He was now officially curious to try this milk-less milk chocolate.

"Have a nice day," said Library Guy, as he handed Seth his brand-new card.

As much as Seth wanted to know what was up with Ivy, figuring out his home situation was more pressing. The phone call was to see about getting his tent and hammock back.

The super sounded genuinely happy to hear from Seth and promised to bring his belongings when the shift ended, which was two hours away.

In two hours, the library would be closed.

"The library? Seth, where are you living?" The super asked.

Seth wanted to tell the super it was none of his beeswax, but he needed the tent, so he mumbled a lie about having a friend who was going to store it for him.

While he waited for the super to arrive, Seth used his new card to get access to the internet on one of the library's computers. He typed Ivy's full name in the search bar.

Bingo.

And damn.

Ivy wasted no time making headlines. She had already "allegedly" assaulted and robbed someone. A toll booth camera picked up the license plate of the victim's car and a grainy picture of Ivy in the driver's seat. Her hair had grown out. Indistinct as her features were, Seth recognized the dark eyeliner around her eyes, her red, red lipstick, and bared teeth that looked like they had just taken a vampire's bite out of innocent flesh. Ever the rebel, she had her arm out the window, a middle finger to the toll booth camera. She was coming for him, no doubt, just as she said she would. Ivy could never let things go.

When the super arrived at the library curb in his shiny car, Seth had a party of squirrels and robins zipping about and dive-bombing his bench. He tossed pieces of white bread from the loaf he had scored from the "little" food cabinet that stood outside the library. The pantry provided him with a tin of anchovies in mustard, ramen noodles, cans of baked beans, chili, and peaches in heavy syrup, which Seth stowed beneath the bench.

All the critters scattered when the super threw open his car door. That was what the Green Spirit operators did when the super came around at work, too.

"You're looking well, Seth," he said.

Rather than accepting the compliment, Seth glanced at where his foot should be. When he looked up, he noticed the super had eyes only for Seth's face. What a pro.

"Brought you a present." Out of his trunk, he produced a gift bag with a big yellow smiley face and yellow and white stringy ribbons holding the handles closed. Seth accepted it as the super asked, "Where's your friend?"

Oh, right. Seth forgot his lie about staying with a friend. "He's running late."

"I can drive you to his place." The super had his hand on the trunk, ready to close it. "It's no trouble."

"No, no, my friend will be here. Just put the tent on the bench if you don't mind."

Any ideas about coming clean with the super about the "friend" and asking him to help Seth haul the boxes and tent disappeared in the reality of the super standing before him. Seth had hoped to convince his boss (ex-boss) of his need for space and nature (and whiskey), but now that the super was here wearing that scrunched up look on his face, Seth knew it would be futile. He would not approve of Seth's camping in the woods behind Doe Pond.

The super—or more likely, one of his minions—had folded and packed all of Seth's possessions in two transparent plastic bins. The boss stacked them on the sidewalk, unfolded Seth's camp chair and sat in it, facing Seth on the bench. "Aren't you going to open it?" He nodded to the smiley gift bag. "It's from everyone."

"Uh, sure. Thanks, Boss."

Seth thought he saw the super wince at the word *boss*, but it was only a flicker, and his beaming smile about whatever was in the bag made Seth curious. He squeezed, but the shape gave nothing away. First thing he pulled out was a toothbrush, followed by a pair of expensive-looking athletic socks with reinforced toes and heels.

Seth eyed his boss.

"What? They only come in packs of two," the super said.

The men locked stares for a few seconds before both burst out laughing.

Seth continued rooting in the bag. There was a travel deodorant, granola bars, ChapStick, and a bag of Tootsie Pops. Tootsie Pops were one of Seth's favorite treats, but how the super found out was anyone's guess. The extra charging brick for his phone made Seth smile. One of his co-workers knew him enough to know he wouldn't be leaving the wilderness and had his back. Tight-dress Sage?

The next gift nearly knocked Seth off the bench. A get-well card with $1000 cash inside. There were notes from every operator on his shift.

Seth's eyes bugged.

"We took up a collection," the super explained, "and the CEO rounded it up to an even thousand."

Seth dashed away the tears before the super could see. "Thanks, man," he said.

After sitting in silence for what felt like forever, the super clasped his hands and leaned toward Seth. "I know no one's coming."

Seth didn't meet the super's eyes. He leaned in too close, the way a friend would when he was about to tell you something confidential. Experiencing the super as anything other than a super A-hole boss whose role was to drive Seth to produce ever more steel brackets and clips—well, it was confusing and made his belly twist.

"I can't force you to take care of yourself, Seth." He handed Seth a business card. "Here, my phone number's on the back if you change your mind and want a ride to the shelter. I have a friend who volunteers there. You'd like him. All things considered, it's not a bad place."

"How would you know?" Seth mumbled without looking at his boss. And he derived a small satisfaction from the super's assenting grunt.

"I guess you're right, Seth. I don't know. But this..." He gestured at Seth's belongings in the bins. "...is no way to live. You can't camp forever, Seth, especially with your foot."

Especially *without* your foot, Seth thought. That's what you really meant.

Seth sat like a stone and refused to respond. He could camp for as long as he damn well pleased. He didn't need the super's permission. He was a grown-ass man.

"You're smarter than this, Seth," the super said.

Seth scoffed.

After an elongated silence, the super got in his shiny car and left.

Chapter 4

WHEN THE SUPER WAS there asking annoying questions, Seth wanted him gone, but when he left, Seth's mind turned back to the O-ring failure that was presently his life. *Houston, we have a problem.*

"Or maybe all I need's a drink."

He clapped his forehead, pulling his better angel into his thought process. "Not now. Not until I get squared away."

A gangly teenager who looked as if he'd just run through a sprinkler and smelled of pot wandered by Seth's bench. The kid's sneakers were muddy, but his face was kind, and he wore a bracelet of acorns. His mind seemed to be elsewhere (or under the influence?). Seth flashed a twenty-dollar bill and asked if the kid wanted an easy job.

"Doing what?"

Seth snorted. "It's not enough that it's easy? I'd like you to carry my stuff. I'm...in transition."

The kid frowned as he gave Seth and his bins the once over.

"To where?"

"You up for it or not?"

The kid agreed with little enthusiasm.

Pot had never appealed to Seth, but he was desperate to quell the throbbing in his stump. The kid said he smoked the last of his stash, but there was a guy who hung out near the food pantry who always had weed for sale, better and cheaper than what you could get at the dispensary. Also, the kid told Seth about a secluded place Seth could camp where no one would bother him.

"How do you know I don't want to be bothered? Maybe I like it right here."

"I can take you there, if you want," the kid offered, undaunted by Seth's meanness.

Seth narrowed his eyes. Would the kid lead him into the woods, club him, and steal his few belongings? And his money? Seth had to trust the kid because he had no way to transport his bins and chair into the woods. Or anywhere.

The two made slow progress, with the kid weighed down with both bins and the camp chair and unable to see where he stepped, and Seth's crutches snagging on roots or sucked into mud. There was no path, so Seth memorized trail markers—downed trees or patches of baby pines.

"How'd you find this place?" Seth asked.

"I lost my drone."

"You ever find it?"

"Sort of," the kid answered, but Seth didn't hear because a wet and treacherous-looking creek barred their way.

He halted. "No way."

The kid set the bins down and rubbed his chin as he scanned. "Here." He gathered largish, flat rocks and made a walkway of sorts. "Your crutches can get wet. Put your foot on the stones."

What if the current, weak as it was, took Seth down? He wasn't exactly agile these days, and his liver had metabolized all the courage he'd consumed earlier.

As if the kid read his mind, he said, "You'll make it, no problem, bruh."

Seth did make it.

The site had only one drawback, the kid said. When it rained heavily, the place became a water locked, squishy mess. Well, Seth wasn't worried about rain. Pussies worried about rain. The kid offered to set up his tent, and Seth's burning not-there foot and throbbing armpits were grateful. Unfortunately, the person at Green Spirit who had disassembled his tent left two of the stakes in the dirt, and it wasn't like tent stakes grew on trees. A powerful gust of wind could transform his cozy orange dome into a worthless nylon blanket.

But bingo—the kid used knobby branches as tent stakes and tied the lines as best he could. Seth chuckled because he'd been wrong. Tent stakes *did* grow on trees. Hopefully, he could trust the kid not to tell anyone where he had set up camp. Seth didn't like even one human being knowing where he was.

Even after he was paid, the kid seemed reluctant to leave Seth in the woods with his plastic bins and camp chair. But when Seth dropped his drawers and leaned against a tree to relieve himself, the kid waved and hustled away.

Once the quiet allowed him a moment to think, Seth realized he had never even asked what the kid's name was. Did he play cards? A diversion would be welcome. Ivy had played Blackjack because it was easy, she said. She played Solitaire, too, because Solitaire was what you played when no one loved you, she said.

Poor Ivy. Poor, murderous Ivy.

Sitting on his camp chair with his whiskey bottle cradled in one arm, listening to the rustling leaves, birdsong, and squirrels' chattering, as well as the far-off squeals of children at the city pool, Seth decided the kid had done him a good turn. He would do his best to get comfortable in the forest of Doe Pond. This would be a wonderful place to drink and watch the sun descend through the silhouettes of trees.

Seth napped in the chair with his stump resting on a bin, woke with a raging headache.

"Time to be a Boy Scout," he mumbled to himself, and shakily pushed upright, wincing at the crutches rubbing his already-raw armpits. He hobbled to a tree, leaned his crutches against it, and tossed his ridge line around the knotty bark, catching it on the other side and looping it in his hand. With his other hand, he used his crutch to walk the string to another tree fifteen feet away. The covered area he made with the tarp stretched over the ridgeline would make a fine place to sit, even when it rained. See, Seth was no dummy.

Before his discharge from the hospital, the doctors had tossed out appointments like clowns throwing candy at a parade. Seth was supposed to attend weekly appointments with a physical therapist, an occupational therapist, his surgeon, a prosthetist, a shrink, and even a podiatrist. Now that he had only one foot, he got a doctor especially to care for it? Bah. And there were endless exit interview questions from the social worker.

Where was that girlfriend of his? Did Seth have a ride home? Did he have someone to drive him to his follow-up appointments because, of course, no driving? The social worker neglected to ask Seth if he possessed either a car or a home. How easily the lies had tumbled out, lubed by the extra rations of painkillers he'd charmed out of the night shift nurse. Seth remembered how the social worker had chewed her gum relentlessly and squinted at him. An edge of disappointment tinged her every word and made Seth feel small, like she was an annoyed mom to a bad little boy.

In the end she made Seth sign something.

Fine. Whatever.

The social worker didn't know what she was talking about. The forest made a fine home. And who needed all those stupid appointments? Seth's brain was full of the wonderful fuzz his pills delivered.

As he mentally berated the social worker, he set his crutches against the second tree and looped the rope around, making a taut line-hitch knot.

"Call me a *Man* Scout," he boasted. "That's me, better than a Boy Scout. Seth, the One-legged Man Scout who prepares not too much, not too little, but just right."

A sharp pain pinched his forearm. A buzz sounded. Another buzz, another strike, this time on the webbing between his fingers. He swore and swiped at the instantly materializing and alarmingly growing cloud of bees.

Seth ran.

Briefly.

Away. Or that was his intention. His flight ended when he forgot he had but one foot and tried to use a second.

Down Seth went, face first, which allowed the bees to zap, zap, zap on the back of his neck, his hands, and all the exposed areas of flesh, including (horribly) his cheek and eyelid. What could he do but lie still like a dead man and hope they stopped? Playing possum had been Seth's standard response for as long as he could remember (except for one stupid, out-of-character moment on a cliff with Ivy). Playing dead was far more actionable now that he could hardly walk, much less run. And besides, he knew from experience the little buggers chased you, no matter how fast you ran. Even a man with two good legs stood little chance of outrunning angry bees.

A few more random stings and the bees got it through their tiny heads that Seth was not a threat worth dying for. The stings, bad as they were, did not hold a candle to the pain in a foot that no longer existed. *Phantom limb pain,* the doctors called it. He loved how the words had rolled off their authoritative, suave tongues as if the words themselves could make the experience smaller than it was and therefore could not make you want to shoot yourself to escape it. Phantom. Limb. Pain. Very scientific. Very chill. Why get riled up over a little phantom limb pain?

In Seth's pocket was the prescription for more painkillers. The hospital had called the script into the pharmacy Seth selected, but Seth also had asked for a paper copy, hoping to "recycle" it for double the opioid fun. What was the saying? You miss every shot you don't take.

But in his haste to get drinking, Seth neglected to go to the pharmacy as planned, and now he regretted that decision as the stings throbbed and burned. He lay in the dirt and leaves where he fell and waited to make sure the bees were really and truly done with him. Far off he heard a woodpecker. And farther than that, the sound of the interstate, of trucks belching. The pool must be closed, because the squeals of children had ceased.

Should Seth bother crawling to his tent—or let sleep take him right there? He heard the high-pitched whine of a mosquito.

The tent, then. He dragged himself along the ground, half afraid that if he stood up, the bees would be like, *there be the dude, let's get him.* Ridiculous? Maybe. But why risk it? Leaves and dirt followed him into the tent as he flopped inside. He zipped it closed and was down before the sun.

He would have to be more mindful of his lack of balance.

It was dark when the pain and itch of his stings woke him, and he had to pee. How he wished there were a magical astronaut hose that could come suck away his pee, like the little thing at the dentist that sucked the saliva out of his mouth. How long had it been since he went to the dentist? No matter, his teeth were in decent shape. Nanette had told him how nice they were, how straight and white.

In the darkness, in the acidic sleeplessness of booze, his worries came to mind, visiting him like helpful ghosts. How would he charge his phone? The library. Check. How would he shave? The library. Whew. How would he get his supplies back to his campsite? Without being seen? Hmmm... Unclear. How would he shower? Love's was too far away from Doe Pond.

Well heck, Doe Pond was how he would bathe. Ivy would never find him here, and this was as good a set-up as what he had before the terrible day of his accident. Oh, things were looking up.

But wait. Toilet paper. He'd forgotten to steal some from the library. The leaves were looking brittle and malevolent and—bingo—saved again. The stream. His personal *bidet*, one of those fandangled ass-washers. What a roller coaster it had been, moving. But these woods could work. For every one of Seth's worries, he found a solution. He gazed into the expansive, now-friendly darkness and searched for his friend the moon, hoping for the magnificent rays through the trees, his sign that things would continue to go in his favor.

A sliver of a moon frowned at him. Undaunted, Seth snuggled into his tent and slept. For tomorrow's trip into town, he needed rest. It was a mile's walk after all, on one foot and two crutches.

Everest to him.

Upon waking, Seth gobbled a can of peach halves and hydrated with their heavy syrup. He took an uncoordinated bath in the creek that also served as his toilet and felt refreshed enough to tackle the journey to the pharmacy. The need for painkillers was so extreme he had no choice but to Rocky Balboa himself into the mood for physical exertion.

Seth walked fifty-odd paces when his crutch slipped on a mossy rock and took him down into the creek, bashing his elbow on another rock and soaking his best clothes, his only clean ones that had taken forever and a day to put on. He lay face up in the creek, too stunned to move and unable to scramble to his feet (*foot*, he reminded himself, foot). Maybe a flesh-eating bacteria would get into his wound and put him out of his misery. The idea of death-by-amoeba spilled through his head as cool, silty water flowed over his bee stings. He gazed at the broccoli-like tops of trees and the blue sky poking through here and there, and he wished he could saddle a cloud or change places with a hawk. (One circled, awaiting his demise?) Instead, he used his crutch to push himself standing, gritting his teeth at the pain where his head, shoulder, and hip had struck the rocks.

Luckily, it was only a few paces back to the camp chair where he could drip dry while knocking back what remained of the whiskey (surely this moment called for whiskey). Not having anything to drink (meaning whiskey) would motivate him to try again to cross the creek—later. Why was he in such a hurry? Might as well enjoy the morning, his first in his new home.

The pharmacy, town, supplies, all of it could wait. Seth propped his stump on a broken tree trunk and thanked God for little pleasures. And—he looked at his bottle—big ones.

The day passed, and he never felt up to making the trip into town. Thanks to sitting in his wet clothes, chilled and shaky, he hardly had the strength to pull the tab on the can of baked beans. He got it partially open and tipped the can, drinking the thick, sweet beans as best he could. They got all over his stubbled face and went down his shirt. When he had to relieve himself in the big way, the stream was too far to bother. He tried using leaves, but they hurt, and he found he didn't care. Everything hurt. His skull had ceased to be large enough for his brain, and his skin was one hundred percent sting. Somehow his tongue had also swollen and threatened to choke him. When his phone showed a call from the super, Seth tried to answer, but his mouth wouldn't make the words his brain wanted. A warmth between his legs turned cool and then cold. Though the sun picked its way through the trees and should have made for a warm day, Seth shivered. Dimly, he heard branches snap under someone's feet.

The kid returned.

Thank you, Kid.

He shook Seth's shoulders and leaned over him, snapping his fingers, the acorn bracelet swinging, his body blotting out the sky and leaves, which revealed to Seth that he was lying in the dirt, face up this time. Somehow. He didn't recall how.

"Bruh. Bruh? You alive?" the kid asked.

Seth groaned.

Chapter 5

THE SECOND HOSPITAL STAY was worse than the first, if that could be believed. The nurses were nice enough, but the social worker—Seth finally bothered to get her name, Mavis—was bossy as all get out. And angry. Oh, was she angry.

"The woods, Mr. Olivern!" She wagged a knobby finger at Seth. "Who *does* that?"

He gave her the side-eye. "People who like trees."

"You can't just plop down a tent wherever you please. You have physical therapy and follow-up appointments with the surgeon, the orthopedist, wound care, and—"

"You're making me want to drink, Mavis. Can you go away?" Seth pulled the white hospital blanket over his face like a child, and he didn't care. He could see her through the knit holes, hands on hips, deciding.

From under the blanket he said, "Please."

"Hmph."

But she turned on her heel and left. Bingo.

The kid came to visit, which was nice. Turns out he had a name, too. Weird-ass one. He brought a get-well card with a smashed joint inside it, signed *Noldy*.

"Noldy?" Seth asked, forgetting to thank him for the joint.

He shrugged and looked out the hospital window. "Arnold, but who wants to be called Arnold? My friends call me Noldy."

The kid had taken the time to show Seth the woods, had returned to save his ass, and now...a gift. "Well, Nold...y. I owe you one." He shoved a tear off his cheek with the fleshy part of his palm. Kid was an angel.

A knock on Seth's door turned his attention to the super and a hulkish Black man in the doorway—dude had the sculpt of a repo man. Guilt being Seth's reflex, he shoved the joint behind his back. He knew this made him look guiltier, but he couldn't stop himself. Neither could he cool the heat in his cheeks and ears that undoubtedly made them glow red.

"Bruh, it's legal," said Noldy. "No stress."

Just the same, Seth left the card tucked behind him as the men entered. The super had a shopping bag full of chips, candy bars, and drinks, all nonalcoholic.

"The cashier from Love's sent this." He held it out. "She said to tell you she misses you and hopes you feel better." A devilish grin played on the super's face.

"Nanette sent this?"

"Is that her name?" The super shrugged. "She saw the Green Spirit logo on my shirt and asked why her gorgeous—her word—friend hadn't been around. I told her I was on my way to see you."

Now the heat in Seth's cheeks was a four-alarm fire. Nanette knew about his accident. Augh. Not that Seth ever planned on laying eyes on her again, but he wanted to be whole in her memory.

"Seth, I'd like you to meet Miles," the super said.

Miles extended an enormous paw to shake. Seth squeezed as hard as he could, which, in his condition, wasn't hard at all.

"I hear you enjoy the great outdoors," Miles said. "Me too."

Seth narrowed his eyes at the super. Any convo that began with, *I hear you do X* made Seth's skin crawl. He couldn't exactly say why, except that he didn't want to be anyone's topic of discussion. It had never boded well for him.

"Miles and I backpack with a group of guys once a year," the super looked to Miles.

He picked up the thread, "I heard about your accident, and I guess you could say I try to find people who need a leg up—um, bad phrasing there...people who've fallen on hard times—"

"Fallen...get it? The one-legged man, fallen on hard times?" Seth's flat delivery made only Noldy chuckle.

"Hard times rolled over his foot?" Noldy added. "Couldn't help myself."

Again, no one laughed.

Miles cracked the tiniest smile at Seth. "Sure, however you want to put it. Here's the thing, Seth, when I needed it, a brother was there for me, and I vowed to do the same. I have this place..."

Seth listened to Miles's offer, wondering if his own eyes were growing as large as Noldy's were.

This XY supersized version of Mother Teresa offered Seth access to his fifty-nine-acre property, a patch of woods to camp in, or a furnished guest room, whichever suited him. Miles would transport Seth to his doctors' appointments. The only catch was that Seth had to promise to have a meal with Miles and afterward do a life coaching session two times a week.

"Life...coaching?"

"A study," Miles said, "From the GOAT."

"He means Jesus, bruh," Noldy chimed in.

Seth rolled his eyes.

"…and be sober for it," Miles finished. "What do you say?"

"Nuh-uh." Seth answered automatically.

Miles's face fell, but he made no response. Seth felt like Miles—and the super and Noldy—expected an explanation.

"Religion sucks," is what came out of Seth's mouth. Church had always felt oppressive and shaming, a space dedicated to power-grabbing and mind control. And dumb-ass rituals, weird smells, weirder chants, and nobody Seth knew had been better for it.

"I'm not offering you religion, Seth, I'm offering you an opportunity to get your life on track. Getting on track is figuring out what your answers are to life's questions."

Seth stuck out his tongue and pretended to throw up.

Miles continued, smiling, "Oh, I see you, brother, but your accident is a call to slow down and take stock of yourself. You're uniquely, providentially situated to make actionable changes in your life."

Seth hated when people used big words.

"Fine," Miles said, "I'll say this as nicely as I can. If you don't get off the sauce and start taking care of that leg, you are screwed, my friend."

"Camping and whiskey, like PB & J, they got to be together." The truth was, Seth didn't mind small doses of sobriety (everything in moderation), so long as things were going right in his life (which they hadn't been). The idea of talking about deep stuff made Seth uncomfortable, especially with this stranger. It was like sharing sex strategies with the dude sitting beside you on a public bus. No. Just…no. Seth became aware he shook his head *no* along with his thoughts.

"I hear you," Miles said. "C'mon, you can manage two times a week. Oh, and I almost forgot the best thing. A guy I know makes prostheses. I asked him if he'd look at you."

"Bruh, you take him up on the *life coaching* or I will," Noldy said.

Nobody laughed.

"I'm not asking you to convert—it's just a meal and we read afterward. Think about it, and if you decide you're interested, call me. If you want to quit after a month, you have my word that you can continue to stay at my place until your prosthesis is finished, no strings." He handed Seth a business card.

Miles Lionson, Embalmer. Bogdan Funeral Home.

"Bruh..." Noldy whispered. "Don't be a dumbass."

To Noldy, Seth said under his breath, "He embalms people."

Miles's face flickered before he flashed a disarming, toothy smile. "It's good money. No customer complaints."

"Seth, you just won the lottery. Take the man's offer," the super said.

With two days to think while lying in his hospital bed, Seth considered Miles's offer. What could this saintly linebacker want from him? His offer was too good to be true. And Seth had learned that anything *too good to be true* was a landmine beckoning him to sit on it.

Seth gazed out his hospital window at the cars and the traffic lights, the people coming to visit loved ones. Seth had no loved ones. As he considered his new state of helplessness, of what life would look like one-legged, his future was boulders crushing him, demolishing his options.

As he lay in bed stewing, his perspective shifted. The bad thing—losing his foot—had already occurred, and accepting Miles's offer couldn't be worse than that, could it? Seth had lost his forest home—well, first he lost his apartment, then his forest home, then his foot and job. What more did he have to lose?

Other than the fact that religion was his own damn business, there was nothing objectively terrible about study. Heck, with Ivy on the loose and Seth being crippled, he wondered if this was God, fixing to apologize for the mess The Almighty had allowed Seth's life to become. On the other hand, God should know Seth needed all the whiskey he could get. But wouldn't it be great to have a room *and* a place to camp out? Maybe Miles's guestroom had a bathtub. What house didn't have a bathtub?

That did it.

Seth called Miles with a compromise.

"I'll read your book—over a small amount of whiskey," he offered.

Probably, he and Miles had wildly different ideas of *small*.

When Miles didn't answer, Seth pressed, "Stopping alcohol cold turkey can make a guy crazy, you know."

Seth had stopped drinking plenty of times, and had no such worry for himself, but why suffer when he could have his cake and eat it, too?

"I don't know..."

"Hey, all things in moderation, even moderation."

Miles laughed and said "Alright, bro. It's a deal."

A deal.

Commitment didn't sit well with Seth. He found himself texting Miles a renege, then erasing it, texting the renege again and holding his finger over the send arrow. Like with Noldy (who turned out to be a nice enough kid), Seth wondered what was in it for this Miles character? The man was an embalmer, after all. Maybe he wanted Seth's kidneys to sell on the black market. Well, the joke would be on Miles, because Seth's kidneys were shot. He did have other decent organs, though.

In the end, Seth stuck with the deal because...what choice did he have?

Until he received disability money or a payout from Green Spirit, it was a halfway house or Miles's house.

Chapter 6

Two days later, Miles arrived at the hospital in a silver Jeep Wrangler with no doors. Seth had to be lifted and deposited into the seat by Miles and the valet, and his crutches stuck out over the top crash bar. G-forces and jostling made Seth grab for his seat belt until he settled into the idea of a painless, high-impact death in Miles's Jeep. The music reminded him of Metallica (but wasn't because *Jesus* was in the lyrics). Miles blasted it at a volume that prevented conversation, which was cool with Seth, who enjoyed watching Miles nod along with the beat. The man liked to take his turns at tire-squealing speed. In no time, they left traffic lights behind, then neighborhoods. After long stretches of unlined roads with cornfields and farms and here and there a grove of trees, Miles slowed and turned onto a winding gravel road Seth realized was the driveway.

"Cows," Seth pointed, as the Jeep bounced over a rut.

Miles cut the music. "Dairy cows. They're my neighbor's. Those cows make the best ice cream in Huntsville. No, the best you'll ever have. We'll go to Flanning's for ice cream when you're up for it."

Seth's jaw dropped as the rest of the house came into full view. A kidney-shaped pond spooned the front of the home, reflecting the timber siding and stone masonry in shimmering glory. The entire front of the house was a collage of square and triangle windows, and a tiered wrap-around porch followed the water's edge. As they got closer, Seth could make out half a dozen cats lounging on the outdoor couches or sleeping in the bars of sunlight. One cleaned itself with its rear leg stuck in the air.

Miles beeped at a cat sleeping in the driveway. It stretched before skulking away in the unhurried manner of felines.

"So...embalming. Did you go to school for it?"

"Why—you want a job?"

"Maybe."

Miles chuckled. "Sorry if I misled you, Seth. I joke that it's for the money because I've learned over the years that people can't make sense of it otherwise. The truth is, I enjoy my job."

"You love handling dead bodies?"

Miles chuckled, then grew serious. "I consider it an honor to be trusted with the last experience a family will ever have of their loved one. It's not just the body, Seth. It's the whole experience of saying goodbye. I design and oversee that last impression."

The last impression.

Caskets.

Funerals.

Memories.

Seth gulped at the memory of Ivy holding his hand, no—crushing—his hand as they stood before a coffin. Their *loved one* had been put back together enough for an open casket. Sixteen years ago, someone like Miles had done miraculous work to make that happen. Was that person proud of the design? Pleased with the artistry of the last impression? Would Miles have been embalming at that time?

The casket memory had long ago morphed into a recurring dream of Seth and Ivy in a hushed but heated argument on the altar in front of the coffin. To make her point, Ivy stabbed the top of Seth's hand with one of her long and painted fingernails, pushed it into his flesh like a tack, and yellow-green embalming fluid leaked out of the puncture. The horror of bleeding embalming fluid invariably shocked Seth awake.

"Bro?" Miles had parked the Jeep and was staring at Seth with raised eyebrows. "You good?"

Seth shook his head to clear it. "Yeah, sure. So how do you afford this place—you got a side hustle selling organs?"

Miles's face fell. "Brother, you are a piece of work. You see badness everywhere."

"Show me otherwise, *Brother*."

Miles snorted and exited the Jeep. He didn't answer where he got the money, and although Seth considered pushing, Seth had his own secrets. Maybe Miles was a good guy. Maybe not. But Seth had limited options. He'd go along with this strange-ass plan while keeping an eye out for trouble.

A drink was in order.

On the deck were plush chairs that almost audibly begged him to sprawl on them. Beside one chair, Miles had placed a squat, wooden table perfect for setting a bottle of whiskey on, and—and now Seth was really fantasizing—a crystal rocks glass.

"Hungry? I smoked a couple of pork roasts yesterday." Again, Miles interrupted Seth's daydreaming.

"Er…"

"Before you answer." Miles put up his pointer finger and dashed into the house. He came back with a bottle of Maker's Mark and—holy cow—a rocks glass. "Don't take this the wrong way. I think you may have a problem, friend. But a deal's a deal. I'm considering this an experiment."

The two men took their meal, an early dinner on the back deck, seated at a stone table with wrought-iron chairs and cushioned seats. The smoked pork shredded easily and melted in Seth's mouth. He almost cried at how delicious everything was and only once wondered if Miles had laced his whiskey with poison and planned to perform Frankensteinian experiments on him or whatever horrible things embalmers could dream up. For the life of him, Seth could not imagine what would motivate a man to take in a homeless, crippled stranger.

But from what he could tell, Miles was as gentle as his many cats and liked sweet tea the same way Seth liked whiskey.

Over dinner, Miles gave a rundown of his schedule and where supplies like towels, toilet paper, and bug spray were located. Yes, he did have a tub, a clawfoot tub in the guest bathroom. Seth wasn't exactly sure what that meant, but he couldn't wait to find out.

"Do you think you'll be more comfortable camping on the back lot, or sleeping in the barn?" Miles gestured with his fork to the barn across the lake. "You're welcome to stay in the main house, but I thought you'd be more comfortable with your own space. Plus, it's easier to get around the barn with your crutches because there are no stairs, and there's a gravel path that takes you to the woods."

As wonderful as the woods were, Seth's throbbing missing foot wanted the softness of an actual bed. It wasn't the woods he craved so much as isolation. Privacy. Silence. A place where Ivy wouldn't find him. Hell, Seth would study the bottom of Miles's feet if that was what it took to earn a vacation in this paradise. Now that he was here, he couldn't believe he had almost declined the offer.

After clearing the table, Miles came back with cigars, one for each of them. "You smoke?" he asked.

"Sure...thanks." Holy cow, whiskey *and* a cigar. The crickets were singing their songs. Dragonflies made a low buzzing, and occasionally the plop of a frog and its burp punctuated the stillness of the evening. Miles didn't mention studying. Maybe he forgot that part of the deal.

But no, Miles simply had other commitments. "Good evening, Seth." He left the Maker's Mark. "I trust you'll find your way around."

Through the screen door came a mellow light and the comforting sound of Miles loading the dishwasher. Seth availed himself of the Maker's Mark and crutched to the guest house before it got too dark to find his way.

The "guest room" was a suite attached to the back of the barn garage, and although the barn blocked the view of the lake, the living area had two sets of sliding glass doors that looked out into the woods. As the sun set, birds flitted high in the trees. Squirrels jumped from branch to branch. Even deer nibbled at the flowering bushes—a doe and two speckled fawns.

But the cats. He'd never seen so many cats in one place. Three cats lay on the outdoor couch. In the grass surrounding the deck, a black cat chased a bug, trying to paw it. Another cat strutted along the deck, winding around the potted herbs and flower arrangements before flopping on its side in the floodlight affixed to the barn. Miles had provided a hutch for them, with boxes and cushions and toys and food, as well as a water fountain. The hutch looked empty though, the cats preferring the human spaces.

Inside the guest house, macrame and nature-inspired art decorated the cedar paneling. Seth opened the coat closet and found rolled-up area rugs had been stashed inside. Snagging his crutches on one of those rugs would have been zero fun. Seth marveled at Miles's thoughtfulness.

The fridge was stocked with shaved turkey, roast beef, cheeses, olives, juices, hard-boiled eggs, apples, oranges, and salads of all colors and textures, all in clear containers. A note with a key taped to it said that Seth could help himself to food from the main house as well. These Jesus-people, they were always trying to woo you with theatrical acts of generosity, and once they had you where they wanted you, they hit you with the fire and brimstone—the wooden crucifix on the guesthouse wall reminded him. Seth knew how to keep any accusing inner voice at bay (whiskey), and he knew how to be stone cold sober if the situation demanded (such a situation hadn't occurred for a while).

First order of business: a bath. *Clawfoot* apparently meant deep as hell, and *bingo*—did it look wonderful. There was a bag of Epsom salts, too, eucalyptus and lavender scented. Seth used the sink as a parking place for his crutches and to steady himself as he undressed, a dicey and disorganized process. First, he tugged down his sweatpants and pulled his bad leg through. Then, because he couldn't put weight on one side (a fact he forgot too often), he had to fold into a sitting position on the floor using only one leg, which meant he leaned heavily on a wall or in this case, a sink, to ease himself down so he could pull off the second leg of his pants. Underwear had been jettisoned from his post-amputation wardrobe because it was just another annoying thing to do.

With the help of the sink and the side of the tub, Seth pulled himself back to standing but misread the slipperiness of the porcelain and his hand fell in, bruising his armpit and ego and forcing curses from him.

On his next try, both hands gripped the tub more carefully, and he sat on the side. He swiveled left then right and used his good right foot to lower himself into the warm, scented water. It burned when he accidentally let his stump touch the water and the salts hit the wound, but the rest of Seth felt divine. This was how a king bathed. There was even a special place to put his rocks glass, which was halfway full of a neat pour.

Too bad the glass was three feet away, on the sink. Argh...

Not to be deterred from the perfect bath, Seth made the effort to get the whiskey, telling himself that it was good to do hard things and his physical therapist would be proud. And...bingo. He did it.

The water warmed his muscles, and the whiskey warmed his throat.

A new man stepped out of the tub and found the zero gravity chair Miles had placed outside the sliding doors, close but not so close as to block the view from the living room. Seth took his third whiskey in that chair, watching the fireflies light up the open field behind the house and around the lake. Thoughts of Ivy buzzed around his head, but he batted them away and focused on the way the bugs swooped and swirled and were brighter than he'd ever seen in the woods behind Green Spirit, or anywhere, really. Must be they liked tall grass. The moon through the trees looked crisp and bright.

When his need for sleep outpaced his need to sit and appreciate the night air, he went inside. On the bedside table sat a colorful glass lamp, a Bible (of course), and a cube-shaped plug to charge his phone. Seth could hear the night sounds through the screen of the sliding door. The wind's gentle reach into the room put him in a mood to sleep. It was all the wonder of camping and all the comfort of not.

Chapter 7

AFTER A KING'S DINNER of grilled chicken, buttery corn on the cob, and baked potatoes, Miles read from a tattered, gilt-edged book. Dog-eared did not come close: the thing looked grizzly-bear-mauled.

"You use that to beat the truth into people?" Seth joked.

"Only when they disagree with me."

Seth searched Miles's face for clues he joked, but Miles was deadpan.

"Bah ha ha!" Miles stamped his feet. "I'm just messin' with you. Bah ha ha!" He got himself under control and opened the book to a page near the end.

Seth balked. "Bruh," copying the kid Noldy's exclamatory phrase, "Why are we starting at the end?"

"Hmmm...I remember thinking the same thing when someone told me to begin my journey here." Miles closed his eyes and smiled. "All the best stories begin *in media res*, which is Latin for in the middle of things. Make no mistake, this is a true story, but even true stories are told best when they begin in the middle of the excitement. You with me?" He opened his book. "Besides, look here." He pointed at the page and read, "'In the beginning was the Word and the Word was with God, and the Word was God.' See? We're starting at a beginning, just not at *the* beginning."

When the study ended, Seth went home and opened the Bible on his nightstand to page one. *The Old Testament* interested him for a few pages before it turned into lists of names and other boring stuff. Turned out, Miles was right about starting in the middle. He had issued Seth "homework" to read between their meetings. It was through his homework that Seth learned that Jesus (like Seth) also went into the wilderness.

The next time the two men met for study, Seth happily pointed out the similarity between himself and Jesus. "My kind of guy, goes into the wilderness."

"To be tempted by the devil," Miles added.

"The man made wine," Seth insisted. "He kept the party going."

Miles's brow furrowed. "At his mother's request."

"I like that he made *quality* wine," Seth said. "And getting my feet—foot—washed by lady hair. I could be down for that." Seth sighed.

As the days progressed, they fell into a routine of doctor appointments, dinner, and study, usually three days a week, depending on what appointments Seth had. After two weeks of moderately buzzed studying, Seth arrived to dinner sober and declined a pour of bourbon.

Miles tried to hide his smirk.

"What?" Seth bantered. "A man can't change his mind?"

"Course a man can," Miles answered.

With Seth's own private space and the woods and the lake and fireflies and nature hugging Seth every minute of every day, he found he didn't want to drink—and he enjoyed the reading and Miles asking what he thought about this or that. Hardly anyone ever asked Seth what he thought. About anything. Whiskey made him silly if he had too much (and having too much was a given). Plus, whiskey turned his stomach into a cauldron of acid, which he assumed was his normal state, but he realized he had feel-good days when he didn't drink and belly-aching days when he overdid the booze.

In Miles's Cat and Cripple Paradise (as Seth thought of it) he relaxed, no longer expecting to see Ivy waiting for him around the next corner (she didn't know where he was) or sitting on his car (thank God he didn't have one) or on his stoop (again, didn't have his own front door). Ivy had not disappeared, but she ceased to exist in enormous technicolor, taking up the entire canvas of his brain. Even when he had the chance to look her up, when Miles took him to the library for books, Seth chose not to. Instead, he checked out a book Miles suggested about a badass guy who ran in the Olympic games and later became a fighter pilot and had the terrible luck to crash his plane into the ocean and became a POW during the Second World War. Louis something was his name. "True story," Miles said. "You'll like him."

"Dude's had a lot of bad luck," Seth said. "Like me."

"Your luck changed when you met me—not that I believe in luck."

Seth chuckled. He believed *only* in luck. Miles was a bit of a fool for giving away his food and his home and his time. But Seth wasn't about to correct him.

Three times a week, Miles drove Seth to his physical therapy appointment, and they ate dinner and read and talked afterward. They were six dinners in, and Miles had yet to repeat a dish. *The man could cook.* And he never pushed Seth to talk or make a declaration about God. He simply asked what Seth thought about this or that passage and prayed at the close of their study. It took an hour, in which time Miles downed three glasses of sweet tea.

In the two weeks since Seth had come, no visitors or friends came by, only a lithe and smiley house cleaner who wore her hair in a braid and hugged Miles like he was her oxygen. She arrived at nine in the morning wearing no makeup and too-long gym shorts (to her knees). While she scrubbed the bathtub or washed whatever dishes were in the sink, she hummed tunes Seth didn't recognize—maybe hymns. Seth was too shy to say anything other than "hello" and made himself scarce while she cleaned by taking a *wobble* as he referred to his woods walk that made his crutch-holding arms ache. When he returned, he found the girl lounging in his zero-gravity chair, using her cross necklace as a cat toy and giggling as the cat in her lap pawed at it.

He remained in the woods and hoped she hadn't seen him spying, hoped she would leave because she was prettier by far than Nanette and Ivy, and Seth was a crippled loser. End of story. And, damn.

That night after dinner, Miles went on and on about how everyone was equal in one way: they needed saving. And anyone, no matter how bad, was worth saving. This was the wonderful thing about Jesus, Miles said.

And that wasn't fair at all. Ivy did not deserve saving.

But since Seth refused to mention Ivy, he blurted, "You keep saying how good God is, well duh. You got this mansion and a lake and a hot little Merry Maid. Don't tell me you're not hitting that."

Miles gave Seth such a stare that Seth instantly wished he'd kept his mouth shut.

After a few seconds Miles said, "Wow, that's a strong feeling, Seth. Where'd it come from?"

Seth shrugged. "My fucking leg, maybe."

"Honesty is a beginning," Miles said. "You can be mad at God. I know I was. And for the record, I am not 'hitting' Monroe." He made air quotes with his fingers. "I met her at a soup kitchen."

"Hmph. Are there more like her there?"

Miles shook his head. "Are you for real?"

"Jesus said I should be truthful."

"So…"

"So she's hot. You want me to pretend I don't want to hit that?"

"I want you to see Monroe as a fellow human, not as a place to park your rig. Do you know a single thing about Monroe? Have you bothered to talk to her? Have you asked her what she studies?"

"What do you mean?"

"At the community college, and I take that as a *no*. And the reason she comes here is to take care of her cats."

"*Her* cats?"

"Monroe worked at a no-kill shelter until about a year ago. The owner died, and she asked if I could take some cats, and we made the deal that I'd take all of them if she'd care for them and try to get them adopted." He waved a hand about. "You see how the adopting part turned out, but I don't mind…Her cleaning the guest room is an extra favor. I figured with your leg and all…" Miles sighed heavily. "She's not my maid, Seth."

Wow. Fucking wow. Seth felt like a five-year-old.

After a guilt-inducing silence, Miles asked, "This isn't about Jesus, is it?"

"No," Seth admitted.

"It's about Seth. What can Seth get out of this?"

"Why's that so bad?"

Miles closed his eyes and, more importantly, his Bible. "Some people think you can say magical words and make all your problems go away."

He shook the book. "This isn't a lamp we rub and get our wishes granted."

Seth couldn't bring himself to tell Miles that he dreamed of Ivy murdering him when he closed his eyes at night, and that he saw the past like a movie rewound and rewound again. Instead, he asked the question he had been noodling since he met Miles. "What's in this for *you*?"

"Exactly," was all Miles answered.

Chapter 8

ON THE RIDE HOME from physical therapy the next morning, Miles asked if Seth would mind a stop at the funeral home to pick up a package that he had accidentally delivered there.

"No need to come in. It'll just be a minute," he said.

Fine by Seth. He was still mad about being made to feel like a freak for having normal dude lust for a hot girl who cleaned in his vicinity.

But after twenty-five minutes, he was boiling in the sun. What could be taking Miles so long? He managed (thank you, physical therapy) to get out of the Jeep without breaking the good leg, and he navigated the three steps in his crutches (go him).

As he pushed the door open, the sound of rushing water greeted him.

From somewhere in the building's lower level, Miles yelled, "NO—turn it the OTHER way!"

"Miles?"

"Here, Seth. Be careful—a pipe broke and there's water all over the floor."

"Need any help?" Seth asked without thinking it through. What sort of help could he give, in his state?

"No man. I'll be a few minutes. Feel free to wait in the chapel."

Seth shivered at the idea, but the chapel was merely a spacious room with plush carpet and ornate mirrors decorating the walls and which, most importantly, did not contain a coffin. Seth took a seat at the back and noted how empty the front looked where a casket and flowers would normally be.

In the foyer, a clock ticked.

The central air turned on, ran its course, and shut off again.

From somewhere, a phone rang a few times and stopped.

Seth's belly did a starvation dance.

With a grunt, he pushed himself upright. He followed the sound of voices and found Miles and another man wrestling with a PVC pipe behind a wall in what looked to be an office. The water was an inch deep and had soaked their pant legs. Both men's backs were toward him.

Miles must have heard Seth approach. Through teeth gritted with effort, Miles said, "Seth, this is my boss, Grant Bogdan."

"Nice to meet you." Grant flicked his eyes Seth's way but remained focused on holding the pipe so Miles could wrap it in electrical tape in what Seth assumed was a makeshift washer.

"Need any help?" Seth asked, hoping the answer would be different now that he was here, but more hoping Miles would say they were almost finished.

"We've got it, but thanks, man. I have a pint of Flanning's in the mini fridge in my office if you're hungry."

Starving. And...Flanning's.

"Office is downstairs," Miles said.

"What's the flavor?"

Miles responded with an angry snort.

Whatever the flavor, Flanning's was worth a couple of stairs. The cows that sometimes strayed onto Miles's property made the milk in the most delicious ice cream Seth had ever tasted, his favorite flavor being peanut butter chocolate chunk. Yes, he was sure because he had tried samples of all twenty-two flavors. Seth hobbled down the hallway, pushed open the STAFF ONLY door and conquered another small flight of stairs.

He pushed open a second, heavier, metal door that also said STAFF ONLY. Something smelled...off. Like pickles burning. Or perfume going bad.

But, Flanning's.

Two doors were at the end of another short, tiled hallway. The mood in the lower level was more hospital, more laboratory. More stinky and horrible and goosebump-inducing. Seth's phantom foot ached from the exertion of the stairs, even though he didn't use it to get down said stairs since it was gone and hadn't helped him do anything since it got rolled over by a tow motor.

Seth yelled, "Which door?" but of course he got no response. He was in the dungeon of The Bogdan Funeral Home. Miles worked here. Monday through Friday. Yuck.

Seth considered the two doors before him and recalled a riddle about two doors—one leading to life and one leading to certain death—and two guards and how one of them always lied and one always told the truth. You had to pick which door to open, but if you picked the wrong one, BAM. Dead. Dead like whatever was making this horrible smell. And the riddle went like this: *What single question can you ask the guards to know which door to choose?* More importantly, which door has a mini fridge with the Flanning's ice cream? Seth could never get the riddle right when he tried to tell it.

"Eeeny meeny miny moe," he said, shoving open the door to his right before he lost his nerve.

Wrong.

The door had a spring action assist and swung open, revealing a stainless-steel table (empty thank God) and a disturbing tray of pliers, scissors, knives, and "S" shaped pins that made Seth's skin crawl. No mini-fridge—but the room was colder than the air-conditioned hallway. And the smell hit him like a rogue wave.

Seth tried to pull the door shut but was unable. He inched further into the lab to get better leverage. As he cleared the threshold, his crutch fell, and he had to let the door go to retrieve it.

A second stainless steel table came into view.

Chapter 9

The embalming room tipped sideways...tipped...tipped. No, it was Seth doing the tipping, the *falling*. He choked and hugged his crutch to his heart. Barely managing to keep himself upright, he leaned heavily on the crutch. All the oxygen disappeared. His mouth opened and closed with no satisfaction. OPEN. CLOSE. OPEN. CLOSE. No air. OPEN. OPEN. Finally, he realized he hadn't inhaled. He took in a bite of air and gagged, which gave him the presence of mind to crutch-walk backward and yank on the metal door while craning his neck, trying not to see and yet unable to tear his eyes away like a carnival gawker. The other embalming dude fixing the pipes with Miles—Seth lost the guy's name in the shocking scene before him—must have been *working* when the water pipe broke.

On the second table lay a mummified corpse of questionable sex and age, with a two-inch slice in the neck. From the spread flesh protruded a metal gadget and a black tube that spiraled off the table and ended an inch shy of a floor drain.

The human body was seventy-five percent water. That's what Seth learned in high school biology, and what he joked to himself when he was hungover, that he'd peed out all but five percent. But no. NO. This was what a body looked like without its seventy-five percent of H2O. Like a little kid, charred and shriveled. Why was it so brown?

And upon closer inspection, and once the room stopped tipping sideways, Seth made out that the corpse was a woman because her long, dark hair had suds in it, and was dripping into a sink of sorts, a space cut out of the stainless steel tabletop to catch the water and shampoo.

No, not shampoo. Dish soap. The bottle was on the table.

Oh, wait.

It was a man with long hair. Seth's body electrified with horror at what death and time had perpetrated against the male genitals. He could only resist the urge to cup his own balls protectively because he needed both hands to steady himself on his crutches.

Cremation.

Cremation would be the way for Seth. He decided in that instant. Or nuclear evaporation of his body. May he never end up on a stainless-steel embalming table.

"Seth, what are you doing in here?"

Miles, his khaki pants wet to his thighs, a wrench in one hand, glanced beyond Seth to the table. "My office is across the hall. Fridge is on the file cabinet…You good, man?"

Seth shook his head *no*. Not good.

Miles guided him out of the lab and back upstairs to the chapel, telling him, "One more step. That's it. You're almost there. Want that ice—"

"No. Hell no. How can you eat—ever?"

Miles gave a small snort. "Man's gotta eat, Seth. I'm almost done here. Give me five minutes, okay?"

Not like Seth had a choice. Miles was his ride. And his digs. And his priest or whatever you called it. And the man worked with grossness like that every day. The man ate breakfast and transitioned—bingo—to scooping organs out of dead bodies. The dude got hungry while "decorating" (his word) naked dead people. He ate lunch and returned to that cool stench and did not toss his cookies. And he didn't even drink alcohol or smoke weed.

Freakish.

Freakish as fuck. Seth wanted a bottle of something amber-colored. He'd take anything that would calm the prickly vines his nerves had become. As his mind came back online, he became aware of the fact that he was hyperventilating.

Miles appeared. "All set." He zeroed in on Seth and declared, "You're whiter than usual, my friend. You see a ghost?"

Seth rolled his eyes.

Miles's Jeep rocketed over the country roads blasting Christian metal music. The wind gusts cleared Seth's head and blew away the smell of death. White clouds. Blue skies. Fields of corn. Cows dotting Miles's property like moving boulders.

Hard to believe that on this perfect day a dude was stretched out on a tray getting the ultimate oil change and a last hair wash with dish detergent.

"How about a drink before dinner?" Miles offered. "Let's sit on the deck."

Seth could feel his nerves lurch at the prospect of booze. That Miles didn't say anything else was the only thing that kept Seth from bowing out of their arranged dinner/study. The man touched dead people. Yes, Seth knew that before, but it was more of a hazy idea, a pastel vision of what it might be like. Like dolls. Or those people-sized things they used to teach CPR. The thing on the table was insulting.

The two men sat on the deck in silence, petting the many cats as the sun folded into the tree line. A pitcher of tea sweated on the table, half gone. The whiskey was a quarter gone when Miles got up to prepare dinner. He had his hands on his hips. "What you saw today—it was a shell. Nothing more. What made that person a person is gone. Nobody likes to think about it, but we're all going to die, Seth."

"I'm not—"

"What? You're not going to die?"

"—hungry. I was going to say, 'not hungry.'" Seth stood to leave and took a couple of woozy steps before falling into a different chair. Keeping a hold of the bottle and using his crutches proved harder than he expected.

"Right. Well, I am hungry. A man's gotta eat. And a man's gotta work."

Seth pouted and absently played with the nearest cats while Miles worked on dinner. He'd planned on leaving as soon as the room stopped spinning, but the smells from the kitchen were too powerful.

Miles brought out warm, crusty bread and spiced olive oil. He set the board down with more force than was necessary. "What I don't understand is, for a guy who finds death so off-putting, why are you chasing it down?" He gestured to the bottle.

Seth swore under his breath and took another long pull all the while giving Miles the stink eye and not taking any bread, although the yeasty smell made him salivate.

"Well?" Miles asked.

"If you want me gone, just say so," Seth replied.

Miles sighed. "That's not what I'm saying."

"I'm creeped out. Dead bodies creep me out."

"In my experience, it's the live ones you got to worry about. Eat."

Seth barely nodded.

The dinner of Chicken Alfredo and bread sobered him enough to stay awake. Before the dinner, Miles took the bottle and replaced it with coffee, setting the cup down hard enough to tell Seth that there would be no arguing.

Later, Seth interrupted Miles's reading. "I don't get it. Why would anyone want to spend all day, every day in a room with...with...THAT?"

"With what?"

"Dead people."

Miles looked up but kept the book open in his hands. "You're one heartbeat away from *that*. We all are."

"I don't want to study anymore. Kick me out if you want."

Miles inhaled and gently closed the book. "Mind if I ask why?"

"I don't know," Seth said. But he *did* know.

Miles's words: *you're one heartbeat away* from the other side, so get your spiritual ducks in a row—was what Seth heard. His reaction was a deep sense of injustice. There were people who did not have time to get their ducks all teed up nicely before they were summarily, violently yanked out of life and turned into a naked raisin on Miles's embalming table.

"Is this anger about God? Or me?"

Seth shook his head. Either he didn't have enough liquor to engage with Miles or he had too much. Or maybe there was no perfect amount to make it easy to ask the question: Why was there so much tragedy in the world? Why did bad things happen to innocent people? Seth wanted to know, specifically: *How in the hell could God allow Ivy to—*

"I'm not going to kick you out, Seth." Miles interrupted.

Three days later, Seth's question about the origins of tragedy remained unanswered, but he won the figurative lottery, twice.

First was when he met Miles's prosthetist friend, or the limb fairy, as Seth thought of him.

And the second was the $250,000 settlement check from Green Spirit.

The super and Connor, the coffee-loving Green Spirit representative who had visited him in the hospital, delivered the first installment to Miles's house. Seth would have to sign a book-sized document to get the rest of the dough.

He couldn't say, "Give it here," fast enough.

As he held out a hand for the pen, Miles put a beefy arm in his way. "Hold up," Miles said. "Does this mean his medical bills are his responsibility from here on out?"

Seth hadn't thought of that.

Connor started talking, answering Miles's question, but Seth couldn't make heads or tail of what the man said. It felt like when politicians "answered" questions, talking in spirals on and on.

Miles looked to Seth and asked, "You following?"

Seth shrugged.

"Would you gentlemen like some tea?" Miles offered.

The four men moved to the large table on the deck. Seth knew serious talk when he heard it, even if he didn't understand all the legalese. But in true super fashion, Seth's boss made small talk, the same kind he used before making an abrupt tack into Seth's work performance. As Miles poured tea, the super mentioned he had not seen Miles at the golf course.

Miles shrugged and gave a half-hearted smile. "You enjoying being number one on the green, Bob? Don't get used to it."

"How about Monday morning?" The super asked.

Seth had a doctor's appointment Monday morning. Was that why Miles hadn't been golfing lately? Surely the man wouldn't give up golfing to ferry Seth around town? He had already given him a place to crash and meals and an A+ clawfoot tub. Seth knew, if the shoe were on the other foot, he would be like, *Miles, you gonna have to figure it out cause...golf. I got golf.* And with that, a small, squiggly, discomforting feeling awakened inside Seth. He squashed that feeling and focused on Connor.

Out of his briefcase Connor pulled one of those electric tablets and a little plastic doodad shaped like a pencil. With it he pointed to the screen. To Miles, he said, "Right here, it states that any and all medical bills that are a result of the work accident have been paid to date. The settlement check is well padded to accommodate future medical bills."

Miles and the super exchanged a lot of talk about attorneys and workers compensation, and although Seth tried to follow it, he was out of his league. They kept using the words *party* and *parties,* but nothing sounded fun. Nothing made sense. At one point he was certain they were discussing his private parts.

"NOW HOLD ON," Seth interrupted. "Repeat that, what you just said."

"If you die before the final settlement payout," Connor said, "the remainder of the money is forfeit."

"No, the other part."

"That *is* the other part." Connor swiveled the screen so Seth could see, but it didn't help.

"Green Spirit is assuming you don't have a will," Connor said.

Miles added, "They don't want the money tied up in probate if you don't live to receive it all. An intestate is someone who dies without a valid will."

There it was. Testicles. And probate sounded like something swingers did.

But Seth believed the super was a genuine, trustable dude. Miles, too. This Connor was on the slick side, but Green Spirit had done Seth dirty by taking his leg. The money was an apology. A damn big one, and he would accept it.

"If you're offering this much, he probably deserves more," Miles said. Seth heard that part. The ears of his mind perked up. *More?*

More money than this?

Connor started to tuck the check away. "We added the money we'd save on legal fees, plus a generous amount for future medical outcomes directly resulting from the amputation—which our consultants say is low. Their statements are on the affidavit on page—"

Miles raised a hand. "I'm reading it, thanks."

Connor picked cat fur off his pant legs. "If we go to court, we'll offer him far less." To the super, Connor said, "Tell him."

"Tell me what?" Seth asked.

The super leaned back, rubbed his bald head in that way he had of doing. "This is by far the largest payout Green Spirit has ever made for a work accident. Company legal counsel advised against this transaction."

Miles took a few more minutes with the text, nodded, and looked satisfied. "I normally would tell you to get your own lawyer, Seth, but I agree this is a *huge* voluntary payout. I think Green Spirit wants to pay you instead of their lawyers."

Seth whispered to Miles, "Should I ask for more?"

"With an amount of money this large, you can live comfortably off the interest. If you ask for more, they may rescind the offer, and you'll have to hire a lawyer. You'll have to wait for the courts to grant you a settlement. It could take months or years to get a payout. And the lawyers take their cut. You follow?"

Now he followed.

And signed.

And became richer than he ever imagined possible.

He tried to give Miles a thousand dollars. And a week later, tried to give another thousand to the limb fairy. Neither man would accept his money, which confused him.

The limb fairy, a Mr. Mitka, promised Seth he would, in a few weeks' time, receive the "miracle" of walking. First, the prosthetist sent him home with a shrinker sock, which lessened the phantom pain, illogically. Seth told the limb fairy he wore it "religiously"—all day and all night. For the minimum one hour a day he allowed his skin to breathe, because he knew that the sooner he shrank his stub, the sooner he'd get a new foot.

His efforts paid off. In five weeks, the swelling went down sufficiently, and the limb fairy rewarded Seth with his very own SACH foot, which made him think of Sasquatch.

Miles and Seth walked the property in Seth's new "foot," a cup with a pipe and a rubber foot with toes eerily the same size and shape of the ones Seth had lost. The limb fairy said it was a temporary prosthesis, but oh my, did it feel amazing. Seth could walk and swing his arms and feel like a man again. Against the limb fairy's advice to take it easy, Seth walked and walked, relishing what once he took for granted. That afternoon, he drank to celebrate but kept it secret from Miles, who had been in earshot when the limb fairy admonished Seth about interactions of alcohol with his newly prescribed pain medications. Now that he was re-learning to balance without crutches, he would hurt in different places, the limb fairy said. The meds were to be used sparingly.

Bah.

High in the trees, the cicadas added their songs to the crickets'. Their electric bug sound heralded the sweltering August heat, but this day was unusually mild. Seth strolled along the pathway in the woods, grateful for the ability to walk. Enjoying the feeling of sweat on his skin, the fluidity and freedom of walking, he circumvented the lake.

Who would have believed putting one foot in front of the other could be so wonderful? He never thought to be thankful for the ability to walk—until it was taken from him.

With no dinner and no study scheduled for that night, Seth was free to spend the whole night drinking in his zero-gravity chair by the light of the moon. He woke in that chair at two in the morning when a cat jumped into his lap. The sudden awareness of himself included the acid in his stomach, a full-to-bursting bladder, and an elephant standing on his head, digging in its toes. How the Kentucky hug could turn on him! He peed in the grass beside the front door, swaying like a metronome before stumbling inside and falling into bed, not bothering to remove his prosthesis.

The next morning, Monroe came to clean while Seth was still in bed. His wound stung, chafed by the prosthesis, no doubt. He hobbled to a stand, closed the bedroom door, and slurred a greeting. She answered in that cheery way of hers, and he could hear her soft singing as she moved about the living room and kitchen area.

Seth brushed his teeth and chugged two glasses of water. A shower was in order, but that would involve taking off the prosthesis. He could get it a little wet—rain and mud and such—but the prosthesis should not be immersed in water, and that included showering. Deodorant and a shave sufficed. Rather theatrically, Seth swung open his door and made a show of strutting and swinging his now-free arms to show Monroe his new self. She smiled warily and began loading his dishwasher.

"Notice anything different about me?" he asked.

"You shaved." Monroe suppressed a smile as she turned back to the sink.

Seth let out a gust of irritation.

"And you have cat fur on your shirt," she added. "Looks good on you."

Seth shook his head and left. He walked the trail into the woods, wishing Monroe would wash his feet with her long hair like the woman did for Jesus. Jesus had the babes. Seth had nightmares of Ivy and a closet of skeletons. Unfair. But as he wandered the woods and contemplated his good fortune at meeting Miles, the fresh morning air blew away the cobwebs of hangover.

He had an epiphany.

Smacking his forehead, he backtracked as fast as he could with his temporary prosthesis, wincing at the pain where it didn't flex like an ankle.

He flung open the door with the same extravagant flourish as before. "Monroe, I can do my own dishes now."

She turned to him. The golden cross necklace glinted in the sunlight streaming through the window. Her hands were buried in the bubble-filled sink.

He approached her. "Thank you for helping me these past few weeks. I know you're really doing it for Miles, but I appreciate the cleaning and your...." He waved his hand around as if he could pluck the right word from the air. *Hotness* was the word he didn't want to say. And it wasn't exactly what he meant, either. There was more. He searched his mind for it.

And latched upon, "...I appreciate the way you smile, even when you're doing shitty tasks, like dishes."

Monroe's face softened. "That's sweet of you, Seth, but I don't mind cleaning. It's honest work. And Miles is paying me lawyer's wages to do it."

There it was again. Miles the saint. Miles the embalming, cat-rescuing saint.

"Well...can I help?" Seth ventured.

"Sure."

Monroe washed and Seth dried. Together.

"I've been meaning to ask, Monroe, what are you studying in college?"

She lit up. "Business. I'm getting an Associate's degree mostly for the accounting classes. I want to open a cat cafe."

"Sounds like you've planned it out."

She chatted about her college classes and the cats and their odd or endearing behaviors. She smiled shyly when their eyes met or their arms touched because of the small kitchen area. A few suds got on Seth's hair, and she petted them away, with the same gentle strokes as he'd seen her do with the cats. A strand of her hair fell loose from her ponytail, and Seth decided it was time for boldness: he tucked the lock of hair behind her ear.

She didn't flinch or lean away. A smile played at the corners of her lips. They finished the dishes.

Chapter 10

Working alongside Monroe gave Seth an inexplicably wonderful feeling, like he had Thanksgiving dinner in his soul. It was more electrifying than being the object of Nanette's flirtatious attentions and more spiritual than walking in the woods. He sought out Monroe whenever she was at Miles's home and asked if he could help with the cats. The tables had turned. Seth cleaned cat dishes for Monroe, gave the cats baths, clipped cat nails, even (yuck) emptied the litterboxes.

One of Seth's favorite morning noises was the soft crunch of tires on the gravel driveway that announced Monroe's arrival. For that reason, Seth enjoyed his first cup of coffee on the chair outside his suite, hoping to hear that happy sound.

This morning, he had barely taken a sip when something else caused him to perk up his ears: a steady, pitiful meowing. He followed the cries to the toolshed.

When Monroe pulled up, Seth was on hands and knees using his best kitty voice to coax the cat out.

"Not again," she rolled her eyes. "Charcoal."

"How do you know?"

She jokingly scoffed. "How does a mother know her babies? Their meows. Plus, Charcoal likes to hide. Last week it was the wheel well of Miles's Jeep."

Seth waded a little further into the space between the flooring and the ground, still creaky from sleep. Rakes, shovels, chicken wire, tiki lamps, and various ceramic pots made it difficult to get far. Two glowing eyes peered out of the tool jumble.

"Come out, Charcoal," he called.

Monroe knelt beside Seth. The morning breeze brought her soap or perfume to his nose. The two of them tried every note of "here, kitty, kitty" and other feline-friendly petitions. The meows stopped, but the glowing eyes didn't budge.

"Coffee?" Seth asked, when it became clear Charcoal wasn't listening, even to her beloved caretaker.

"I'd love some."

They sipped coffee to the background "music" of Charcoal.

"Do you think she's stuck?" Seth asked.

Before Monroe could answer, Seth's phone jangled with an incoming call from Miles.

"Hey Seth, I apologize for the late notice, but I can't make it back to take you to your appointment."

"That's okay, Miles. Everything alright?"

On the other end of the line, he chuckled. "Everything's fine. I've got to stay for the plumber, is all. Hey, maybe Monroe could give you a lift?"

"Nah. I'll cancel." *Let's see…PT with a humorless drillmaster or the day with Monroe? Tough choice.*

After Seth ended the call, Monroe's phone sounded with a notification. She put it in her pocket and stood up. "Let's go," she said.

"Seriously? Miles texted you?"

"Yep."

"What about Charcoal?"

"Something spooked her. She needs time to settle down."

"What would spook her?" Seth scanned the property.

Monroe shrugged. "Dunno. Cats are skittish."

"That's why they have nine lives."

"Afterward, we can go to Flanning's," Monroe offered. "My treat for all the help with the cats."

Usually, the post-PT aches and pains caused Seth to hobble or limp to the reception area, but because of Monroe, he didn't let on about the screaming of his muscles.

"Still up for Flanning's?" she asked, looking like she had just stepped out of a lake. Running the few feet from the car into the office had soaked her good. Her hair clung to her face and neck, and her shirt had become transparent enough to be distracting.

"I don't mind a little rain," Seth said.

At Flanning's, they ordered sundaes and coffees. Monroe asked if they could eat outside at the picnic tables beneath the awning because the air conditioning was too cold.

Seth noted her goosebumps as he held the door.

They had the eating area to themselves. At the driest table, they huddled side by side and watched the thunderstorm, the drops percussive against the metal roof, the splashes reaching well inside the pavilion. In the pasture across the road, cows lowed and frisked, enjoying a break from the summer heat.

"This is the best ice cream I've ever had," Seth mused.

"Don't you and Miles come here often?"

"Yes."

Even when Monroe raised her eyebrows Seth didn't elaborate that the ice cream tasted better because he shared it with her. The shape of her cross pendant showed through the drenched fabric of her shirt. Seth did not allow his gaze to drop further, but maintained eye contact or stared off at the cows as if they were enthralling.

"What do you want to do?" Monroe asked.

"I don't know—dishes, cat chores?" He answered, assuming she meant after the ice cream.

"With your life, once you get on your feet."

Seth felt his mind go blank. Trick question. What on earth could she possibly mean, *do—when he got on his feet*? Seth was strictly a day-at-a-time guy. A survive-another-day guy. Even this, this ice cream with a pretty girl, was an alien experience. It was innocent and delicious and erotic (thank you, rain) all at the same time. Why should he focus on anything but this?

"Oh, I'm sorry. I didn't mean for it to come out like that."

She thought Seth's silence was about his foot.

He swallowed his lust, shook his head, and waved off her apology. "It's not that. I haven't given much thought to what's next. I know I can't stay in Huntsville forever, but I like the...area. I could see myself renting out the barn, if I can convince Miles." He fished for her reaction with that last bit and hoped she'd show excitement at the idea of him staying. But he also genuinely loved the hills and fields and the solitude.

"Don't you want to work?" she asked.

Not the reaction he'd hoped for. "I have enough money from my settlement."

She shrugged. "Still..."

Her face scrunched in confusion, possibly over his inclination toward sloth. Work, at least the kind he had experienced in his thirty-six rides around the sun, didn't give him joy or fill him with purpose. Work was something one *had* to do. Why would he work if he didn't need money?

"Don't you think you'll get bored?" she asked.

He looked earnestly at her. "Not with you around."

She rolled her eyes, but there was heat in her cheeks.

The rain stopped as they turned into Miles's driveway. The two muddied their already-wet knees as they peered beneath the tool shed to make sure Charcoal had let herself out.

"Meow...meow," came the response.

Either Charcoal had no interest in coming out or she was trapped between the ground and the subfloor.

"Charcoal...here girl." Monroe held a tube of something that smelled strongly of tuna. To Seth she said, "Cats can't resist these."

But Charcoal didn't come out. Her cries became more frequent and pathetic. Monroe left and returned with a broom. She taped the tube of cat treat to the end and pushed it under the shed.

"Ouch!" she scrambled back. A bee fluttered and fell from a welt on her forearm. She tweezed the stinger out. "Bees. Shit."

"The princess doth swear." Seth couldn't help himself.

Monroe growled. "Cats can get stung."

"That would explain why she's not coming out," Seth ventured. "She probably disturbed the nest." Seth's bee ordeal was fresh enough in his mind to make him wince.

Monroe looked thoughtful and frightened. "Be right back." She dashed to the main house and came back wearing too-big rubber waders, a rain coat, and a balaclava.

Seth tried to hold his face together, but the giggles erupted. At her indignant look, he rolled onto his back and belly-laughed until he cried.

"Unhelpful, Seth," she said through clenched teeth.

Rage made her even more beautiful.

"I'm sorry." He wiped the tears from his eyes. "It's just...the bees will find a way in. You know that, right?"

Her narrowed eyes said she didn't know that.

"I disturbed a nest, once. Bees get trapped in your clothes, and in their panic to get out, they sting you. They go for the face for some reason. Wearing that thing will only make them focus on your eyes and mouth. There's no way I was going to let you go under there dressed in that...but I shouldn't have laughed. I'm sorry, Monroe."

It took a few seconds for her face to soften. All the while Charcoal made sure she wasn't forgotten. "Meow, meow, meow, meow, meow..."

Tears welled in Monroe's eyes. "I can't leave her there till Miles gets home."

That did it. Saint Miles was not going to save the day this time. Bing-fucking-go.

"I'll get her out." Once Seth's pride tossed those words out, he instantly wished Miles would magically arrive home to stop him from having to follow through. He took a deep breath and listened for the sound of Miles's Jeep.

"...meow...meow...meow..."

What he could do was prepare himself properly. "Hold on a sec." It was his turn to stalk back to his suite, toss several gulps of bourbon down his throat, and saunter back, letting the booze fill him with I-don't-care.

"You just made yourself tastier, you know that?" Monroe crossed her arms and tried to look angry, but Seth could tell she worried for him. Reluctantly, she handed him a tube of kitty crack and gave him a kiss on the cheek. "Thank you."

"Don't thank me yet."

As Seth crawled lizard-like beneath the shed, he listened for buzzing. The adrenaline-powered rush of his blood and Charcoal's meowing forced him to stop and concentrate every few seconds. Gingerly, he lifted the rakes and shovels and shifted them, stopping to listen for bees before setting them down out of his way. As Seth pushed a roll of chicken wire aside, he caught the sound of buzzing.

He froze.

Monroe asked how it was going.

"This might take a while," he whispered, so as not to make the bees mad. Did talking make them mad? He didn't know. Why chance it? Of course, Charcoal had been meowing her fluffy head off, and she was still here, so maybe it didn't matter. Seth prayed that he might be able to pull off this cat rescue without becoming a depository for a nest's worth of bee venom. He asked God to tell him where to put his hand, when to stop moving, which way to drag himself toward Charcoal.

And he made it. Charcoal's "meow" was so close, Seth felt hot, kitty breath on his face.

"I got her!" Seth called out.

Pulling Charcoal out with him proved harder.

Nothing like dragging an unwilling, scratching, hissing, terrified cat by the scruff—backward over the exact (please no bees), *exact* route he had entered. She thrashed and contorted in his grip, raking his arms and face and neck. This was tough love, he decided. And it wasn't too far from hatred.

"Seth...?" Monroe called out.

He could not see her or bother to answer. If he let the blasted cat go, all would be for nought. As he backed closer and closer to the edge of the shed, light spilled in, allowing him to see the bees before hearing them. A handful darted around, sounding angry, but none had struck him, yet.

A screech told him the same wasn't true for Charcoal.

As he pulled her out and handed her off to Monroe, a sharp pain zapped Seth in the calf. Then another. A lance on his ear sent him running off like a canon. Monroe, too. She ran while clutching Charcoal to herself.

Seth, Monroe, and prisoner-Charcoal careened toward the pond, taking stings all the way. Even the muck didn't bother Seth, who thanked God he had his prosthesis on, which made running possible, unlike the last encounter with bees. At the last moment he removed the prosthesis and hurled it away, taking a sting for his trouble.

Rescue complete.

They sustained a handful of stings and spent the remainder of the day floating on rafts in Miles's pond, slopping baking soda paste onto their stings and immersing themselves over and over again into the soothing coolness of the water (except Charcoal, who Monroe tended to and kept in the shade in a dog-sized crate). Monroe dabbed antibiotic ointment on Seth's deepest scratches.

"This is an old one." Monroe pointed to the scar on Seth's wrist, the one he never looked at or thought about.

Seth gave no explanation. He looked away, hoping she'd let it go.

"This water is terrible for cuts," she said.

"But it's great for stings," Seth countered playfully, relieved she did let it go. They splashed each other and volleyed a beach ball back and forth from their rafts. He wanted this part of the day to last forever, but he knew it couldn't. Three o'clock was way past the time she usually stayed at Miles's. She had studying to do.

She thanked Seth again and gave instructions for checking on Charcoal as he walked beside her to her car. Her hand was on the car handle.

"I know what I want to do," Seth blurted.

She stopped and looked innocently up at him. "What?"

How could she not know he wanted to kiss her? How? Seth had a dance he did, with women, a choreography that served him well when his goal was hit and run. That dance would be unfamiliar to Monroe.

Without a technique, Seth locked up.

She smiled, got in her car. "Whatever it is you want to do with your life, Seth, if you show the same grit as you did with Charcoal, you'll be a rockstar."

The next morning Monroe came earlier than usual—and usually she only came every other day. Seth was glad he hadn't spent the night celebrating his rescue of Charcoal over a bottle of bourbon. With a steaming cup of coffee in his hand and his stump in a compression sock on a folding chair, he watched her car approach.

"Morning, Seth. How's Charcoal?"

"Good."

Monroe had a mischievous smile. She traced Seth's scabbed-over cuts with her finger. He looked up at her, at how the sun behind her put him in her shadow, her hair red at the edges from the light.

"Come inside, Seth." She kissed him on the lips this time. "I have something for you."

Now he wished he had his prosthesis. He had to use the crutches to follow her inside. She pulled a wrapped box out of her purse.

"Here."

Seth felt himself blush. Receiving gifts was not something he was accustomed to.

"Well, open it."

Inside was a bracelet made of black stones, some with green marbling. It had a decidedly masculine look and was tied with a piece of leather.

"The stones are Jasper...to keep you safe from bees and...everything."

He slipped it on and tightened it. "What will keep me safe from my feelings for you?"

She smiled, thinking he flirted. But it was true.

Because it was all he knew and he did want her, he kissed her mouth, tasting silk. As his hands began a reflexive, hungry trek down her neck and shoulders, he felt a stab of something—what was it? He shoved whatever it was down and focused on the delicious curve of her waist, her hips.

All he had been through, Seth would do it again to arrive at his moment, be in this room kissing Monroe. He let his imagination run. And his hands.

Someone threw open the front door, banged it hard enough to shake the entire barn and dislodge the wooden crucifix from the wall. It fell to the floor in two pieces. Both Seth and Monroe jumped and pushed off from one another.

Ivy stood in the doorway.

Chapter 11

Seth blinked and rubbed his eyes with the fleshy part of his palm.

Standing in his doorway was a wrinkled, dilapidated *version* of Ivy—her mother. Ivy's mother had grown out her hair, and—but for wrinkles and a slightly hunched posture—Dazey Wotterich was a replica of her daughter. In one fist she held a black cat, shaking it by the scruff. "These things are terrible luck." She dropped it unceremoniously and crossed the threshold as it dashed away.

Seth spread his hands out like seatbelts between Monroe and Dazey. It had been sixteen years since Seth had laid eyes on Ivy's mother.

Dazey's bottle-black hair thinned into wiry points like singed paint brushes. Her ink-lined, bug eyes ranged over both him and Monroe. After all these years, to have this maternal nightmare stand before him in tight, holey jeans and leather boots, braless in a plain white t-shirt that was more of a tissue—Ivy's mother was even more ugly than he had remembered.

Dazey's gaze dropped and paused on Seth's prosthetic foot. She pursed her lips. "Ivy told me you were damaged. Not gonna lie, that's karma if I ever saw it. And you got off easy compared to what she got—" Dazey locked eyes with Monroe. "Who the hell are you?"

Monroe stepped out from behind Seth's outstretched arms. "I'm the—I'm...none of your business. Don't shake the cats."

There was a three-way silent showdown where time crawled. Dazey settled her glare from Seth to Monroe and back to Seth, where it remained decidedly longer, as if she were piecing together a puzzle.

"This is *not* your girlfriend?"

Seth took one of Monroe's arms and guided her around Dazey and toward the door. "We'll talk later, Monroe."

"Monroe?" Dazey bellowed. "As in Marilyn? Oh, *please*."

Monroe stopped and gathered the broken crucifix. With her eyes on the pieces, she breathed, "Rude." Then she met Dazey's challenging stare, but Monroe was significantly shorter than the older woman, so she had to crane her neck.

Dazey gave a sideways glance to Seth, and he knew he'd better dispatch Monroe before Dazey did, so he hustled her out the door and barely jumped back before Dazey slammed it closed, even harder than she'd thrown it open.

Like a crazed linebacker, she rushed him, pinning Seth to the wall and pressing her cupped hand against his neck, choking him. With her foot, Dazey rammed his balls hard enough to double him over, had she not held his neck.

He grunted, yanked his head away, and felt a burning sensation on his neck as her fingernails raked bloody tracks into the skin.

"Nice to see you." He doubled over and cupped his balls.

"You never visited her."

Seth was sober, and the adrenaline did not feel adequate for this moment of reckoning. He wanted to wave a magic wand and disappear this woman. He blinked, hoping she was a hallucination.

But...no.

Dazey stood before him in Miles's guesthouse, not at all mythical or dreamlike. Her lipstick had smeared when she wiped a hand across her mouth, drawing a reddish slash on her cheek and teeth, which were presently bared.

"You never answered her letters," she pressed.

Because her daughter was a monster.

That a mother would side with her daughter, Seth could understand. The Dazey Wotterich he knew was an absentee-mom biker-chick with the maternal tenderness of a crustacean.

This woman was a new creation, to use some of Miles's Jesus language, but not *good* new. Bad new. Very bad. Dazey was a harbinger.

On the horizon was cold revenge—sixteen years' cold.

Dazey strutted the short length of the kitchen-living area, peeked into Seth's bedroom, out the sliding door, and finally plopped onto the sofa. She slammed her black harness boots onto the coffee table, smashing the television remote and popping out the battery. "Oops." She cupped a hand to her mouth.

Could he take her on? Dazey was trespassing. She had broken in. Did he have the physical strength to best this woman who could, theoretically, be a grandmother, hand to hand?

Bingo, if this little meet and greet had happened *before* he lost his foot. The months of inactivity and—let's face it, lethargy and—let's face it some more, drinking—had done him no favors. He felt as insubstantial as her t-shirt.

"Still can't get a word in edgewise with you, Seth," Dazey stretched one tattooed arm on the sofa back. "I told Ivy not to trust the silent type. Too bad it was that other kid who bought it and not you."

Seth could barely believe the tears he felt stinging his eyes, would not have believed it—if Dazey had not been blurry because of them.

"You're fucking crying? Would you have cried if it was my Ivy, eight feet under the ground? I don't think so." Dazey chucked a coffee mug at Seth's head.

He ducked, and it shattered on the wall behind him.

She didn't know, and he wasn't going to tell her coffin holes were six feet deep, not eight. Seth had done a short stint working for a cemetery. Thirty minutes with a back hoe, and the job was done. *Six feet under*, as the saying went. As it went for Seth's friend, Woods. Because Woods couldn't leave (ever, again), it felt right for Seth to be where Woods was buried, especially in the years after high school when others their age had gone off to college, and Ivy had been sent to prison.

Dazey patted the space beside her on the couch, as if Seth should come sit next to her and they'd have a talk. From her jeans pocket, she produced a vaping pen and sucked deeply on it.

"What? Don't tell me you quit? Pot's not a crime anymore. Well, for Ivy it is, but voting's a crime for Ivy." She gave him a sharp sideways look. "And I blame you."

Seth did not join her on the sofa. The past froze his mind and paralyzed his body. It was no revelation that Dazey blamed him for her daughter's sentence. Seth's testimony was key in the prosecution's case, and Ivy blamed him, too. She had written Seth as much before he changed his address and did not leave a forwarding.

Dazey took a second hit on her pen and laid her head on the sofa back. With her eyes closed, she murmured, "Ivy's going to kill you, Seth. You know that, right?"

He did. Know that.

A knock on the door startled him.

Dazey didn't lift her head.

Seth feared it was Ivy. But the knock was…well, a knock. And a polite one at that. Monroe? Yes, and Miles. He wore a black suit, white shirt, and a grey tie. The trainers on his feet didn't match. He must have thrown them on to walk over. He also wore a deep frown, the likes of which Seth had not yet seen.

In one beefy hand he held the pieces of the broken crucifix.

From behind him, he heard Dazey rise from the couch. "You must be the sugar daddy," she said.

Monroe's eyes narrowed.

Miles was a statue. "I am the owner of this house," he said.

"Well, I regret to inform you that you have a cat infestation."

Miles's face scrunched up, like he smelled something bad. To Seth he said, "This your mom?"

"Oh, *please*," Dazey said.

"Are you his guest?" Miles countered.

"Yes," Dazey said.

"No," Seth said. "This is my ex-girlfriend's mother."

"Oh," Miles said. He shot a stern, magisterial look at Dazey. "We don't hurt cats, here."

In a sing-song, mocking voice, Dazey repeated, "We don't hurt cats, here." To Monroe, "Are you for real? You went and tattled like a little baby, that I hurt your cat?" She lowered her voice. "I held it by its scruff, just like its mama would. You'd know that if you knew anything about being a mother." Dazey's throat seemed to close off. Her eyes glazed and she screamed, "Nobody knows pain like Dazey fuckin' Wotterich, thanks to *him*." She sprang forward, pointing at Seth, her finger inches from his face.

It was now or never for Seth. "Leave, Dazey."

She didn't move.

"You heard the man." Miles gestured at her with the broken cross.

She stared at the crucifix as if seeing it for the first time. Coming back to herself, she blinked, dropped her accusing finger, and shook with sobs.

"Miss Dazey," Miles softened as he approached her, "Whatever you have suffered, the Lord Jesus knows it. He loves you. He—"

"DON'T YOU DARE GIVE ME THAT GOD BULLSHIT."

Miles halted, fixed his eyes on her and spoke in what felt like a whisper. "All I have to give you, I give you. Call it what you want."

"I call it bullshit."

"Now I know you're upset, but—"

"Fuck you. And your god."

Miles took a deep breath. "Miss Dazey, I'm asking you—nicely—to leave."

"And I'm telling you to fuck off. I'm talking with Seth, and I'll stay till I'm done."

Miles's demeanor changed.

Monroe glanced at Miles and cringed.

He crossed the living room in two of his linebacker strides, grabbed the Bible off the coffee table, and held the book to Dazey's face, shaking it.

"Ooooh, I'm so afraid of your big, fat book." But for the first time, she eyed the door.

Miles theatrically made as if to check a wristwatch. "Well, looky here, it's time for a come-to-Jesus meeting."

Dazey crossed her arms over her chest and widened her stance.

Miles opened the book, "The book of Leviticus, chapter one..." He didn't read like when he studied with Seth, and he didn't begin in John or even Genesis. Miles added no emotion to the text, but droned out the words in a bored, authoritative lecture. "...the Lord said...bring the blood...splash it against the altar..."

Minutes elongated.

"...skin the burnt offering..."

Minutes of loud, toneless reading.

"...slash it to pieces..."

Chinese water torture with a Bible.

Monroe backed quietly out the open door and didn't shut it. Seth watched her walk across the gravel toward the main house, shaking her head (and laughing? –hard to tell). Seth wanted to leave, too, but it was because of him Dazey was here. Miles slowed his reading pace but articulated each word, even louder. "THE PRIESTS SHALL ARRANGE THE PIECES...THE HEAD...THE ENTRAILS..."

Dazey thunked her boots on the hardwood, adding to the din.

Miles read and read, without so much as a glance up from the text. Five minutes' more droning.

A battle of wills.

Until Dazey reached some critical mass of frustration or boredom and swaggered out the door, slamming it and shaking the walls again.

The silence was...what Seth might call holy. The most churchlike moment of his life to that point. More reverent than Woods's funeral or the stuffy, stained-glass Sundays he could barely recall from his childhood. In the glorious absence of Ivy's mother (and Miles's reading), Seth wanted to break out into song, to sing something cruel and loud. Ludo's "Love Me Dead" came to mind.

"The Word is *sharp*," Miles said, mostly to himself. He set the book on the couch arm, folded his big self into the small couch, and grinned mischievously. "...sharper than a two-edged sword, which I just used to prod that...*woman* out of my house."

Seth joined Miles, plopping into the cushions on the opposite side of the couch. They listened to the crunch of boots on gravel, the motorcycle revving, until there was no sound of her. She must have coasted down the driveway in neutral when she had arrived because her bike was loud.

"Interesting, what you did there," Seth said.

"I had to get creative." Miles touched the book.

"Sorry about the cross-thingy," Seth said. "I'd like to fix it."

Miles handed it over and thanked Seth. All traces of Miles-the-weirdo-preacher vanished. Seth did not like that version of Miles, but he was glad to be rid of Dazey.

"Should we expect to see her again?" Miles asked.

"I hope not," he answered. *But it's not her I'm worried about.*

Ten minutes later, Miles left for work. Seth walked over to the big house to find Monroe, but she had gone.

Usually, he enjoyed having the property to himself, but not today. Every time a car drove by on the country road, Seth froze and listened for the sound of tires on the gravel. With the garage door open so he could listen, he fixed the wooden cross with Gorilla Glue and held it together with clamps while it dried. As he worked, his mind raced.

Ivy wouldn't make a grand but stupid entrance like her mother had. She would surprise him. Like sixteen years ago, the epic surprise of Seth's life. He had vowed never to be blindsided like that again.

All day long, Seth jumped at the sound of trusses settling or even cats meowing. When the air conditioning ticked off, Seth froze and listened, scanning the nearest window or doorway trying to see Ivy before she saw him. He wasted the afternoon absently petting cats and ruminating or searching the house for Ivy, hidden under a bed or in a closet. The ache of hunger and the chafing of his prosthesis made him wish he was in a dark bar somewhere far, far away. Instead, he grabbed a bag of pretzels, a six-pack of beer, and the whiskey bottle and dropped into the zero-gravity chair. He knew he was about to numb himself silly with liquor, nature, and cats. "To hell with it," he said to himself and guzzled straight from the bottle. He removed his prosthesis and allowed his chafed skin some needed air. As soon as the urge to pee hit him though, he remembered how much of a pain in the ass it was to use the crutches, which were inside the house. Seth hopped inside and said a thank you to God and to karma that he didn't lose his balance and eat floor.

Every time he got up to grab more food, he felt imprisoned by his missing foot.

Imprisoned.

Jailed.

Prison.

Ivy.

She would come.

Of course she would. No way had Dazey come on her own. Ivy told her mother where Seth was and sent her. The gig was up. Being drunk was probably not Seth's best idea. Intoxication impaired his reasoning and dulled his ability to parse threats. Because he and Woods had been wasted that night, they didn't see the danger signs until it was too late. Not seeing the signs was Heywood Johnson's—Woods for short—last mistake.

Seth alone had walked away that night, alive and able to make more bad decisions. Like this one: he tipped back the bottle.

Chapter 12

The first thing Seth noticed upon waking at three a.m. was the air on his face—air that, while refreshing and cool, should not be there. Also, a cat licked itself at the foot of his bed, Peaches the disheveled calico, if his eyes could be trusted. The sliding glass door was open, both the glass and screen doors, and the sheer white curtains billowed out into the room like ghosts.

Explained the cat.

But what could explain the open door?

Seth had drunk himself silly, but not so silly that he would forget to close the door. No amount of alcohol could make him *that* careless. He specifically recalled closing the sliding door and locking it, and even wishing for blackout curtains on the doors so the sun wouldn't claw at his eyes, which he knew from experience would be dry as deserts.

The next thing Seth noticed was that his prosthesis was not resting against the wall in the corner nearest the bed. Hadn't he set it there when he swapped it out for the crutches last night?

As frantically as his crutches allowed, Seth ransacked every room of the guest house, every closet and cabinet, the hamper, the bathtub. He checked the area outside the sliding door, in case he had dropped his foot in the grass. Could the cats have gotten it? Would they?

As the morning minutes ticked by and the fuzziness of sleep burned off, a sinking clarity replaced Seth's befuddlement.

Which was confirmed when his cell phone rang with a call from Miles.

It was the flies darting all around the mailbox that got Miles's attention as he left for work. The red flag was raised, but Miles knew he hadn't placed anything in the box for the postal carrier.

"So I opened it...Only reason I didn't puke is on account of my job. One of the cats, probably Lavender—"

(*Probably?*)

"—was stuffed into the mailbox. And there's more, but I gotta go. I'm the only director here, and we have two funerals today. We'll talk when I get home," Miles said.

"Wait, what about if Monroe comes—what do I say?"

"Nothing. Keep quiet. I brought Lavender to work."

"Ew."

"I had a grocery bag. Listen, Monroe was just there yesterday. I don't think she'll come by, but check around the property in case. I don't want her to find anything like what I found." Miles said.

"My prosthesis is gone."

"You sure?"

"Pretty sure. The door was open when I woke up."

Miles swore. It sounded strange coming from him. "I'm calling the cops."

"No...I can still get around on the crutches. I'll look everywhere, I promise." Seth assured Miles he'd scour every place Monroe would go, and when Miles returned from work, they could account for all the cats.

"It's not just about the cats, Seth. People who abuse animals are capable of—"

"I know what they're capable of. *Please.* Don't call the cops."

"You just make sure, man. Monroe loves those cats," Miles said.

Oh, Seth knew how much she loved those cats. He had the scars to prove it.

"And I *am* calling the cops," Miles added.

"What?! No! Maybe someone else ran Lavender over and put her in the mailbox for safekeeping. We don't know for sure."

"Brother, she stole your prosthesis. Do you have any idea how much those things cost?"

Losing that thing cost Seth his mobility—that was what he knew. But he was more disturbed that she broke in while he was sleeping to steal it—that she broke in and did nothing more.

The crutches put the *pain* in painstaking as Seth scoured Miles's property looking for (and hoping not to find) more dead cats. He checked the cat hutch, the deck, searched the area between the guesthouse and main house and every other place on the property Monroe might go. He began counting cats off in his mind as he saw them, but truthfully, he didn't know the names of some of the shy ones. They were like birds to him. Or squirrels. Did he even know how many cats there were?

Not a chance.

Seeing Monroe play with her cats—the joy the spry and moody critters brought her—well, it was contagious. And thanks to Seth, one of her furry darlings was dead. Seth's good deed with Charcoal had just been cancelled. He had better memorize her kiss because it would be the only one he ever got.

And he didn't have his prosthesis anymore.

That gut-wrenching, rage-dialing thought—that he no longer had his prosthesis—was what decided him on drinking. Today's libations would be taken on higher ground. Seth wanted to face the road, to face everywhere, all at once. Since that was not possible because Seth was not a housefly with compound eyes, he decided the second-best option would be to station himself on Miles's deck. By the time Seth had finished combing the property for dead cats, it was after lunch. He dragged a chair to a spot where he could scan the road and most of the property. What a stunt it was, Seth pulling the metal chair without his prosthetic foot for balance. He held onto the deck railing and hopped, tugging the chair along inch by inch. By the time he got it where he wanted it, his arm had a pincushion's worth of splinters and he was exhausted.

And parched.

He parked himself in his chair, gulping some hair-of-the-dog. The patio was the best place to see cars enter the driveway. The sunshine, the birds and frogs and cats—and the right amount of alcohol in his blood—lulled Seth into a fuzzy peacefulness.

Every time he had to grab another beer from the fridge, he was reminded of his missing prosthesis. He drank because he was bitter, and he drank because Miles would be home at some point and would ask questions. With anyone else, Seth could lie. But with Miles? After all the Jesus talk? *The truth shall set you free* and *blessed are the truth-tellers* and all that jazz. Miles's convictions had wormed their way into Seth and made him question what was up and what was down.

Several beers and some Maker's Mark sloshed inside his belly when the cop car pulled into the driveway.

Argh. Miles.

Same cop, he could tell by her tattoos.

"Mr. Olivern, I didn't expect to see you here." She took impossibly long and authoritative strides, a walk he envied and might have considered attractive if he could erase the uniform and clothe her in a skimpy bikini with those tactical instruments strapped around her bare waist.

He made a half-hearted effort to rise, but the hand he wanted to use for leverage held the bottle. He set it down with a thunk and pulled himself unsteadily upright.

"Hello," he nodded with his best good-boy face. "I'm Miles's guest."

"Yes, he told me." She leaned against the railing, her back to the driveway. "Miles also said you got some fucked-up enemies. My words, not his."

Of course, the sainted Miles didn't swear around the ladies. The cop liked Miles. Seth could tell by how dreamily she said his name and how her hand drifted from her firearm and onto her belly. What was up with Miles? Good guys were supposed to finish last. Certainly Woods, the goodest guy Seth had ever known—his saintliness had done him no favors.

"...Mr. Olivern? Yoo-hoo....Earth to Mr. Olivern."

"Oh, sorry."

"What can you tell me about this..." She checked her notebook. "Dazey Wotterich?"

"Nothing."

"Nothing? That's not what Miles said." The cop pulled a chair over, easy, like it was a piece of plastic. Seth glanced at his red palms full of splinters.

"Mr. Olivern, I know you don't think I'm on your side, but I am. Miles said your prosthesis was stolen. I'd like to help you get it back, but I need you to help me help you."

Seth snorted.

The cop made a you're-testing-me smile.

"You don't catch the shmart ones," Seth slurred and hiccupped.

"We caught your ex-girlfriend, didn't we?"

She knew about Ivy. Blasted cops. Always knew more than they let on. Had she read about the trial? Whatever. She already knew all she needed to know, what everyone knew or thought they knew about him and Ivy.

She gave Seth a steely stare. "What happened to you? I read the Affidavit. You were confident and articulate—for a kid. You had a scholarship to a good school. Should you have been there that night? No. Hell, no. But cut yourself some slack. Your brain wasn't finished developing." She patted his shoulder. "Don't shut out the people who want to help you."

Seth's prosthesis was long gone, either at the bottom of Miles's lake or in a landfill somewhere. Ivy didn't dick around. This cop was like all the others, detectives who had used Seth to get Ivy arrested but were of no help when she was out on bail, like when Ivy stole the dried flowers off Woods's grave and put them in Seth's car. She lit them on fire, but because there were no fingerprints and no proof (like anybody had doubts), Seth was out a car. That might have been the moment Seth knew, when it came to Ivy, he was on his own.

And this cop, no matter how pretty or how much she tried to use her verbal judo to get Seth's cooperation, was not on his side.

Seth played his favorite card. He shut his mouth.

The cop eventually left him alone. He watched her inspect the property, probably looking for clues she would not find. She got in her cruiser and left.

Miles returned home earlier than usual.

Good thing Seth had the foresight to put his empty beer cans in the recycling bin and put away the whiskey. From the deck overlooking the pond, he waved, but Miles's footsteps dragged, and his shoulders drooped in tiredness. He handed Seth an envelope smeared with mud and maybe blood. "That woman's deranged," he said.

Except Miles thought it was Dazey who was deranged.

"What's it say?" Seth asked but made no reach for it. He absently crushed the can in his hand and became aware when beer ran onto his fingers.

"I don't know. Your name's on it, not mine."

Seth guzzled what remained of the beer, took the paper, and touched the holes where Lavender's canines had been used like staples. Without looking at Miles, he slurred, "I'm sorry about Lavender."

"You're wasted, aren't you?"

"A little." Seth hiccupped.

"Well, open it," Miles ordered.

Seth opened it. The familiar, loopy girl-writing made his mouth dry up.

Seth, this is what a letter looks like. We write them to people, especially people who are in prison. When someone in prison writes and asks you to write back, this is what you do unless you are a complete asshole, which you obviously are. Clearly you have never met one of these before, because IN 16 YEARS YOU NEVER ONCE SENT A LETTER BACK!!! How many times did I write? Never mind that it's your fault I was there in the first place.

Your cat scratched me when I tried to get it to deliver this letter. They eat cats in Japan. - Ivy

Over Seth's shoulder, Miles also read. "Dogs," he said. "They eat dogs in China."

"Ivy can justify anything," Seth replied.

"Sixteen years?" Miles asked. "What's that about?"

So, the cop knew about Ivy, but Miles didn't.

Where to begin?

Miles had taken Seth in and shown him kindness. More than anyone had in a long time. Since Woods. And look what Miles got for his generosity? He didn't deserve this, and neither did Monroe. Seth considered asking Miles to sit, maybe pour each of them two fingers (to start) of bourbon, and confess the events that plagued him night and day for sixteen years.

For all of two seconds, Seth considered it.

Instead he said, "I made some bad choices when I was young, before my brain was finished developing." (*Thank you, pretty cop.*)

"You don't say."

"My ex-girlfriend..." Seth waved one arm dismissively. "...she was pretty."

"Pretty?"

Seth shrugged. "I saw signs that she was messed up in the head, but I ignored them."

"Hmmm..." Miles took a deep breath. "With a mom like that, your ex had it rough as a kid. Hurt-people hurt people, you know."

"Oh, I *know*."

"It doesn't excuse bad behavior, but what Ivy and Dazey need is Jesus."

Seth rolled his eyes. "Bad behavior? *Bad behavior?* You don't even know what she did."

"I don't have to know."

"Why can't you hate them like I do?" He knew the booze had loosened his tongue.

"Part of you doesn't hate them, Seth."

"Whatever, man." Seth turned his head and retched over the deck railing onto the dahlias. Shit timing, he thought, as he wiped the back of his mouth with his hand.

"I can't talk to you when you're like this." Miles strode off and slammed the door.

Seth skulked off to the guest house.

In the middle of the night, Seth screamed himself awake, his nightmare more vivid than ever before. The details of sixteen years ago came back to him as he lay pinned to his bed like a bug shot through with a needle. He recalled the smell of Woods's sweat, the suffocating darkness in the cramped chest freezer, the last swig of beer they shared nonchalantly before the boys realized how bad things were going to get.

Miles must have heard because there was a knock on the door and Miles was on the other side, asking if he was okay.

"Trying to sleep," Seth growled.

Miles used his key to enter. "You sure?"

"Go away." Seth covered his face with his blanket.

Miles sat on the edge of the bed, and the whole thing felt very childlike, very Peter Pan with Miles holding a gilt-edged book and asking whether Seth would mind him reading? It was how he put himself to sleep when times were tough, Miles said. If Miles believed a bedtime story could work some sort of religious voodoo and turn Seth into something good, he would be sorely disappointed.

Seth thought Miles was a whacko if he was entirely honest.

But he let him read his holy book. The man had done him only kindness, after all, and Seth planned to repay Miles for his generosity in the only way he could: by hightailing it out of there as fast as his one foot would allow. Come morning, Seth would leave.

Chapter 13

SETH CRUSHED AND THREW his paper missives across the living room of Miles's guesthouse with ever-increasing annoyance. Writing a goodbye letter was the least he could do in order not to be a shit, but it was impossible to come up with what to write. His heart got all melty and uncomfortable no matter what order the words took, and they didn't reflect his feelings. *Words don't do it justice* took on new meaning.

His initial attempt: *Miles, At first I thought you were a whack job like all the other religious people I met over the years, but...*

Then he tried: *Miles, I always thought Jesus freaks were no fun, but you have a surprising sense of—*

His last effort: *Somehow you made a million-year-old book interesting, and the burgers were the best—*

Ivy was right about one thing: Seth sucked at penning letters. Later, Seth would write. He'd get himself settled in a new place in a galaxy far, far away and he would be inspired to pen his true and honest thoughts, maybe even tell Miles about Ivy. Monroe, too. He would tell her that ice cream in the rain was his favorite thing.

With Seth's bank card, pre-loaded with the backlog of Green Spirit settlement payments (that would continue to pay out every two weeks until who-knew-when), he had options he never had before. Like ordering an Uber.

Seth tidied his guesthouse, feeling nostalgic (and irritated, as it was more difficult without his prosthesis) as he put the dishes away. A last look out the back door was all he allowed himself. Getting in and out of the zero gravity chair with only the crutches was a pain in the ass, so he opted to stand by it one last time, cataloging everything wonderful—the way the sun cut bars through the trees, the cottonwood bitties swirling in the light, the cats chasing one another or laying in the little circle pillows they made when they curled in on themselves.

His possessions consisted of a duffel bag with clothing and toiletries, a phone charging brick, his stainless-steel camp flask full of whiskey, two bottles of water, and a box of peanut butter granola bars. He left his camp supplies bins in the closet with the rolled-up rugs. He had money now. As he walked out the door, Seth touched the wooden cross he had glued back together. No harm, no foul.

A car turned into Miles's driveway—the Uber was quicker than he expected. But...no. His heart twisted at the sight of Monroe's car.

"What are you doing?" she stepped out, frowning.

"I'm going...out for a bit—er—for a while."

Her eyes narrowed.

Did she know about Lavender yet? Surely Miles told her. If she knew, then the right thing for Seth was to give Monroe his condolences. If she didn't know, then the right thing to do was get the hell out without mentioning whiskers or tails or meows of any kind.

He regretted drinking too much last night.

Monroe advanced, searching him. Because he leaned on the crutches, his hunched back put his face at the same height as hers.

She knew about Lavender.

"Monroe..." Seth didn't know what to say.

"You're leaving, aren't you?"

He swallowed and managed to nod. Something caught in his throat. Words. Words caught in his throat.

"Without saying goodbye—why?"

He shrugged and choked out, "I'm Irish?"

Monroe bit her lower lip. A storm brewed behind her eyes.

Seth tried for levity. "Irish goodbye? Ever heard—"

"Keep your jokes, Seth." She rolled her eyes.

"I've been a burden."

"Says who—you? Miles deserves better, and you smell like a bar."

Seth's hands tingled. Magnets in his soul pulled him toward Monroe. He envisioned dropping the crutches and wrapping her in a bear hug, picking her up off the ground and kissing her cheek. He wanted one last smell of her hair.

Instead, he threaded his right hand through the crutch and extended it to shake. "Bars don't smell too bad. I kinda like them."

Monroe let out a frustrated sigh. "Is this about that woman? Miles asked me to stick around after work today. What happened?"

He gave up on the handshake. "You don't know?"

"Know what?" she asked.

"About...about..." (He waited for her to say it: *Lavender*.)

"About what?"

The Uber car pulled into the driveway. Maybe Jesus *was* looking out for Seth. "I gotta go. It's been nice knowing you, Monroe. Real nice. And I'm sorry. I am."

She frowned.

"You'll understand. Later. I mean, when I'm gone."

"That's it?" She grabbed one of his crutch bars and stopped his momentum, swinging him around and taking him swiftly down onto the driveway. "Oh, gosh, I didn't mean to..."

Seth looked at her. The sun made Monroe into a black silhouette, the kind they used as pictures, before actual pictures. Her necklace was so close he could see the etching on the silver cross, block letters: MON-ROE. He squinted at the brightness and the pain in his hip that had taken most of the impact. Shame boiled up, shame at being knocked over by the pixie-sized Monroe.

She tried to grab his wrist and assist him. The Jasper bracelet dug into his flesh, then released, the leather string snapping, the stones making rain-like pings on the gravel.

"Oh, shit," Monroe said absently. Then, "The princess doth swear." She extended a hand this time, to help him rise.

There it was: pity.

Didn't she get it? The one thing he couldn't stand from her was pity. "Get lost, Monroe. I can get up by myself."

In the side mirror of the Uber that smelled of air freshener, Seth watched Monroe's reflection get smaller and smaller. She stood in the driveway, not waving. He had been shitty to her, and she didn't even know the full extent of the shittiness yet. It was better to be gone before her anger turned to tears over Lavender.

It was best to forget Monroe altogether, actually.

First stop, even before the hotel: the limb fairy's office. Although Seth wasn't due for his prosthetic check-up for two weeks, the office was open, and money could get him practically anything—even a new prosthesis.

"I'm here for a replacement foot," he told the receptionist.

Her eyes widened. She looked Seth up and down and pursed her lips, click-clacked on the keys of her laptop and made small, judgmental noises as she looked at whatever was on her screen.

"Hmmm...hmmm..." She ducked her lips and swished them to the side. With a flourish, she took a piece of stationery and scribbled a figure. "This is assuming your insurance covers the office visit." She pushed the paper toward Seth.

"Eighteen thousand dollars!" Seth slammed his hands on the reception counter. The crutches fell and so did he when he tried to catch one, but he braced himself by leaning heavily forward, his face inches from the woman's.

From the back offices, Mr. Limb Fairy appeared. "Hi...Seth?"

"Your secretary says a new foot will run me eighteen K because I lost my other one. No way it cost eighteen K."

"That's right. It cost you nothing, but a flexible transtibial prosthesis does run about twenty thousand dollars if you include the visits for fittings. What happened to the one I gave you?"

"Stolen."

"Oh, no. I'm sorry. Where's Miles?"

When Seth hesitated, Mr. Limb Fairy guided Seth into his office, told the receptionist he would be unavailable for a few minutes, and closed the door.

"What happened?" he asked.

Seth told him about Dazey and Ivy (the short version) and that he believed the Jesus thing to do would be to leave Miles and the cats because it was him Ivy wanted. Miles was a friend, and Seth didn't want to see all that Jesus-kindness repaid with harm. (Seth wasn't positive, but the limb fairy gave off the same Jesus vibe that Miles did, and he didn't miss the limb fairy's slight smile at the name of Jesus.) Seth added some flattery on how hard it must be to make such expensive small appliances and finished with, "I know you already did me a solid, and I'll pay for the replacement, but eighteen thousand? You got any coupons?"

"Seth, I'm not charging you. God has blessed me—"

Bingo.

"—and I want to pay it forward."

Seth thanked the limb fairy and used his real name, Mr. Mitka, but it felt strange on his tongue. The limb fairy instructed him to make an appointment for a fitting and handed the receptionist his file. He shook Seth's hand, and Seth felt like a VIP. He had marched into the office without an appointment, and got seen by the doctor (prosthetist, not doctor, the limb fairy corrected, but Seth couldn't pronounce that).

Now, the receptionist looked at Seth with respect as she addressed him, "Mr. Mitka would like you back for the fitting in three weeks."

"Three weeks?!"

She sighed ever so slightly. "What day of the week is good?"

"Any. The first available. And can you call me if it comes in sooner?"

She said she would, but Seth didn't believe her.

For his temporary living situation, he chose the Eastbridge Inn because it had an indoor pool, washers and dryers, a little store with munchies, complimentary breakfast, free Wi-Fi, and computers in the lobby.

"How much for three weeks?" He asked the bright-eyed desk clerk.

She reminded him of Nanette, but younger and innocent like Monroe. "Let's see…" She began typing. "Do you want a room near the lobby? Or the pool?"

"The pool, please."

She eyed him, taking note of his crutches. "And they say flag football's not dangerous—you scored, I hope?"

Seth looked at her, bewildered.

"Oh, I assumed, because of your crutches and…"

The shirt he wore had a graphic of a teal-colored bull crashing through a China plate. The "pieces" were the shape of footballs. It was one of Miles's hand-me-downs.

"I take it you play?"

"Er…"

"Football," she said helpfully. Her reddish curls bounced when she spoke.

When Miles had offered Seth the shirt, he said he accidentally ordered the wrong size. He didn't say where the shirt came from.

"Yeah, I play." It was easier to lie. All she could see were his crutches. She perceived him to be a whole man with nothing more than a broken bone. How he wished it were true.

She quoted the price for the room, gave him his key, and drew a smiley face and double underlined the desk phone number. "I'm on the afternoon shift, if you need ice or anything."

Was she being flirty?

"For your injury," she added.

He wished he could stop time and not have to walk away. She'd see him for what he was.

"I get around fairly good. Thanks…"

She pointed to her name tag. "Cheryl."

"Cheryl." He wished for a distraction, prayed for something to take her attention away from him so he could walk away without her seeing his stump.

The sliding doors swished open and the autumn air brought in a few leaves. A bus parked outside had a mob of sporty-looking teenagers spilling from its door. A man, clearly the coach, led the way. Seth gratefully hobbled to the side. Cheryl winked at him before turning to welcome the group.

"See you around," she said.

Two days later, Seth lounged in the "sunshine" coming through the thick, floor-to-ceiling glass of the indoor pool, watching the brown, crinkled leaves swirl in the grass and flowered landscaping outside. The pool temperature and chlorine-infused humidity made it comfortable for shorts and a t-shirt, and the hum of the pool filter kept him company as he searched the local police blotters and headlines for articles about Ivy. Nothing more had been printed.

His phone vibrated. Miles.

The day he left, Seth had texted his goodbye and resolved not to have any more conversations with Miles. Even when Miles texted to ask whether Seth wanted his camp gear, he did not respond. Crap move? No doubt about it. Miles had been good to him, but if Miles's own words could be believed, he would get his reward in Heaven for helping Seth. And the truth: Seth didn't know what he wanted Miles to do with his gear. He never planned to see Miles again.

Cheryl entered the pool area. Seth grabbed the towel his stump rested upon and bunched it to make it look as if it had been haphazardly tossed over his foot. He pretended to be fascinated by the squirrel outside, but in his peripheral vision, he watched her approach.

In her hand, she held a dog-eared book. "How's the football player?" she asked.

"Super."

"Mind if I sit?"

"Please." Seth gestured to the empty lounge chair beside his.

"It's wet. Do you mind?" Cheryl reached for the towel that was bunched up by Seth's foot, the towel that was doing the very important job of concealing the lack of Seth's foot.

What to say? No? No, Cheryl, sit on the wet chair. He threw out his hand like he was stopping traffic and tried to come up with an excuse as to why he couldn't simply hand over the towel. Oh well. It was nice while it lasted.

He handed over the towel.

His stump caused her to flinch. Her eyes widened. The book and towel fell into his lap.

"Oh, my gosh. I'm sorry." She cupped her hands to her mouth.

Sorry for dropping a (thankfully light) paperback into his groin? Or sorry to see he didn't have a foot?

"No worries." He tried to sound nonchalant.

"I thought..."

He waved away her concern with one hand and offered the towel with the other. She dabbed the water and sat, pushing past the elephant of his missing foot by gushing nervously. The book in her hand was one of the best she had ever read. *Watchers,* by Dean Koontz, had been left behind by a guest, and she thought Seth might enjoy a good "beach" read if he hadn't read it already?

His deer-in-the-headlights feeling must have shown on his face because she continued, "I always wanted a dog like the one in the book, and I identify with the main character's love of the outdoors."

Now she had his attention. "The outdoors—like, camping?"

She practically bounced on the lounge chair, causing Seth's stump to do likewise. "Minister Creek is my go-to. We stick to national forests because they're free."

"You can get a campsite for free?" Seth asked.

"Not campsites, exactly. In a national forest, you're allowed to camp wherever you want. I use a hammock because I like sleeping off the ground."

Seth liked the idea of *wherever he wanted*.

"They have some free sites in the state forests, but you have to sign up for them, and sometimes they're booked. Besides, Minister Creek has a great vista."

Vistas. Brought Ivy crashing into Seth's consciousness.

"Hey, you good?" Cheryl asked.

Seth turned over the book in his hands, pretending to examine it. "Yeah," he said, but he was *yessing* to the idea of camping, not books. He would investigate national forests. Reading had never been his thing. That was why he hadn't been keen on studying with Miles, but—thank you, Miles—Seth found reading wasn't as boring as he had remembered. Still, what could motivate a person to read a story that wasn't even true? His doubt must have shown.

"You don't have to read it. I just thought—"

He clutched it to his chest. "No, I'm...thank you. I don't see hiking in my future, is all."

"Don't sell yourself short. Amputees are famous for doing all sorts of crazy things."

Seth raised his eyebrows. "Like what? Who?"

Cheryl pushed out her lips and considered. "Like that Paralympian runner. Can't recall the name…"

Seth shrugged. "Ilene?"

She rolled her eyes. "The guy, the one who shot his girlfriend."

Seth grimaced.

"She was a model or something. He shot her through the bathroom door, told the jury he mistook her for an intruder hiding in his bathroom." Cheryl snorted. "And he got away with it because his girl wasn't alive to testify."

"That's motivating."

"And Captain Hook, he was an amputee."

"So I can be a pirate, a book character."

"This is America." She gave him a flirty wink, "You can be anything you want."

He was too slow with a witty response, so she continued, "Some book characters are more alive than people. You know why I like books? You can close them whenever it gets too much. If you don't like what the story is doing to you on the inside, you don't have to read it. Give *Watchers* a go. It won't disappoint."

Seth made as if saluting her. "Aye aye, Captain. I'll give 'er a go."

"Call if you need anything," Cheryl smiled dazzlingly, and Seth began to wonder if his missing foot was weirdly attractive, like he was the three-legged dog every empathic girl wanted to adopt and rescue. As much as Cheryl had a generous vibe about her, and she was objectively beautiful, she couldn't compare with Monroe. While holding the un-opened book in his lap, Seth catalogued every woman he had ever known personally, and some famous ones too, even *the* Marilyn Monroe. None of them held a candle to his Monroe.

His phone vibrated with a call: the limb fairy's office.

"Hello?" Seth was instantly wary. Mr. Limb Fairy had never contacted him before.

It was a woman's voice. The receptionist. She wanted to know if Seth could make a trip to the office. Mr. Mitka had an update, and it required a second fitting.

"What for?"

"I'm not sure..." (typing sounds) ...looks like he's ordered you a second prosthesis. (more typing) It's pending a patent, and you match the criteria for the trial. (typing) ...a cycling prosthesis.

"Cycling? As in bikes?"

"Looks like it."

Seth on a bicycle, after all these years. Could he cycle around the country with a hammock, camp for free in the national forest, like Cheryl? He could live that way forever, maybe. No one would find him in a national forest. No supers would make him pack up. No tattooed cops would toss him into the back of a cruiser or take his liquor. And most important: there would be no ex-girlfriends in a national forest. He thanked the receptionist and ended the call.

At first, Seth flipped through *Watchers*, deciding whether to give reading a go, but he was not in the mood for pretend stories. Instead, he Googled national forests and cycling and ultralight backpacking. He lost himself in developing a plan, a great adventure that was definitely not him running away from Ivy. He was running toward something. And it would become clear in time what that thing was.

It took only a week for Seth to know all the staff at the Eastbridge Inn by name. Most of them he liked—with one exception. Sonia.

Surly from a hangover and the annoyance of crutches, Seth had yelled at her, "Couldn't you at least look before you assumed it was trash?"

Sonia stood before him, hands on hips, her hint of lip mustache quivering with rage. "Sir, it was *in the trash*. We have drawers for undergarments. We provide laundry bags."

What Sonia didn't understand was, it was his favorite pair of underwear. He could order more boxer briefs now that he had the settlement money, but he liked that particular pair. It wasn't too squeezy on his legs like some brands and didn't ride up his thighs, either. They were his sweet spot pair because they were washed and worn the right number of times. And now...gone.

"I want my underwear back," Seth insisted.

"That won't be possible, sir."

"Go get them. Please."

"I'm sorry. They're gone."

"They're not gone. They're somewhere. Where do you put the garbage?"

And Sonia huffed and stomp-led Seth to the front desk where Cheryl was enjoying something on her screen. The glow lit up her face. She smiled brightly before her expression fell at the sight of Seth and Sonia and their twin steely frowns.

"What's up?" she asked.

Sonia opened her mouth to speak, but Seth cut her off. "She threw away my clothes. I'd like to get them back, please, if it's not too much trouble."

"Miss Cheryl, our gentleman guest placed his...personal item in the trash."

"On accident," Seth countered.

"No problem," Cheryl said. "We'll replace the item."

Seth tried not to sigh. He didn't want to admit it was his underwear. He liked Cheryl, and it was embarrassing, and also it would piss him off if she couldn't empathize with the importance of men's underwear.

"Or we can reimburse you." Cheryl offered.

He plastered a smile. "I want to look for it, if you don't mind."

Cheryl explained that hotel dumpsters were not your average garbage, that Seth might want to reconsider. Seth wasn't poor anymore. Buying ten pairs of underwear was within his means. But...walking. Seth would have to order an Uber, crutch around a store, maybe get a pair that he liked, maybe not, Uber back. Hell and the no.

To Sonia, Cheryl said, "Do you know which dumpster it went into?"

Sonia shook her head.

Seth loved how the underwear *went* into something, like it had a will of its own. He would have phrased the question: Sonia, which dumpster did *YOU* put the underwear in?

"I have a break at three and can help you look," Cheryl offered. "What'd you lose?"

"No thank you," Seth answered.

"His *underwear*," Sonia said.

"Oh." Cheryl blinked back a chuckle. "That feels more like a *you* thing."

Zero understanding of the importance of underwear. Seth flashed both women a "smile" that felt altogether Jack-Nicholson-here's-Johnny. As if Cheryl wouldn't go dumpster diving over a lost pair of Victoria Secrets? Come *on.* And not like Seth didn't have his fill of chafing with his prosthesis. What Seth could control was his underwear—no thanks to sloppy cleaning ladies.

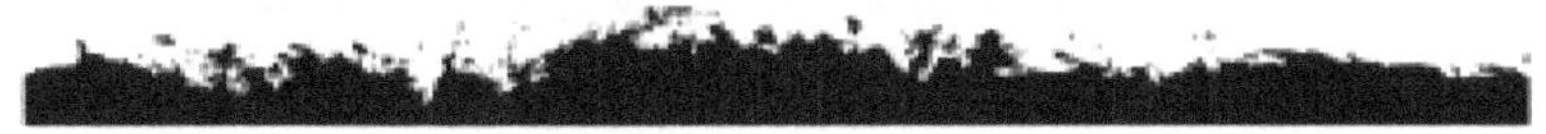

As he approached the dumpster, Seth could see that the only way to access it was by hanging over the side or by climbing in. Neither option looked promising. Leaning over meant he had to support his body weight by touching—ick—the dumpster sides, which wouldn't allow for a thorough search.

So it was that he found himself wholly inside the receptacle, trying to mouth-breathe as he crawled upon the clear bags of horror the cleaning workers had tossed in, praying he wouldn't accidentally rip one open. Worse than the trash bags were the other hideousities: plastic bottles of urine, poopy diapers, spoiled chocolate milk, a million ants in a Skittles bag, a torn-open bag of dog poo—all coalescing into a foulness the likes of which Seth had never experienced.

A text notification sounded. Oops. Seth had meant to remove it from his pocket. No way could he touch his phone.

It might be the limb fairy, texting. Seth vigorously wiped his hand on his shirt, regretting that he'd have to wash said shirt, and then he pinched the phone with his finger and thumb, touching it as little as possible.

Miles.

He pocketed his phone. "Sorry Miles. I'm in Hell," Seth said out loud. People said Hell was hot, that Hell was on fire. Maybe, but given the atmosphere in this dumpster, it now made sense that Hell would reek, too. It reminded Seth of when Miles took him to a sauna to help his sore muscles. Seth had slipped on the wet tile floor (of course). As he struggled to stand, he noticed an awful stench coming from the floor drain. Exponential grossness. He remembered asking Miles to smell it, to tell him if dead bodies smelled worse than the floor of that sauna.

"Bro, I am not sticking my nose down there," Miles answered.

Seth was pretty sure he had teased Miles about that, telling him Jesus would have smelled the drain.

Would Miles have helped Seth look for his underwear, like, in the name of Jesus? Hard to say. On one hand, Miles had given Seth a place to stay, temporarily. But Miles had also given a posse of cats a place to stay, temporarily. Just because Seth wanted to slog through this awfulness with the goal of finding his best pair of skivvies didn't mean anybody else was obliged to join him. Still, it would be nice to have a friend in Hell.

Something came out of nowhere and smacked Seth in the head—a mostly empty paper bag. The McDonald's someone had hurled into the dumpster startled Seth.

"HEY," he shouted reflexively.

The person screamed.

Seth apologized. He was the one trespassing, after all. It wasn't every day a dumpster yelled at you when you tossed in your trash. Just then...Seth hooked his finger on a bit of fabric that looked familiar. His beloved boxer briefs. "Bingo!" he shouted.

Footsteps hurried away.

Hefting himself out of the dumpster was a five-star delight. He was fairly sure he had pulled a muscle in his shoulder. His underwear smelled like burned coffee. His phone continued to buzz with notifica-tions—four texts, all from Miles.

Bro, R U really gone? Like 4 good?

Monroe's ok she strong

How about saying goodbye?

U R not responsible 4 Lavender, U know that right?

(Here the great Miles was mistaken. Seth was 100 percent responsible for Lavender.)

Seth rubbed first one palm then the other on his shirt, juggling the phone. As he made his way across the parking lot, a last text came in.

Jesus isn't done with U

Seth rolled his eyes.

It was Ivy who was not done with Seth. Couldn't Miles see that? The wise and dashing embalmer was blind to the fact that wherever Seth went, Ivy followed. With sixteen years of prison time to strategize, Ivy had plans for Seth. He knew she was the vengeance type, which was why—months ago—he somewhat intentionally let his car payments and rent lapse, so he would be less findable. *Somewhat intentionally*, as in, does the rent get paid or does the booze get bought? Booze. Booze. Booze. Booze.

Bingo, booze.

As the time for Ivy to be released drew closer, Seth had chosen booze over rent money, knowing at some level that having an address would not be his best bet. The tow motor taking his foot had been an unforeseeable wrench in the gears of Seth's machinations, but now things were work-ing again. The little patch of woods beside Green Spirit had been Seth's practice. Like the underwear he had balled in his sticky hand, forests were a little dirty, but comfortable. They were vast and dense and full of hiding places—and chaotic like his mind.

Seth wasn't finished with forests.

Chapter 14

Canon City's historic district was the perfect place for Seth to try out the new prosthesis he had stolen—Robin Hood fashion—from the limb fairy. The aroma of yeast drew him into a brewery where huge steel drums dwarfed the bar and dining areas, and tree trunk slices covered the walls. A jacked bartender set a beer before him, nodded at his prosthetic foot, and said, "On the house."

Seth opened his mouth to object, but the bartender held up a hand.

"I'll be offended if you don't take it."

Seth didn't want to insult the titanic dude. Plus, the beer was amazing. He ordered a small pepperoni pizza.

Hard to believe Seth had traded in his crutches for two, count them, *two* prostheses. Straight from the limb fairy's office, he hopped on a bus to Canon City, Colorado, to the Royal Gorge Bridge (far enough away and Cheryl's suggestion AND the highest bridge in the US of A).

Seth drank to drown the bad feelings about not following through with the limb fairy's trial for the "novel prosthesis." Instead, he focused on what a great destination Cheryl helped him choose. He had dispatched about half the pint when the bartender thumbed to the news on the television.

"Can you believe this horseshit? 'Merica's got boots in every corner of the globe and paying for it with my tax dollars—" he brought a fist to his chest and thumped it. "Mine. Don't get me wrong, I appreciate your service, but we done enough fighting."

Keeping his eyes in his beer stein, Seth said, "I don't follow that...horseshit."

"Yeah, why would you? You lived it. Hey, I hope it's not an asshole move if I ask what happened?"

Seth blinked.

"With your foot...if it's not too personal or anything."

Or anything.

"It got run over."

The bartender waited for more, but Seth didn't give it. Instead, he tacked. "I have a bicycling prosthesis I'm looking to try out on the trails. A friend told me this is a good place for trail riding."

The bartender stopped wiping the counter. "A friend, huh? Have you ever done singletracks, before your injury?"

"Sure," Seth lied.

"'Cause these trails are double-black diamond."

Seth didn't know what that meant. As a kid, he rode wherever he wanted. Trails, sidewalks, highways, you name it.

"Just don't go to Squiggly's for a bike," the bartender continued. "They're crooks. Century Wheels will hook you up. Tell them Dave sent you," he said.

"I appreciate the tip, Dave." Seth put out a hand to shake. "Seth."

Turned out Dave had a little brother deployed to Iraq in '05, never to return. Seth looked like Dave's lost brother, and bingo—the free beer made sense, as did his feelings on war. Dave recommended the Royalview Lodge, a little hotel that was mere steps away from the bar.

"Come back, and I'll hook you up—adventure of your life." he said, mysterious-like.

Adventure?

The bus ride and the beer and pizza made Seth too tired to ask. "See you later," he said, and left a fifty percent tip.

The Royalview Lodge wasn't cheap. Good thing Seth had his settlement egg, but he'd burn through it in no time in places like this. He was here for one reason: Cheryl. If she were to be believed, the highest bridge in America would "blow his mind." Crossing the wood planks suspended a thousand feet above the Arkansas River had been the "holy experience" of her life. (Seth wondered what Miles would say about that?) Cheryl had grabbed onto Seth's arm like a little kid and yanked on it, until he promised to visit the Royal Gorge. The web page she had printed out with a park map and her notes was in the pocket of his backpack.

Tomorrow, Seth would follow through on his promise to Cheryl because he had a shiny new foot from the limb fairy. For tonight, he was flush with prostheses and full of complimentary beer and delicious pizza in Canon City, Colorado. Ivy would not find him, a man who could zip all over the country as he pleased, camp anywhere there were trees. That calming thought put him to sleep.

Seth woke in his hotel bed to the sound of roosters. A goat stared at him through the window, its tongue lazily working at the dried grasses in the screen tracks. Beyond the goat was a basketball half court with spiky weeds growing in the cracks. The breakfast buffet had personal touches: brightly colored serving dishes. Fruit salad. Cinnamon-raisin bread that smelled freshly baked that morning. There were hard-boiled eggs and eggs cooked-to-order. Seth feasted and returned to his room, thinking he would get an Uber or a Lyft to the gorge. When he arrived, he found a bicycle parked beside his window. No one was around, but whoever left it had skewered a note through the handbrake.

Thought you could use this while you're here. I've got lots of these lying around. - Dave

The bike had thick, knobby tires and a tiny seat—big enough for one of Seth's ass cheeks. His bicycle prosthesis had two options: One that could thread through a regular bicycle pedal, and one that looked like it clipped onto the crank arm directly (bypassing the need for foot and pedal). What Seth didn't like was that—unlike his regular prosthesis, the cycling one was basically a steel bar. He chose the more human-looking prosthesis and took a spin around the parking lot. The disk brakes were so sensitive he almost flung himself over the handlebars.

Wow, what a bike. Seth marveled at the kindness of strangers. He pedaled to the bar and thanked Dave, who said he could borrow the bike while he was in town.

When was the last time Seth had ridden a bike? Never with a prosthesis. The fabulous foot slipped neatly through the slots in the pedal, and the shaped tread secured his foot. This differed from his memory of pedaling because it allowed him to pull back on the pedal and push forward. All this time he had used only half the circuit. No wonder racers were so fast.

On Main Street, Seth catalogued the coffee shops, antique fronts, gift stores, pizza joints, and liquor stores, each adding a unique flair to the street-facing brick masonry. The place had a decidedly western vibe, what with the mountains rising up as a backdrop and the long, straight street with cars parallel parked in every available space. In the outskirts of town, he pedaled faster and enjoyed the speed and wind in his hair. Sweat kept him cool as he toured around the neighborhoods, waving to dogs on tie-outs, and passing by people tending gardens or mowing lawns. What would that feel like—having a garden to grow things in? Or a lawn to mow?

Constricting.

Like he was a dog on a tie out.

Ivy could find him, and God forbid if he had any pets.

Seth shook his Ivy-thoughts away as he passed a sparkling stream, twiggy trees with spindly leaves, cactus plants, and a plump lizard the same orange-red color as the ground and rocks. He tooled around Canon City until his belly told him it was lunch time. Once again, he enjoyed a pizza (half this time) and two beers with Dave before calling an Uber to take him to the Royal Gorge Bridge & Park.

Upon hearing the cost for admission and gondola tickets, Seth made a joke that he was already missing one foot and could not afford the arm and leg they were charging.

The teenage embodiment of ennui did not laugh, so Seth reluctantly handed over his bank card. Another park employee overheard their exchange. The pretty, buck-toothed girl with a thousand piercings and two thick braids giggled and offered Seth a ride in a golf cart to the gondolas. And while he didn't need the ride, thanks to his prosthesis, he felt like royalty as they sped by the walking tourists.

That gorge, though.

In his amazement, Seth practically tumbled out of the golf cart, eyes glued to the scene before him. He patted the girl's shoulder, and without taking his eyes off the gorge breathed, "thank you for the ride."

"Right?" She agreed. "Gorgeous. Get it? Gorge-eous. Enjoy." She zoomed off.

The phrase *took my breath away* came to mind. Apparently, there were things in the world that were so blazingly magnificent, they shocked the nervous system, hitched the breath, and then...AND THEN...remained so overwhelming and awe-inspiring...Seth felt he had transcended the ordinary, physical world. Not unlike being buzzed, Seth decided. But better, infinitely better.

The chasm stretched down, down, down to what looked like pieces of Christmas tree tinsel, but was actually the sun-lustered Arkansas River twisting far below.

Seth pressed his face to the gondola's glass. The river glinted with the sun's golden reflection. The car swayed, reminding Seth and his fellow riders their lives were in the hands of human engineering.

After the gondola, Seth stood before the ticket booth and considered shelling out more money for the Sky Coaster. Money no longer stopped him, but he had trouble shaking the scarcity mindset. Plus, he was a little scared.

A beauty wearing hiking boots and playful socks saw him considering the tickets and assured him the ride was worth every penny. She had just purchased a ticket for a second ride on the Sky Coaster, and—did he want a partner? She convinced him to purchase the package deal so he could also ride the zipline afterward.

As they were hoisted by nothing more than a cable and body harness to the top of the ride, Seth held onto the chest straps. When he assumed they were almost to the top, he tried to look over his shoulder, but the harness prohibited it. Up and up and up they went, far beyond how it looked from the spectator's perspective. People were ants. Specks. It was SO MUCH HIGHER than it looked.

"Are we almost to the top?" He tried to sound nonchalant, but his throat was full of terror.

His riding partner laughed.

Interminable seconds passed before the lift finished and locked into place. Once there, the ride paused for a second or two as they dangled over the canyon, *nothing between him and the gorge but air,* just like he "wanted."

Funny how he couldn't trust what he wanted. This was frightening as fuck. Was it too late to bail? Seth was about to ask—but the sudden, extreme sensation of pressure on his face and throat and heart as they pitched forward and went into freefall cut off all thought. His stomach danced a g-force jig. Reflexively, he joined the screaming of this fellow rider as they plummeted toward the canyon bottom and gradually began to arc, swinging like a pendulum over the river. Both screams morphed into laughter as the intensity mellowed and they swung back and forth over the gorge, the wing-shearing speed prompting Seth and his partner to fling out their arms.

"Zipline?" his new friend asked, before they had removed their harnesses.

"Hell yes."

They spent the afternoon taking in the sights and purchasing more rides. His new, crazy-socks friend reminded him of Monroe. Were it not for all the excitement, the similarity would have made Seth's heart ache. Maybe that was why he invited Kimmy to grab dinner at the park's taco place. Nachos, quesadillas, and margaritas filled Seth's belly, and Monroe's doppelgänger soothed his senses.

That evening, Kimmy joined him in his hotel room. He stationed himself in the single chair, and she sat cross-legged on the bed.

"You remind me of someone," he said.

"Anyone but your mother," she replied.

"Ha. No. A friend. After my accident, I met these Bible thumpers."

"Bible humpers?" Kimmy asked.

"Thumpers," Seth corrected. "Bible *thumpers*."

She dissolved into giggles and kept repeating, "Bible humpers...Bible humpers..."

"I take it you're not religious," he said.

Kimmy held up a baggie of dried mushrooms. "My religion," she said.

Bingo.

Seth ate one and learned how stunning the motel light fixture could be. They went outside and lay on the weedy basketball court. The clouds. They spoke wispy, epic tales. He and Monroe, no—Kimmy (her name was Kimmy)—laughed for what felt like hours. But who knew how long it truly was? Time stopped existing for a spell. Although he could get used to a place like Colorado, Seth didn't want to put roots down anywhere. There was too much to see now that he had the means to do it.

During their mushroom trip, Kimmy thrilled him with tales about all the exciting places he could visit if he had a decent bicycle to go with that special prosthesis of his. There was a trail dedicated to cycling across America, the TransAmerica Trail. There were offshoots, too, if he wanted to go to places like Las Vegas or Death Valley. Kimmy whetted his appetite for adventure (and made him miss Monroe more). Nothing happened between them other than talk, not that Seth hadn't allowed his eyes to graze Kimmy's taut yet curvy figure. She had sent him green lights with her mischievous eyes and playful touches, but Seth didn't bite.

"Meet me for lunch and a bike ride tomorrow," she said, as she hesitated in the doorway of Seth's room.

"You mean today."

"I guess we stayed up pretty late. Today, then."

It took three weeks of research at the Canon City Library, and Kimmy, who worked at the sporting goods store, to outfit Seth for long-distance cycling. He purchased a set of panniers, as well as lights and all sorts of goodies for outdoor living, aka camping. The weather turned colder, and Seth wanted to head south. He and Kimmy planned a route while sharing pizza and beers.

Dave came out from behind the bar and shooed the server away. "I got these two."

"Dave was the first friend I met when I got into town," Seth said. "He tried to kill me on the singletrack."

"Told you it was double diamond. You didn't believe me," Dave said.

The truth was, Seth had no idea that double-diamond meant taking a bicycle over roots and boulders and ramps and making the bike fly. The double diamond track hugged steep cliffs that meant death if not perfectly executed.

"Hey, I completed a double-diamond trail," Seth put a fist to his chest.

"Walked. You walked a double diamond," Dave countered. To Kimmy he said, "You should have seen this guy with his steel pirate peg lugging my fat tire bike over most of the ten miles of the Royal Cascade trail."

Seth laughed at himself. "Fucking double diamond. Dave cured me of mountain biking."

"Happy to help." Dave gave Seth a chummy slap on the back. "Meal's on the house, friends."

Seth tipped him enough to cover more than the meal and a tip.

As they hugged goodbye, the last thing Kimmy said was, "And to think, you never tried anything with me." She kissed his cheek. "You gay, Seth?"

He smiled.

And almost called Miles to tell him what Kimmy said, how it hadn't even occurred to him to sleep with her and she was hot. Smoking hot. Gay check. No? No. What was happening to Seth?

Chapter 15

Seth swerved his touring bicycle into the middle of the county road that would take him to the North Lakes Route and eventually on to Sleeping Bear Dunes, where the sand trail to Lake Michigan had views "to die for." Always hooked him, that phrase, *to die for.*

Seth met the cyclist who suggested he visit Sleeping Bear the way he met most of his cycling friends: at a small-town diner. At the bar while wolfing down waffles, fried chicken, and scrambled eggs, they struck up a conversation about the weather, their muscles, where they had been, where they were going, and because the sky opened up and poured rain, they even got around to confessing their *why*—why cycle across the country? Seth's standard answer was that he had a settlement check and a special prosthesis and neither should go to waste. The Sleeping Bear cyclist was a high school teacher who used his summer break to see the country.

Every long-distance cyclist had tells. One, they walk-hobbled, usually straight to the john upon entering the establishment. Two, they ordered two full entrees but were lean and leathery. Three, a pitcher of ice water sweated beside them that was refilled several times and eventually poured into water bottles.

The math teacher also sported the camphorous aura of Tiger Balm. Sore muscles were a given for long-distance cyclists. The wiry teacher finished his breakfast by tossing back half a pecan pie. With pictures, he clarified how the Dunes Trail had deep, soft sand that infiltrated every kind of shoe or sock, yet it was too hot to walk barefoot. Because of this, the four-mile trek felt longer, especially on the return trip. He offered a disgusting picture of his blistered feet and a video of him dumping a cup of sand out of each shoe. Right then, he noticed Seth's prosthesis, and his face screwed up.

"It'll only be half as bad for me," Seth joked.

The teacher clapped Seth on the back and mumbled something about half-full cups with a mouth full of sweet pecans. He excitedly insisted Lake Michigan, the secluded beach at the end of the Dunes Trail, was worth the blisters, of which Seth would only have half. That was enough to convince Seth.

And here he was, *en route* to Sleeping Bear Dunes in Michigan.

Having an end point to look forward to was how Seth passed the time on the bike, when the road was smooth and easy. In the ten months since he set off from Mr. Limb Fairy's office, he met cyclists of every age. Some were running from grief, having lost a husband or wife. Some were running for a cause like leukemia or cancer. Some had hordes of fans on social media (those, Seth steered away from, not wanting his picture out to gazillions of strangers). Cyclists wanted to see the country, slower than in a car. Faster than on foot. Like Seth's teacher friend.

After the unpaved, treacherous eighty-five miles of C & O Trail in Pennsylvania, Seth was down for some flat Ohio. His single earbud piped John Denver's "Country Road" into his head, and he breathed in the sweet, grassy scent of straw, noting the bales dotting the fields. He played a little game on roads like this, that of keeping his front tire threaded between the painted yellow lines. The road had an expansive silence that allowed him to hear approaching vehicles in time to slide over to the shoulder.

Was it dicey to ride in the middle? Maybe. But cyclists got made into meat pies even when they obeyed road rules, so why not have fun?

He had started at the East Coast Greenway in Richmond, Virginia, dodging the heavy traffic sections labeled *high stress road/extreme caution* on the cycling maps. Seth's months of cycling had taught him: Country roads, bingo. Gravel, semi-bingo. Desert (with plenty of water), if-you-must-bingo. Tunnels and bridges teeming with distracted, phone-holding idiots and without road shoulders, HELL-TO-THE-NO-BINGO.

There were cooler and more respectable ways to die.

Mile after mile, Seth traveled. Since he set out on his bicycling journey, Miles had texted a handful of times. Sometimes it was a **How U doing?** Or an encouraging verse, a link to an article, or a GIF on Seth's birthday. (How did Miles know it was Seth's birthday?) Seth didn't answer. Any communication opened the possibility of more communication. *How are you?* would turn into *Where are you?* And Seth didn't want anyone to know. Cell phones could be used to find people, he wasn't sure how, but because of that possibility, he kept his phone turned off when he wasn't using it for directions. Truth was, he missed Miles. And Monroe. He missed her more.

After a full day of cycling, Seth could count on sore muscles and a fall into a deep sleep. On the rare occasions he splurged on a motel, he took a bath. Fine. Bath*s*. His bathing ritual would cost the motel more than a room's worth of hot water. And he made sure to ask ahead whether the rooms had bathtubs. Some didn't, he found to his utter disappointment.

Might as well camp if he couldn't soak his aching muscles in eucalyptus and mint Epsom salts.

Seth used a GPS program he had downloaded from the library in Wytheville, Virginia. A fellow cyclist created it because there were stretches of the TransAmerica Trail that were without cell service where Google Maps cut out. Seth, the cycling version of Lewis-and-Clark, surprised himself by answering questions from other cyclists, offering tricks and road wisdom he had picked up along the way.

Trick number one, lubricant, specifically Chipmunk Butter. Seth could kiss the Ironman athlete who introduced him to the tin of miracle salve that smelled of cacao and protected his nether parts from chafing. Trick two, snacks. Not just any old granola bar would do for the energy needed to cycle. Seth had his favorite kinds and flavors, but not every gas station stocked them. So that he didn't have to languish on what was basically candy bars with oats tossed in, a small canister of his favorite shake powder and a bunch of high-energy bars were tucked in his panniers. And trick number three, a wide-ass bike seat. Priceless, if he didn't want to become a eunuch. The tiny seats used by triathletes—no. Just, no.

Seth's goal when he got on the road at 7:30 this morning was to arrive at Peace Lake by sunset. An entirely doable goal of mostly flat Ohio miles with an effort level of C+. The weather promised to be rain-free. Seth was tan and lean. His ball cap and aviator sunglasses protected his eyes from road dust. He had allowed his hair to grow and kept it from getting into his eyes with a crimped ponytail he threaded through the plastic clasp. He still shaved, but only when the scruff made his face uncomfortably hot. There were days he looked in the truck stop mirror and barely recognized the angular-faced man with sun-bleached curly hair who stared back—some days clear-eyed, some days almost healthy-looking.

With enough road between Seth and…anybody, he felt more at peace. Every road was different, and every road was familiar. Most had yellow lines and white lines. Most had roadkill here and there, litter on the shoulder, potholes, bridges, culverts.

Houses or farms or fields changed in small, cosmetic ways, but also, they didn't. You could tell an area where tax dollars didn't pay for trash pickup by the rusted-but-still-standing swing sets, the junk piles in the yard, the ancient cars half-digested by weeds sinking into the earth. There were the rural communities that didn't remove the signage for long-forgotten political races, the people and their promises bleached out by sun and warped by precipitation, the paper peeling in confetti-sized pieces. America was a big-ass country, with lots of places to disappear into. When the grit of the road and camping and blisters got to be too much, Seth found a little cozy hotel to lie low in for a while. His last hotel had a deep bathtub and a balcony overlooking a little creek.

The outdoor pool had cushions on the lounge chairs, and it was there that Seth read *Watchers* for the third time while enjoying Red Fox cheddar cheese and chasing it with sparkling water. He downloaded *Watchers* onto his Kindle because he wanted to keep the story with him, and it made more sense to carry the Kindle as opposed to paper books, though he preferred them. Novels had opened a new escape hatch for Seth. He could lose himself in other worlds and other lives and not even be hungover in the morning. *Bingo.* Audiobooks were great for listening while on his bike—days when the road dulled his senses and he needed a voice in his head that wasn't his.

The only hard copy book he carried with him was a Bible, which he needed to thumb through and jump around in whenever an existential question had him in its grip. Sometimes he yearned to call Miles and get his take on whatever Seth had been ruminating on—mostly when he drank too much. Although drunkenness happened less often, too, because keeping and carrying a heavy glass bottle and liquid was too much trouble. On a bike, every pound mattered.

Sometimes fortune—he called it fortune—handed him a pithy phrase that landed exactly right, or a book he needed to read, like the time he accidentally downloaded an audiobook he never would have chosen on his own.

Because he had mistaken the white facial tissues on the book cover as clouds in a blue sky, he found himself listening to *Maybe You Should Talk to Someone*, assuming the *Someone* was God. Turned out it was a lady therapist. The book was her memoir. He had nothing against therapists of any stripe (did he?). His intention was to swap out the accidental book during his first break, but the author's voice was engaging, and her story piqued his interest. What could it hurt to give the book a listen for a few more miles? And thus hooked, Seth listened to therapist/author/patient Lori Gottlieb on the gravel roads of Pennsylvania, his eyes blurring at the tragic and revelatory end of her story. Seth had to shut it off, so his tears didn't run him into a ditch. Gottlieb's memoir showed Seth he wasn't the only man who lived with relentless guilt, and he wasn't the first person to use alcohol to drown it. Coping was tricky. There were endless ways to numb out, but some ways were better than others. The book confirmed for Seth that the quiet thrill of long-distance cycling was more than a diversion. He revered the road and the sky and the wind on his face, his body strong and capable as he took himself wherever he wished to go.

When he wasn't piping a book or a song into his head, scenes from his past turned over and over in his mind. His titanium cycling foot held up brilliantly, and he mentally thanked the limb fairy. On the heels of his gratitude was a pang of guilt for his Irish goodbye. Months ago, Seth had agreed to participate in the trial for the cutting-edge, state-of-the-art, might-as-well-be-bionic cycling foot. He had wanted to be honest with the limb fairy about his intentions, but if he had confessed his plan to get out of Dodge that very day, he knew he would not get the foot, and he absolutely needed both the foot and to get out of Dodge. For Miles and Monroe's sake and his own. Could he help it if the world—Ivy—conspired against him and made him lie? No, he could not. He was trying to achieve damage control, was all. And survive.

Most days he wanted to survive.

Other days, he did not. Like when he woke from a nightmare with the smell of freezer mold in his nostrils and the muscular yank of gravity in his belly—on those days his body thrashed against the sheets and launched him out of bed as he re-played the night all those years ago—the bolt of adrenaline, the surge of strength, the bracing, the impact, the broken bones, the screams (his), the silence (Woods's), and the gurgle of the creek, the shards of moonlight reflected on the water.

And far above, Ivy, peering over.

He'd wake to find himself on the floor, having fallen out of bed.

Getting on the road was the best way to shake off the nightmare. A few miles of cycling to Rob Zombie or Metallica, and Seth left his anxiety behind.

It was one such morning after his recurring Ivy nightmare that Seth congratulated himself on his healthy coping.

"BINGO!" He shouted and raised a fist to the sky, juiced about shaking Ivy from his head—when his tire blew out with a malevolent hiss.

Chapter 16

In the scratchy, littered grass beside the road, Seth unloaded his panniers and set his bike upside down. He pulled the new inner tube out of the box, only to have it fall apart in his hands.

Lucky for him he had another. Checking the Boy Scout box was all he'd been doing when he purchased two extra inner tubes from a hardware store that had hand-written price tags and a 1950s vibe. The tubes were older than he was.

And useless.

The second tube ripped when he filled it with air.

"What the hell?" Seth tore the boxes into tiny pieces and tossed them in the air while grumbling at his terrible fortune.

Seth made sure his prosthesis was visible as he attempted to wave down passing motorists. As asshole after heartless asshole passed by, his growing rage made its way into his fervent arm motions. He knew he looked like a crazed aircraft marshaller, but he didn't care. Why was it so hard to get a lift?

He gave the truck driver the bird.

He screamed at a mother and child who slowed but didn't stop.

After an hour, Seth sat down beside his bike and asked God why he hated him.

A minute later, a rusty pick-up truck that looked older than Seth skidded to a stop before him, kicking up a cloud of dust. The white-haired driver offered to take him to a shopping plaza.

Seth raised an eyebrow to the sky.

The man had a tablet around his neck with a little notepad and laminated cards. One read: I'm mute.

Seth yelled a "thank you."

The man turned the card over. It read: I hear fine.

"Nobody stopped for me," Seth tried not to yell.

The man pointed to himself.

"Yes, you did. I appreciate you."

The man pointed up and smiled.

"Yes, the weather is good. That would have sucked balls if it was raining, but being stranded like that sucked pretty darn bad anyw—"

The man squeezed Seth's arm and pointed to a hardware store.

"Yes. That one's fine. You're a life saver."

The man pulled up to the curb.

"Thank you," Seth said.

He drew an invisible cross on his chest and pointed up.

With the time lost, there was no way Seth would make it to Peace Lake—a KOA campground that had a pool and sauna AND woodsy tent sites. As the sky purpled, Seth scaled back his aspirations and hoped only to reach a motel before dark. After another mile, he adjusted his goal to the even lower bar of not becoming roadkill. It was a moonless night on a country road, after all.

Wicker Hills was the home of The Frog Jump Festival, or so said a welcome sign. Seth had noticed the flattened black blobs on the road, and sometimes he spotted a live one, jumping. One unlucky Wicker Hills frog managed to jump into his tire spokes. Seth pulled over, sighing as he waited for the traumatized amphibian to free itself. It was only a matter of time before this frog joined his friends in the asphalt.

It was the near-miss with the bat that was the last straw. Seth wasn't sure if it was his sweat that attracted bugs, which attracted bats, but one rude little sucker almost smacked him in the face, and he barely managed to right the bike and prevent a collision into oncoming headlights.

Time to pull over. He chose a little patch of woods to *commandeer*, as he liked to think of it. Cheryl's pirate, that was Seth. He had been Nanette's Mystery Man. Kimmy's gentleman. Monroe's...what?

Anything but cripple. He didn't want to be defective in her eyes.

The dense patch of trees framed the back portion of an empty lot and looked big enough to have a house of its own, but providentially, it didn't. The deal was sealed when Seth almost swerved into a drainage canal. Swearing, he hopped off the bike and waded (gingerly) through a garden of wildflowers and vegetables, steering clear of the gardening spikes jutting above the growth and the nets and the aluminum pans swiveling in the light breezes.

What a boon to find a fire ring and two hammocks already strung up deep inside the treed area. He secreted his bike behind a tangle of bushes and struck camp. In the darkness, he could only guess how well hidden he was from the road and from the homes on either side of the wooded lot. Hopefully, it wouldn't matter. Seth planned to wake before the sun and be on his way—no harm, no foul.

Chickens made low, guttural noises from a little shed in the backyard. Ooooh, eggs. Seth could grab a couple and fry them up right there. He had his camp stove, after all. Chicken people always had more eggs than they could eat.

First order of business was to set up his stove. He'd sleep in one of the two hammocks they so kindly had ready for him. Seth's cycling prosthesis could be walked upon, but dirt clogged the pedal grooves, so he mostly kept it for cycling. Tonight, he didn't bother changing out of it because the nighttime suburban hush amplified every noise.

Lights were on in the houses on either side of him. His watch read 10:14 PM.

As he moved toward the chicken coop, Seth listened for sounds from inside the house and was rewarded with a loud television show. Through the part in the curtains, he could see cartoons. The comforting scent of dryer sheets puffed from a vent. The back patio had a huge, open umbrella, but the stuffed couch beneath it was empty. It was a beautiful night to sit outside, and Seth was glad the homeowners were not taking advantage of the warm weather.

He stole through the yard, taking care not to step into the shaft of light thrown by the kitchen window. The chickens' run spanned the length of the property. He could see the wire outline and fencing against the wispy clouds, but chickens put themselves to bed when the sun went down. It was Ivy who had taught him this when they were kids. Ivy knew how to steal eggs and how to turn them into delectable omelets with cheese and pickles because her mother had those two items on hand and not much else.

Please, let there be outside nesting boxes. If Seth had to go inside the coop, he'd have chickens screaming at him. Noob chicken people kept their nesting boxes inside the coop. Bah. You had to step in poo, around chickens, and God help you—get past the rooster—to take the eggs. Better to have nesting boxes that could open from the outside. Better for thieves like Seth. And...*yes*. These were savvy chicken people. Seth pocketed the three cleanest eggs (as far as he could tell in the dark) and closed the lid. As he made his way back across the yard, he froze at the sound of a sliding door on its tracks. He dashed clumsily to the nearest tree, flattened himself against it, and dared a peek toward the house. Sure enough, a man stood with a can to his lips and a vape pen in his other fist. He surveyed the doorframe and looked at the steps leading from the deck to the yard.

"Hon, we can pull it out the back. I won't need the chainsaw."

From inside the house, a woman's voice said, "Trash pickup's tomorrow."

The man said to himself. "Nah...I'm going to burn it."

When the man stepped back inside, Seth hightailed it into the relative safety of the woods. Now was not the time to light the camp stove in case the tiny blue flame gave him away. He'd break open his Maker's Mark and sip a while, till everyone in the world was asleep.

Bingo.

With whiskey flossing his thoughts, he lay in the hammock and noted the tree shadows against the starry night sky. Every so often, he glanced at the sliding door and the windows. After a while, the man reappeared, this time hefting a piece of furniture through the open door. An overstuffed couch. He wedged it back and forth, shimmying it through the doorway and grunting with the effort. The woman helped from the other side. He gave instructions for her to push this way and that. Once the couch was through the door, each grabbed an end.

"Let's burn it right now," the man said.

Seth looked at the fire ring by his feet, a mere three feet in diameter. He didn't risk making his watch glow with the time, but it had to be pushing midnight.

"Not tonight, okay?" the woman replied. "I'm exhausted, and—Kibeth! Get back here."

Kibeth?

A dark, ferocious-looking shape bounded out the back door and jumped onto the couch as they held it aloft.

"Kibeth, down," the man ordered.

Kibeth, stay, Seth prayed. *Stay on the couch.*

The dog was enormous and had a K-9 look about it. If Seth could have stopped his own heart from beating, he would have. He held his breath, didn't move a single muscle. He prayed for an invisibility cloak. For a miracle. Please, let this dog not smell him.

Which was when Kibeth came barreling toward the woods, snapping and woofing, his tail wagging like mad. He began to pick his way through the brush in Seth's direction until a beep sounded, followed by a yelp from Kibeth, who turned tail and fled back toward the house.

"Told you we don't need a fence," the woman said.

"Told you we don't need a fence," the man sing-songed in mimicry. "Shock collars are cruel, darling, like you."

She kissed him. "If it isn't rough, it isn't fun." The woman patted Kibeth's head as he obediently tramped inside the home. She shut the slider. "Let's leave it for tonight."

The man made a sexy growling sound.

They left it.

Soon after, the television went dark and the lights, too. Seth felt lonely. He wanted a woman to banter with him. He wanted Monroe. How often had he talked with the imaginary Monroe in his head? Often. They spoke about this or that book and about whatever cats Seth happened to see on his travels. And Jesus. Sometimes Seth questioned Monroe on what Jesus would think of this or that. Like tonight. Tonight, he asked her whether Jesus would be angry that Seth took the eggs.

Imaginary Monroe said, "You're hungry, Seth. Jesus knows you're hungry."

Seth noticed that the Monroe in his head didn't say that Jesus wouldn't be angry, just that he knew Seth was hungry. His ability to conjure Monroe grew in correlation with the quantity of alcohol he ingested. Tonight, his envy for the couple made him want a LOT of Monroe. He was hungry, yes, in more ways than one. All he could feed was his belly, so he soft-boiled the eggs and ate them with the cheese and crackers. He got drunk while reading. Ivy crashed into his dreams for the second night in a row, the dreams he wanted only Monroe to reside in.

He woke up to a seismic hangover and an alarming sight.

The man, presumably the same one from last night, stood in his backyard wearing camo boxer briefs and black military boots—with his back to Seth, thankfully. Over his bare shoulder was slung a large gun, looked to be an AR-15. The dude's vibe made Seth wish he were not mere yards from the man.

Let these woods belong to the other neighbor.

A pillar of dark smoke rose from the ground before the man's boots. The couch from last night had been lit on fire, and the man gleefully squeezed streams of lighter fluid, causing the fabric to flame up with ever more intensity.

"Hon, you're missing it," he called toward the house. "Would you mind grabbing the marshmallows on your way out?"

Seth watched in silent, frozen horror as the man opened a box of graham crackers and arranged them on the flat-topped rail of his back deck. He garnished each cracker with a piece of what was probably chocolate.

S'mores? For *breakfast*?

"And bring some coffee for our friend, will you?" He turned and looked squarely at Seth. "How do you take your coffee?" He squirted the couch, and the flame burgeoned.

Seth could not get more frozen.

"You *do* drink coffee? Kibeth got into your stash, I'm afraid." He shook his head. "That dog eats anything." And the mostly naked, un-tanned, tattooed Viking smiled and popped a piece of chocolate into his mouth. "I'm Paul. Those are my woods you're trespassing in. That's my wife's hammock. Sleeps nice, doesn't it?"

Seth could not divine whether this Paul meant to befriend him or was about to shoot him, so he chose his usual possum response.

"Can you talk?" Paul asked Seth, as a lovely woman with a braid down her back came out the door bearing two cups of steaming coffee. "We're out of cream." To Seth, she said, "I didn't want to wake you, but people are coming to look at the lot today."

Seth saw the huge FOR SALE sign he had missed in the night. He pulled himself out of the hammock. "I'm...sorry. I ran out of sunlight. I took a couple of eggs, too. I can pay you for them."

Paul waved away his offer.

The woman studied Seth while he pulled on his prosthesis. From the deck, she grabbed a folding camp chair and placed it before the burning couch. "Sit?"

When Seth made no move, the woman looked at the rifle and ad-dressed the man, "Is that necessary? You're scaring him."

Paul laughed (a little maniacally, to Seth's wary ears). "It's more polite than deading him, and he's trespassing. I'm within my rights to shoot him."

The woman looked at Seth and rolled her eyes, "He's kidding."

Seth wasn't sure he was, though.

"Here, before it gets cold," she gestured to the seat and held out the mug.

"Thanks." Seth kept his eyes on the gun-toting Paul as he made his way toward the couch bonfire. The coffee was hazelnut. *Delish.*

The woman explained, "The side lot doesn't belong to us, but we don't want a buyer to cut down all the trees. We plan to buy it, but we need a little more time to save up."

"I see," Seth said, although he didn't.

"We couldn't have you sleeping on our hammocks when the realtor arrives. The couch and...this (she nodded to half-naked Paul with his rifle) is to discourage potential buyers about who their neighbors will be."

"I have music to greet them," Paul said. A blasting guitar riff and "America, Fuck Yeah!" crashed into the quiet country morning. Seth resisted the urge to cover his ears until Paul mercifully shut it off.

The woman's name was Kataeri, she said, and they had spotted Seth last night on their ring camera. It was for protecting the chickens from coyotes, which was why it was trained into the woods.

"Are you afraid of dogs?" Kataeri asked.

"No."

"Hmmm..." She pulled out her phone and showed Seth a black and white image of his own terrified face. "If you're sure...?"

Seth told her he was sure, and she brought Kibeth outside, as well as a bag of marshmallows. They toasted them over the couch and pressed them into s'mores. Not a bad breakfast, after all. Kibeth was handsome in the light, especially when he wasn't mistaking Seth's prosthetic foot for his silicone chew toy.

Of course, the couple asked where Seth had come from and where he was going. He had been slowly figuring out the answers to those questions over the past months as people he met along the way kept asking.

"I started cycling when I lost my foot." True, if abbreviated.

"I'm going until I find what I'm looking for. And I'll know it when I see it." True, in the sense that he had no clue where he wanted to go and no idea what to look for.

Paul asked what Seth now considered to be the universal question. "What happened to your foot?" And Seth gave the answer he had settled on: "Work accident. Not a bad thing, ultimately. I wasn't paying attention, and the company more than compensated me for my trouble. I got early retirement, and I see all sorts of cool places and meet interesting people...like you."

People loved that answer.

By this time Paul had chilled out enough to lay his rifle across his lap. Kibeth sat at Kataeri's feet.

They offered Seth the use of their shower and gifted him with a new, ultralight camp chair that weighed exactly one pound. It was perfect for when you wanted to sit by a fire but didn't have a log or a large rock nearby, Paul said. Kataeri made egg salad with everything bagel seasoning and instructed him to spread it like dip on the seed crackers she put in his pack. It was past noon when he said goodbye. No one had come to see the side lot after all. Or they had seen Paul and turned tail.

"Where's your next destination?" Paul asked.

"I was going to Peace Lake, but now maybe Filmers, since I got to rest here. Thank you, by the way."

Paul knew Filmers State Park. Things got rowdy sometimes, he said. Motorcyclists liked the small sites and were known to arrive in the wee hours of the morning.

Seth's original destination, Peace Lake, was only an hour away. He decided not to hurry through Ohio, to enjoy the pool and beach at Peace Lake and stay the afternoon and night there. Talk turned to which roads Seth would take, and Paul offered a better route, the same distance but more scenic.

"When Route 301 turns left, you go right onto Old School Street, then take 20 west to the bridge."

Paul also gave him directions to a corner store not a mile from their home. Seth wished he had a gift for the couple. All he could give was a handshake.

"You're good people," he said.

At the store, Seth restocked his camp supplies and splurged on marshmallows, graham crackers, and peanut butter cups. Tonight, he'd have a fire and his own twist on s'mores. He would toast to Paul and Kataeri.

Chapter 17

AFTER A HOT AND mostly dehydrated day on Michigan roads, on a byway named Bohemian Road, the Sand spring Community Swimming Pool called irresistibly to Seth. Moonlight reflected off its glasslike water and cast its glow upon cushioned lounge chairs. Someone had left the fence door unlatched, which felt like a personal invitation (like the hammocks at Paul and Kataeri's house). Situated between the pool and street, the pool house would block midnight drivers from the view of Seth swimming naked.

Bingo.

The pool temperature had to be pushing seventy-five degrees. Still, the chlorinated water refreshed him. How great to submerge completely, to do flips in the water, seal swim the length of the pool. While swimming, Seth could leave his prosthesis behind. The only issue was a slight pull to the side when he kicked.

He swam laps, taking care not to splash, although the closest homes were behind a line of trees, and everyone in a neighborhood like this would have their windows shut and the air conditioning blasting. What he wanted was to jump off the diving board, but the splash would make too much noise. Instead, he shaved his beard, being careful to stand in front of the skimmer so his hairs and shave foam would be sucked into the filter. He washed his hair, too, and wished for a shower to rinse the chlorine from his skin and hair.

Bingo.

A showerhead stuck out from the brick wall of the pool house. At first, the water was hot when it came out, but cooler water followed. Seth stood under the refreshing shower, touching the brick wall for balance, letting the water sluice through his hair. How much cleaner and cooler a shaven face felt when the water ran over his skin. In fact, the swim so refreshed him, he didn't bother with bourbon. Instead, he lay on the cushioned lounger with only his soft throw blanket beneath him, bare as the day he was born. He pulled his damp hair into a ponytail and settled in with cold pizza, warm beer, and his Kindle, the soft backlit screen lighting up his face and taking him into the story. The humming pool filter, the crickets' calls, and the random interruptions of higher-pitched insects were his music. The pool had an electrical outlet presently charging his phone, and he had set his phone alarm to give him time to be up and out before the sun.

But oh, five o'clock came too soon. Seth's eyes were barely closed when the phone vibration woke him.

One last swim, to rally him for the ride ahead.

As he pulled himself out of the pool and reached for his towel, the pool house door opened with a squeak. A girl, who couldn't be out of high school yet stood in the doorway, a sly smile on her face. She wore a gauzy white Cami and short shorts with strawberries on them. Her painted toenails stuck out of the black slides. Her septum ring glinted in the light that had turned on when she opened the door—a motion-activated light that Seth had managed not to trip by climbing the fence.

"Hi," she said. Coyly.

Seth clumsily wrapped the towel around his naked self, trying not to hop all over the place. Failing.

"Don't," she said. She pulled the door closed and approached.

With one hand he braced himself on the bricks of the pool house, and with his other he gripped the towel knot. She approached, twirling her sleep-tossed hair. Her highly glossed lips parted in an almost-smile.

"I was just leaving," Seth said, but he did not move. He couldn't, without hopping over to where his prosthesis lay propped against the lounge chair. This girl's behavior was very Ivy, very brazen and sexy. Very fucking scary and electric in a forbidden way.

"I saw you on the ring camera," she said. "I watched you read...and sleep. You're cute when you sleep. What happened to your foot?"

The pool filter kicked on, sucking the water into the skimmers. The sound drew Seth's attention, and the girl took the opportunity to put her hand on his shaven cheek. The touch was as curious as she was young.

"How old are you?" He gently removed her hand.

"Old enough," she purred. "Don't worry. I won't tell anyone. It took me the whole night to work up the guts to come. I saw you. On the camera, swimming...and everything."

"Yeah, you said." Seth gripped his towel knot again.

"I snuck out." The girl hiccuped.

That was when Seth noticed her glassy eyes and how she swayed a bit. Her minty breath, likely camouflaging something. "You drove here?" he asked.

She blinked slowly. "What do you care?"

"Let's start over," he said. "I'm Seth."

"I'm stoned." As if to prove it, she giggled.

"Well, Stoned, it's a pleasure to meet you. I was on my way out."

"Please don't go. I just want to talk. The pool doesn't open until noon."

Why this gorgeous high schooler would want to talk with Seth was anyone's guess. And, looking at her lips again, Seth was certain talk was not all she wanted. He hopped over to his lounge chair, hoping that his ungainly movements would make him less desirable in her eyes.

It did the opposite. She wrapped herself around him and made herself into a crutch. A crutch that palmed his bare chest, presently. Awkwardly, he jumped out of her grasp and motioned for her to take the chair beside his. Like it was his to offer, and not him trespassing in the girl's community pool.

"So how'd you know I was here?" Seth asked.

She sat in Seth's chair, beside him. "My dad's the president of the homeowners' association. He has the camera feed on his phone. I hacked his account so I could watch the animals that trip the motion sensors..." She described the deer she had seen, the raccoons, even a fox.

"Then I saw you—" Her breath caught.

"Uh, yeah...I was hot."

"Yeah..."

Seth shook his head. "No..."

Stoned blinked and seemed to expect Seth to say more. He didn't know what. Staring at the moon seemed like a good idea. He could feel the girl's eyes on him. They sat wordlessly side-by-side for a long while until she sniffled.

"Hey..." Seth oriented himself to better see her.

Yep. Crying.

"Hey...er...what's wrong?" Seth wasn't sure what was going on. As far as he could tell, nothing had transpired that called for tears.

Stoned cried on, silently.

"I admit," he nudged her gently with his side. "I am unqualified to handle tears." He felt her slouch into his side.

Her sniffling stopped.

"I have a friend who would know what to do. He boggles me because he seems normal at first, but he's an embalmer. And he reads the Bible, like, over and over. Very strange. He'd have—"

"I'm strange."

Turned out, Stoned was shy. No—more than shy. She explained that the idea of being with people, especially with people her own age, terrified her. She didn't know why. She liked people, but only from a distance. She had moved in with her father and his new wife a year ago, had no friends, and couldn't wait for the summer to end so she could go back to college, where her class load kept her too busy for friends.

"College, huh? I thought you were younger."

"Thanks." She rammed her shoulder into him. "I graduate in a year. Genetics and Genomics."

"Wow," Seth breathed, "that's a lot."

"I'm autistic, I think."

"You think?"

"My therapist doesn't like labels. He says I'm *more than autistic*, but I think he says that to make me feel better about the fact that I have no friends."

"But look at you—you seem normal." *Except for the spying and scaring the crap out of a total stranger in the middle of the night.*

Stoned sighed. "Everyone thinks if you don't act like Rain Man, you're not autistic."

Seth snorted. "You're definitely not Rain Man."

There was silence. What he meant by *definitely not Rain Man* was that she was easier to look at, but he didn't want Stoned to think he was down for *getting down* with her. Even if she thought she wanted the likes of Seth, she wasn't in the right frame of mind to know what she wanted.

"Rain Man's a little before your time, isn't it?"

She scoffed. "I learn all I can about the spectrum—and everything. I like learning."

"Fair enough."

Stoned twirled her hair as she spoke, choosing her words. "If you had…a headache, how would you prove it? To someone else?"

"I'd tell them my head hurt."

"I don't believe you, that your head hurts," she shot back.

Seth thought about that. How would he prove to someone else that he had a hangover? If they didn't believe him, he'd be at a loss to convince anyone of the painful throbbing in his skull. Hangovers were as real as gravity. And all too commonplace. But could he prove he had one?

Girl had a point.

"I came because of your foot," she explained, "I figure people treat you differently because of it. And you're smoking hot. But that's not the real reason. I want a friend—with benefits…"

Unexpected.

When Seth's paralyzed tongue would not make words, the girl continued, "If that's your thing?"

"You're asking me to have sex with you? Why?"

"You make it sound gross. I just want a friend who's far away, who I can talk to without all the nerves getting in the way."

"Wait. Weren't we just talking about something else? Now we're talking about being friends?"

Stoned grabbed fistfuls of her hair and made an exasperated sigh.

"Sorry. I don't understand," Seth tried to make eye contact by leaning in.

She would have none of it. "Argh—I want someone to write with me. Would you do it—tell me all about where you go and who you meet?"

Seth's smile was cut off by the clang of the metal fence opening. A hulkish kid with blonde, curly hair and red shorts that said GUARD in white letters strode to the pool house and let himself inside.

Both Seth and Stoned jumped up from the lounge chair, and Seth frantically pulled on his boxers, thanking God that he had the sense to put his clothing out the night before, when he intended to be dressing in the dark. Usually and for balance, Seth put on his foot before his clothes.

Stoned held a *shhhh* finger to her lips and eyed the intruder, whose back was to them.

How would it look, Seth with this girl-woman, pulling up his pants? But how would it look, Seth with only a towel for clothing, caught with her?

His stump snagged on his shorts, and he lost his balance and toppled back onto the chair, cringing at the noise it made. But for some reason the lifeguard didn't turn around.

Earbuds. Thank God for earbuds.

The guard hadn't seen them yet, had his shirtless back to them, and was bent over swishing paper sticks in the kiddie pool. A line of text tattooed his bronzed shoulders at the base of his neck—Latin, or something. Three words. Too small to read.

An ear-piercing "HEY!" zapped Seth and sent him flailing back onto the lounger with his bike shorts mostly up his legs. The first guard spun and took in Seth, Stoned, and the second lifeguard.

He touched his earbuds. A knowing smile played on his lips.

"The pool opens at noon," he said to Seth. To Stoned, he said, "Hey, Liberty."

"I'm calling the cops," the other lifeguard threatened.

"Don't," Seth begged. "I was leaving." With his shorts mostly on, he gathered his beer cans and put them in a plastic bag. He hoped that if the lifeguards saw he meant no harm, that they'd turn a blind eye. As he hastily gathered his things, he said under his breath, "Liberty? It's nice. Fits you."

"I like when you call me Stoned," Liberty's voice had a new, sad resignation.

"Stoned, it is," he winked as he pulled on his prosthesis. Without waiting for a response, Seth practically ran out the gate, dropping his bag of cans and pizza box in the garbage on his way. Stoned-Liberty grabbed his towel and followed, asking if she could have his phone number, his email, and could she snap a picture of them together?

"Are you nuts?" Seth hadn't meant to sound harsh.

The little, hurt sound that issued from Stoned-Liberty stopped his momentum. He turned to her, to tell her no—no way was he down for being penpals with benefits.

The male lifeguard caught up with them. "Hey, you dropped this." Seth's phone.

"Oh, thanks."

From the poolhouse, the female guard shouted, "Gabe, he left this, too." She held up his Kindle, not willing to walk it out to the parking lot.

Gabe strode the thirty feet or so to his co-worker and returned with Seth's Kindle. He addressed them both. "You know each other?"

Liberty spoke first, "Yeah, he's my uncle. Uncle Seth. We were swimming."

Gabe clearly didn't believe her.

She added, "Don't tell, okay?"

"I won't, but..." He thumbed back to where his co-worker stood, hands on her hips, watching the exchange.

"I don't want any trouble," Seth said, thinking of the cops and the death glare he was getting from the female lifeguard. She held up her phone, recording them. Gabe followed Seth's gaze, then strode back to his co-worker. The whole time, she seemed to be videoing Seth and Gabe alternately. Seth could not imagine her saving anyone, only yelling at kids who were trying to have fun.

Gabe whispered something in his co-worker's ear. Her jaw dropped open. An angry expression settled on her face. Gabe put out his hand for her phone, and she reluctantly handed it over. After doing something (erasing her footage?) he handed it back to her.

As he returned, he lowered his voice, "Selena's not going to tell. I told her you have access to the cameras, and you recorded what she did last summer."

"But...I don't...know what she did," Stoned-Liberty replied. "I didn't even live here until the end of the summer."

"Doesn't matter because I know," Gabe said. "Your dad gave me access when you guys went on vacation last year and said I should call him if I saw something significant. He didn't want to be bothered every time a deer set off the motion detectors." Gabe let that sink in before continuing. "You better erase the footage," he said.

"Why are you guys here so early?" Liberty asked. "The pool's not opening for hours."

"Swim meet," Gabe thumbed. "Selena was on the schedule to open. When I saw the video, I knew it would be better if I got here first."

Seth imagined Selena walking in on him and Stoned-Liberty. He would be in the back of a police cruiser at this moment, had she been the one to discover them.

Aha...things were getting clearer. This Gabe knew they were here and pretended not to, to give Seth privacy to get dressed.

"Thanks, I owe you one," Seth said, extending a hand to shake.

"Don't mention it." He shook and left them with a wave.

When Gabe was out of earshot, Liberty took Seth's hand, leaned into him and whispered, "I turn twenty-one in a week."

He thought of Monroe, the woman who haunted him in all the best ways. Monroe was older than Liberty by what—seven years? When Seth had met Monroe, he saw only opportunity. Here, he saw a lonely, misunderstood girl, who would give herself to him in return for what? Being her pen pal? He didn't want her to feel ugly or rejected, but he could not accept her offer. How carefully he would have to step. *Careful* stepping didn't come naturally to Seth. His social skills were as crippled as his body.

"A guy who would take your offer—the benefits—is..." He recalled a conversation about Monroe, how Miles had rebuked Seth's offhand comment about wanting *to hit that.* "...well, he's not your friend," Seth said.

Her eyes welled with tears.

Bingo. Rejected. Of course she felt rejected.

Quickly, Seth added, "You're beautiful, and I'm attracted to you and all. Hell, anyone with eyes is attracted to you, Liberty—er, Stoned. But writing's not my thing..."

"I'm not asking for a book, just a text once in a while so I can see the cool places you go."

"I don't think it's a good idea."

"Look at you. You haven't had a "good" idea in a long time. That's why I like you." And she gushed about all the bad guy characters she loved: Loki, the Joker (played by Jared Leto, of course), Christian Bale from American Psycho—"

Seth had to gently stop her when another car pulled into the parking lot, someone helping with the swim meet, no doubt.

"Let's save the picture for another day."

Instant tears.

"BUT...I have an idea. How about I give you my number, and we'll start slow, okay? You know, tell each other what we like to do for fun? What our favorite ice cream flavor is...that sort of stuff."

"Chocolate." Liberty sniffled and almost-smiled.

"Peanut butter," Seth said.

Liberty snapped a selfie and made sure Seth received the text. "Trust issues," she said by way of explanation.

"I get you," Seth replied.

She kissed his cheek.

Chapter 18

IN THE WEEKS AFTER meeting Stoned-Liberty, Seth sent pictures he hoped she would enjoy: the Sleeping Bear Dunes, Lake Michigan, and a friendly dog that followed his bike for several miles. He snapped shots of things he never thought to capture before: rocks piled on the side of the road by previous travelers, signs or billboards that made him laugh, the malevolent turkey that chased him into traffic and got squashed by a semi (edgy, yes, but she enjoyed horror books). Stoned-Liberty always responded with pictures of herself at various locations. The smoothie bar, the fitness trail, the mall, and the library. She'd taken to swimming at the pool, had a tan, and her most recent picture was her standing on the lifeguard chair in a bikini holding the megaphone to her mouth, yelling something.

Seth asked, who was the poor kid getting a bawling out?

balling out???

is that old people speak?

Now Seth was old? He grinned, sent her a GIF of a wrinkled old man, and texted:

who were u yelling at?

She texted back that she was singing. Her next text was a link for the music video, "What's Up?" by the 4 Non-Blondes.

Gabe played it for me

best day evr

Seth had a feeling she had a crush on Gabe. Good for her.

It wasn't always easy thinking of things to write to a brainiac on the spectrum. What Liberty needed was a heart-to-heart with *her* old man. Instead, she had Seth. He told her how—whenever he asked a local person how far it was to the next town—they would respond in minutes, not miles. Car minutes. Seth was often at a loss to decipher how much time it would take on his bicycle. And he'd have to factor in extra time if he had decided to dunk his consciousness in beer or bourbon the night before. The morning routine was considerably longer with a hangover (he shared that with Liberty, as well as a stern admonition not to do as he did). Hangover days happened now and then (usually after an Ivy nightmare, which he did not share).

Stoned-Liberty texted to ask Seth what he thought about her taking a midnight swim, as Seth had.

How to answer? Did she want permission? He told her to clear it with Gabe first since he'd see her on the videos.

duh the point is 4 him 2 see me on cameras

Seth felt a strange protective care for her. He texted:

trust me, he sees u

She texted back:

tell me a road story

She always called them road stories.

Seth did not share what happened in this morning's hangover moment, when he found himself with no choice but to dismount his bike during rush hour on I-90, cars and trucks whizzing by, honking, while he squatted and cleared his entire large intestine into the berm. Used a sock to wipe.

He kept that road story under the hood.

Instead, he told her about a man he had met a couple of days ago who was also missing his foot and most of his leg, who almost got run over while shepherding ducks across the road. Seth included a picture of the man in his wheelchair, sweeping them with his hands, the flag of the USA flapping from a long pole attached to his chair. That was yesterday. Seth offered to buy the bearded vet breakfast, recalling the kindness of the bartender, Dave, who mistook Seth for a vet. Seth told Stoned-Liberty that the vet pulled a mangy Bible out and spent the whole breakfast telling Seth all the times God had protected him from harm.

"Except the one time," Seth couldn't help himself.

"Oh, this?" The vet patted his stump. "This was the best thing that ever happened to me. You know what I mean, don't you, friend?" The man motioned to Seth's prosthesis.

"Er...no...not really." Seth had to ask, "You ever ask God why he let you lose your leg?"

"Plenty of times, friend. He gives me the same answer every time."

"And what's the answer?"

The vet didn't move, didn't answer.

"Well—what's he say?"

More silence, then, "That's it. Nothin'. He don't say a thing." The vet slammed his hands on the table and laughed—way more than the story called for, if you asked Seth.

When Seth relayed the conversation to Stoned-Liberty, she texted: **its true**

what's true? Seth returned.

god is funny Stoned's text didn't quite clarify.

So Seth texted: **trying 2 figure out god**

Her answer: **he knows that**

Seth texted: **u remind me of someone**

She texted back a picture of a gorgeous actress.

But Seth meant Monroe. He meant Stoned's insides reminded him of someone else's insides. Stoned-Liberty reminded him of Monroe and how sure of God she was. Stoned-Liberty was a young woman trying to feel beautiful and valuable, who didn't know she was. But she was darn sure about her feelings on religion. Over and over on the road, Seth met people who wanted to riff about their faith. Some were nut jobs who had no idea Seth wasn't interested in hearing their political opinions or getting rescued "from the jaws of hell." Seth's theory was that the pushy ones were salesmen in some invisible holy corporation that paid strictly on commission. To dispatch those pests, Seth would feign ignorance about all things religion, let them get their talk out, and dutifully repeat the recipe prayer they provided. Oh, the joy on their faces when they clapped him on the back and assured him he was saved. He'd lost count of how many times he'd been saved.

To Stoned-Liberty, he texted: **jesus freaks r attracted 2 me 4 some reason**

There was a pause in the communication. Seth could see the jumping dots showing she was typing an answer, but no text came. Either it was a super-long text or Stoned-Liberty was second-guessing what she wanted to say.

fwiw, she texted **Jeremiah 23:24**

fwiw? Seth looked it up. *For what it's worth.* Right on, Seth thought, as he pocketed his phone and mounted his bicycle. He would look up the verse later. Sweet of her to pick it for him. It reminded Seth of how Miles would use verses like clickbait. Stoned-Liberty's fascination with religion surprised and perplexed him because—as far as Seth could tell—she was as much a lost pirate as he was, stealing what happiness she could and drowning (or in her case, smoking) away her problems.

The road was rough that day, what with idiots and assholes navigating the construction on a stretch of county road. Seth had *to keep a reverent focus* (that was the phrase he used in a text to Stoned-Liberty), in order not to kiss asphalt. The road was his religion, he told her.

Over the many miles, he came to believe there were two choices faced by drivers, two lanes. One was a long-ass snake of cars that had dutifully merged into the correct lane waaaaay the hell back where the sign said to merge. The other lane was empty, except for a few cars that whizzed by, fast-tracking to the front, where they would cut off whoever they needed to, in order to cut the line. One lane was full of polite idiots, and the other lane was full of selfish assholes. Seth, who rode on the shoulder to the right of the idiots, could hear them cursing the assholes from their open windows. One idiot in a BMW almost ran Seth down trying to avoid a collision with a dented, rusty minivan whose driver bullied his way into the lane.

If Seth were in a car right now, which would he be—idiot or asshole? Asshole, no doubt about it.

Miles would be an idiot; he was pretty sure. Monroe, too. What about God? God didn't have to choose because he could magically turn his car into a plane and do a flyover, bypassing the choice altogether.

The more Seth thought about it, though, he didn't think God would do a flyover because that was just another way to be a selfish asshole, to muscle a way out of the common experience, which, to Seth's mind, was an exercise of patience. Waiting for one's turn. God would merge when the sign said to merge. He would wait for his turn. Seth should change his ways and become a person who waited in the idiot lane.

Easier said than done.

At an ice cream stand a few miles out from his destination, Red River Gorge, Kentucky, Seth shoveled a banana split into his mouth while looking up the verse Stoned-Liberty had sent him, Jeremiah 23:24. When he read it, he chuckled.

He read it again from his campsite at the top of the Indian Staircase, a vista overlooking the Daniel Boone National Forest: *Can anyone hide from me in a secret place? Am I not everywhere in all the heavens and earth?*

Chapter 19

THE CHURCH COZIED UP to the corner of two country roads, almost trails really, that once upon a time may have been asphalt, but the creep of vegetation narrowed the road, leaving only enough driveable space for a single car.

Didn't matter because Seth had not seen a single car in many miles.

On either side of the road, tall, ash-colored grass sprawled all the way to the horizon, dotted with a few scraggly evergreens.

What a strange road.

Had he missed a turn?

Seth figured the church doors would be locked for sure, notwithstanding the wooden sign almost entirely curtained by black-eyed Susans, their yellowness a shock in that dry and colorless landscape. The sign read: *Come in. All are welcome.*

Rather than come in as the sign suggested, Seth cased the place. There were no cars in the tiny gravel lot behind the well-kept church. A yellow film of pollen covered the windowpanes. When Seth wiped it clean with his hand, he blinked and rubbed his eyes.

Three stained-glass lancet windows threw dazzling light onto the altar, diffusing the room in colorful bands of brightness. The ornate wooden pew backs shone with care. The sloped ceiling was cedar wood, and the windowed walls allowed the sun to shine all the way into the cathedral. The wall-to-wall red carpet looked as soft as a comforter.

A man reclined upon the altar steps, reading.

He had a faded green t-shirt and khaki shorts, hiking shoes so dusty you couldn't tell where the dirt ended and the sole began. Yet the shoes were not worn out. The reader pulled absently at the elastic of his brown socks. His fingers looked strong, if that was possible, and his lean frame had an ease Seth had never seen before in a human being. As if he were made of breeze, yet as solid as the steps he sat upon, as sturdy as the book in his hand, as ephemeral as the shaft of light draping his shoulders. His hair was about as long as Seth's, curly too, but dark and glossy like the oak pews.

The man looked up from his book and turned toward the window.

Seth lurched back and flattened himself against the church siding like a criminal, trampling the flowers. "Aww...darn," he muttered. After a few seconds he peeked again, rearing back in surprise when he found the man had come to the window and stood inches from the pane.

"Hi, friend," he said.

Caught, Seth waved guiltily.

The man pointed to the door and mouthed words that looked like, "It's open."

Seth nodded and gave a hesitant thumbs-up. The door swung easily, and he was greeted by the comforting scent of warm candle wax.

The man motioned for Seth to join him on the plush altar steps.

Seth hesitated. "Do I know you?"

"Uh huh." He winked. "Please, join me. You've had a long journey and still have a long way to go."

Seth eyed him.

"Even God rested, Seth." He smiled, "but not because he needed to."

Seth remained standing, narrowed his eyes. "How do I know you?"

The man steepled his hands, elbows on his knees. "You know you're dreaming, right?"

"No."

The man raised his eyebrows, as if Seth's answer disappointed him.

"You're familiar, but I can't place where we met," Seth tried again, keeping his distance.

"I have some news I need to share," the man began. "It's not good."

When he didn't continue, Seth asked. "Well...?"

"There was a fire at Miles's home."

"A fire? How do you know? And how do you know Miles? Wait. How do you know I know Miles?" Seth pinched his own arm as he spoke. It didn't hurt.

"The way I know everything I know. It would take a long time to—"

"No. I don't believe it."

"To believe or not is your choice. But regardless, it is true." His eyes were kind.

"*How* do I know you?" Seth asked, this time in a whisper.

"Miles did not survive."

"What...?"

"I'm sorry. I know he was a friend."

Seth dropped onto one of the steps, put his head in his hands. All the times he felt the urge to contact Miles, to reach out and tell him about his travels or his evolving convictions on life and religion, yet Seth had never followed through. And now, could this be true? Miles...gone?

The man put a hand on Seth's shoulder. A pulse of heat and energy vaulted through his body, starting where the palm of the man's hand rested.

Another thought came on the heels of his grief. "Monroe. What's going to happen to her? And the cats."

"Monroe is strong. What do *you* think will happen to her?"

Seth shook his head and scrunched his eyes. "I don't know."

"I want to leave you with one last thing, because I know you'll be angry at yourself for not asking. The answer is: *free will*."

"The answer?"

"To the question you'll wish you asked me when you had the chance."

But Seth didn't have a question.

In the befuddling way of dreams, Seth was transported back to his bike seat and was trekking along the overgrown road that had led him to the church. Only now, he was peddling in the other direction, away from the church.

Running away, Seth, like always.

No.

Seth squeezed the brakes and winced at the sound of burning rubber. He turned his bike around, intending to go back the way he had come, back to the old country church, to grab the reader man by the throat and compel him to reveal where Monroe was.

Not paying attention because the overgrown road was deserted, he turned his wheel onto what became a five-lane interstate. Electric cars were so quiet, especially in dreams. They could be going seventy miles an hour and you would never know.

Unless one clipped your bicycle tire and shot you with a rocket's thrust, not up, but down. Down into the gritty asphalt, yanked hard and fast enough to flatten your skull, crush your rage, erase your grief. Erase everything.

Bingo.

Seth found himself in the morgue, staring into painfully bright lights. The stainless-steel table he lay on chilled his bones. On the table beside his, Miles leaned over a corpse and motioned for Seth to get up, to come closer. Beneath his black plastic apron, Miles wore a Rolling Stones T-shirt (Seth could see the teeth and tongue). Black rubber gloves protected his hands. Faded jeans and rubber boots completed his work ensemble. Between Miles's feet, a hose fed brownish liquid into a floor drain.

Ick.

"You didn't do me already, did you...Miles?" Seth asked.

"Don't be a chicken, Seth."

Chicken? Miles wouldn't call him names. He broke out in sweat. Dead people didn't sweat.

Miles grinned as he worked on the body, a woman. Her shriveled legs looked like tree branches that ended in a pair of high heels. Her feet didn't look right.

Why didn't they look right?

Because naked bodies in a mortuary didn't wear high heels. Dead people on display were covered from the waist down by a blanket.

Years ago, Ivy had asked, was Woods wearing shoes under there? Asked while she and Seth stood over Woods's coffin. Ivy tried to move the blanket to see, and Seth stayed her hand. She scratched him with those pointy, fire engine red nails of hers.

"Ouch!" he had said too loudly and garnered the attention of the room, all of Woods's friends and family who were there to mourn.

Woods sat up in the coffin. "Don't touch me, Ivy," he mumbled, his eyes still stitched shut, but trying to open, his mouth leaking embalming fluid where the jaw-clamping wires tore the flesh. Woods managed to pop one eye open, the stitches tearing through his eyelids. "It's your fault I'm here."

Seth thought Woods spoke to Ivy, but a cold, wooden finger touched him. Woods meant it was Seth's fault.

Dreaming for sure.

Nightmaring.

Ivy didn't skip a beat. "Oh, what do you care, Woods?" She sputtered, "You're dead. You won't be needing your feet or your legs." With a palm to the chest, Ivy shoved Woods back onto his coffin pillow.

"Ivy," Seth said through gritted teeth. "Show some respect."

Woods barely hit the pillow before he turned into Miles, morphed like one of those lenticular cards that shift when you tilt them different ways. Woods-turned-Miles moved at double speed, picked Seth up by his arm pits and yanked him into the casket (which was surprisingly—dreamily—nightmarishly deep. Deep enough that Seth caught the side of the coffin and hung there over a chasm, legs swinging. When he chanced a look down, figuring he'd see Woods's or Miles's body which had to be beneath him, he saw the hundred-foot ravine into which he had fallen all those years ago—the river winding at the bottom, the boulders scattered in the creek bed, the trees lining the sides, the shale sticking out here and there or in piles where there had been washouts.

"Let go, dummy," Ivy said. Her hair hung down and tickled Seth's knuckles as he held onto the side of the coffin. Ivy was Ivy and her small, freckled hands began to peel Seth's fingers from the sides of the coffin. Her manicured nails dug into his flesh.

He could not hold on much longer. About that, Ivy was correct. Seth had been trying to order his world, to reorder his life after that harrowing, broadsiding, neck-breaking, heart-breaking, killing day when he realized—too late—that some monsters were pretty. Some monsters made you feel good for a while. They bit later. Like bourbon.

After squeezing his eyes shut and saying a prayer, he let go of the side and fell. He opened his eyes to...

Woods.

In the casket where he belonged.

No Ivy.

No Miles.

Standing beside the coffin was the mysterious and gentle reading man from the church. "You're this close." He pinched his fingers an inch apart.

"From what?"

"You know 'from what.'" (Yes, that was rebuke Seth heard.)

"I want to know what's true," Seth said.

"What do you believe is true?" The man answered.

"I don't know. Would I have asked if I knew?"

"Yes, you would," Reading Man countered.

Seth hated when people told him he knew things. It made him feel stupid and childish.

"Fine, I meant to ask for justice," Seth said. He liked the word *justice*, because justice involved Ivy being locked up and regularly tortured in a cell on Alcatraz or wherever they put the too-bad-to-fix people. Seth's hate had played a scene: Ivy disemboweled, Seth jumping rope with her intestines while she watched. Even with all the reading and praying and the whole God-forgives thing fermenting inside him, Seth couldn't bring himself to imagine a world where the likes of Ivy was forgiven.

Miles appeared on the other side of Seth and opened his Bible and pointed. In the dream, he and Seth had a long discussion in which Seth raised objections, and Miles and the Reading Man parried them.

"But she killed Monroe's cat. She set your house on fire. She killed you, man."

"I died because I went back inside the house," Miles corrected.

"Trying to save the cats," Seth said, not sure how he knew that fact. "I can't forgive Ivy for what she did. God can't make me forgive her."

"You're right that I won't, but not that I can't," the Reading Man said.

Miles continued, "I should have known better than to go back inside, but...Monroe. You know how she loves those cats."

Seth teared up at an image of Monroe tickling her chin with a cat's tail, sitting in the setting sunlight with cottonwood fuzzies floating around her like fairies. "I'm sorry for what I said about Monroe. I don't see her that way now."

"You mean, you don't consider her a place to park your—"

"Stop," Seth interrupted. "I didn't mean it. Or, I *did* mean it, and later I didn't. Look, the point is, I don't think that way anymore. I don't know why, and I don't know how. Something's changed about the way I see people. Except Ivy. I still hate her guts and would like to see her intestines pulled out while she watches."

"You're this close." Miles held his fingers as the reading man had.

"To the truth?" Seth asked.

"To the bottom of the ravine," Miles answered.

And Seth felt himself back inside the Morley chest freezer. His body slammed into the creek bed at a hundred miles an hour, give or take. Terminal velocity is one hundred twenty miles per hour. Seth woke from his nightmare, just as surprised as when he came to years ago, alive, after the fall that should have killed him, that did kill his best friend.

The nightmare had changed. Was it a vision? Was it true about Miles?

Seth reached for the bourbon flask he kept in the pocket of his hammock, took a huge swig. Morning sun brightened the hammock's seam, then splashed in upon him when he pushed the fabric open, passing the empty flask through the slit in his hammock. He gazed at the treetops and the bluing sky and was relieved to feel the bourbon already working.

To his camp coffee, he added another slosh. Might be a day to lie low at the campsite, drink bourbon, forget himself.

Chapter 20

Seth woke for the second time that day in his hammock, this time to the setting sun, the empty bottle of Buffalo Trace cradled in his arms. Cottonwood fluffs made lazy circuits in the sunlight. Indian Creek Lake stretched out to his right, light diamonds twinkling in its center. The silhouette of a kayaker and a paddleboarder glided into view. Their laughter and conversation made Seth wish for company. He strained to hear their words carried on the breeze, but he caught only snatches. He became aware of his phone vibrating in his hammock sack, soft but insistent. He also became aware of his bladder and his skull, both smarting.

By the time he fished the phone out, the buzzing had stopped. He didn't recognize the number. Before he pocketed it, a call came again from that same unknown number.

Seth answered.

On the other end there was silence. Not a dead line, because there were faint sounds like the caller was in a public place, maybe a restaurant or an office.

"Hello?" Seth repeated.

Something about that silence felt menacing. Seth ended the call and waited, thinking he would get another call, that someone was toying with him. He texted Stoned-Liberty.

hey you call me from a different #?

no Y?

nm talk soon :)

Even though it was evening, Seth made campfire coffee. He opened a new bottle of bourbon, poured himself a mug, and added a splash of coffee. He sipped it by the crackling fire and rested his feet on a debarked log. The lake became placid with the setting sun. Animals or fellow hikers snapped branches in the woods as they trudged within earshot. Every time, Seth would freeze and listen, straining to know whether the footfalls were coming closer or passing by.

Passing by.

He munched on peppered beef jerky and potato chips, feeling lazy because of the day and night he had spent drinking in solitude. He was better than that—that was his goal these days, to be better than a drunk amoeba—but the dream had gotten under his skin.

Seth's phone buzzed again. He delayed pulling it from his pocket in case it was the unknown caller. Let them leave a message. When it stopped going off, he checked it. Whew. Texts from Stoned-Liberty and a video of her coaxing a groundhog. The groundhog warily approached and almost allowed her to pet it before turning tail and running off.

"Don't go," she said to the groundhog on the video. "I'm lonely."

That was how Seth felt. He almost called her, but Liberty was not the person to help him interpret or examine his dreams. Instead, Seth tried Googling for news from the Doe Pond area. He wasn't superstitious, but what could it hurt? Finding nothing would put him at ease. He entered into the search bar: *house fire huntsville.*

And there it was.

Miles's home. What was left of it. The article had been published two days earlier.

"How?" Seth asked.

Free will.

Where had that come from? It came to mind right then, as if it were an answer to a question Seth didn't know he had asked.

The answer to the question you will have wished you asked. The Reading Man said Seth would have a question, but he didn't have a question. He had only grief that felt like a woman's hands, choking his heart. Ivy's hands.

He scrolled, searching, hoping to read that Miles was unhurt. *Body found amid debris in Huntsville County fire.*

No.

Another thought punched him. Monroe? What if the body...a small noise issued from his lips.

He dialed Miles's phone number. It went to voicemail. What fuckery that he didn't even have Monroe's phone number. He tried Miles again, and someone picked up. Not Miles.

"Hello?"

"Who's this?" Seth asked.

"Lieutenant Stacy Kaufman, Huntsville Fire."

"Where's Miles?" Seth could barely get out the question because he knew the answer, but he had to ask anyway, had to hear it. And also, he didn't know what else to do with himself.

"I'm sorry, I can't comment from this phone number...are you family?"

When he couldn't make words in response, she apologized and suggested he contact the police department for more information. She offered a direct number to the chief that would be answered twenty-four-seven, but Seth had nowhere to write it, so he thanked the lieutenant and ended the call.

Why would God allow Miles to die?

Why?

WHY???

Free will.

There it was, the question and the answer. It made no sense, but the words popped into Seth's head, unbidden. He had no idea what free will had to do with a good man like Miles, dying a senseless, random death. Seth wished a tree would fall on him. It could happen. Trees fell on unsuspecting campers all the time. Well, not *all* the time. But it happened. It would make as much sense as Miles dying in a fire. Actually, because Seth wasn't as good a man as Miles, it would make a hell of a lot more sense.

As Seth waited for (and dared) God to judge him with a tree to the head, he peered at the leafy treetops, made golden by the firelight.

The next day, Seth searched the headlines, hoping for a story about the many cats from Miles's residence. All those homeless cats would be a newsworthy story for sure. Seth hoped he would see Monroe, with her cats, in a story showing all the adoptable cats who survived the fire. He waited and waited for the story to appear, but it never did. Nothing about Monroe appeared. Nothing about cats.

Seth could take the suspense no longer and made the call to his ex-supervisor, the super, as everyone called him.

"Seth!?" the familiar, jolly voice, obviously happy but wondering why he was hearing from his ex-employee.

"Hey Boss," Seth said. After the usual how-are-you's and Seth's truncated story of his cycling adventure, Seth got to the point. "Do you know about Miles?"

The super made a pained sound. "So you heard...a tragedy. I didn't know you were still in touch."

"Well, we weren't...exactly...I'm calling about his...friend, Monroe. She had a lot of cats at his place, and I wonder what's going to happen to them?" Seth, Miles's long-lost, cat-loving friend who is *not* losing his shit over the beautiful owner of said cats. Totally believable.

"Can't say I know anything about the cats, but you know who might? Miles's friend, the one who did your prosthesis."

Augh. But of course it would be Mr. Mitka the limb fairy, the dude from whom Seth had stolen his prostheses.

The super obviously didn't know Seth was on Mitka's naughty list. He said, "It's great that you're traveling the country and living your best life. Miles would have wanted that for you."

Seth thanked the super and hung up. He did not want to contact the limb fairy, but his need to know Monroe was okay overrode his misgivings. Even the receptionist recognized Seth. He could tell by the way her voice lowered an octave.

The limb fairy's tone was also uncharacteristically cold. "Hello, Seth."

Seth choked out, "I understand if you're mad—"

"Kindly get to the point, Seth."

"I was calling about Miles."

"Oh. You heard."

"Yes."

He cleared his throat. "What can I do for you?"

You can tell me how the fuck Monroe is. "Um...I remember there were a lot of cats...and...I was told you might know something about how they are. And Monroe. How she is..."

There was a pause.

"Miles spoke of you so often, I assumed you kept in touch."

"He did?" Seth wanted to ask what he said, but the limb fairy's tone dissuaded him.

"Look, I have a patient waiting," the limb fairy got stern, "What you did was wrong, Seth. You thwarted research that could've helped others."

"I know, Mr. M—"

"And leaving like you did was incredibly selfish."

"Yes," Seth agreed.

"Now I have to—"

"Wait. Do you have Monroe's phone number?"

"If I did, I wouldn't give it without her consent. Goodbye, Seth." He hung up.

Googling cat rescue shelters in and around the Huntsville area eventually yielded a person who knew Monroe *and* was willing to speak on the phone with Seth.

Ann, a volunteer who walked shelter dogs, told Seth that she and Monroe were friends, and although she hadn't heard from Monroe since the funeral, she'd pass on Seth's phone number and a message to call him.

Monroe never called.

After a week, Seth reached out to Ann again.

"I can't understand it," Ann complained. "She didn't even say goodbye."

"Really—Monroe?"

"Isn't that horrible to do to a friend?"

"Yes," Seth agreed with a pang. "Horrible."

"It's so unlike her, usually so thoughtful. The shelter took in all the cats from Miles's house, and—because of the fire—we got them adopted in a week. Tragedies do that to people," she said.

That didn't sound like Monroe. She would say goodbye.

"Are you sure there wasn't anything wrong?" Seth asked. "Like, she was in trouble?"

"Monroe? Never," Ann countered. "She's a good girl."

"Yes," was all Seth could mutter.

There was silence while Seth tried to figure out another way to ask the same question about Monroe, hoping for a more satisfying answer. On Ann's end, the barking of a dog got louder. She swore and breathlessly explained that "the brute" nearly yanked her arm out of the socket at seeing some "luscious thing in the woods."

"Okay. I'm concerned about her, is all," Seth said.

"She probably got herself a boyfriend. She was always going on about a man she was waiting for. I'll bet you, he heard about the fire and came. Men are heroic like that—when they're not pigs. You know?"

When they're not pigs...sure.

Ann was fine to give out Monroe's phone number, but warned Seth that it might not be Monroe's anymore, since she hadn't responded to Ann. "If you have any luck getting a hold of her, tell my girl to call me," Ann said.

Seth promised he would. He thanked Ann and ended the call.

Something was wrong. Monroe didn't do as Seth had done. She wouldn't. Every time he conjured Monroe in his mind, the memory of Lavender, shoved into the mailbox, dead and bloodied, came too.

Chapter 21

SETH CYCLED ACROSS INDIAN Creek, cooling off in the spray of water kicked up by his tires. For the second day in a row, he sped along the Powdermill Singletrack in a rented mountain bike. He balanced the tires on the edge of the packed-earth trail, half a foot wide in spots, nothing but a sneeze between him and Woods and Miles and the Reading Man (who he'd not dreamt about in the two weeks since he found out Miles had died, but wished every night that he would because let's face it—Seth wanted the Reading Man to tell him where Monroe was). *Where was Monroe?*

THIS was the question. Free will was not the answer.

Two weeks since the fire. It still didn't feel real that Miles was gone. And what had happened to Monroe?

"Where are you?" Seth would ask the trees, but he always meant Monroe. The roots crisscrossing the singletrack made focus on anything else impossible. Mountain biking was a religious experience, more than road-riding had ever been. It worked like bourbon: made him forget himself. Bingo.

Over and over Seth replayed the Reading Man's words about Monroe.

"What do *you* think she will do?" the Reading Man had said. Or something like that.

Seth didn't know.

And he was angry the Reading Man had not appeared in his dreams to answer his questions. Every night he prayed for answers, and every morning he woke up ignorant as to Monroe's whereabouts. And bitter about it. The Reading Man had only answered: free will. What in *thee* fuck did that mean? That Monroe had free will? Sure. And Seth? Yes. Ivy? Fucking-A she had free will, and she used it to kill.

So, Seth hopped (Bingo—the one-legged man *hopped*) on his mountain bike and swiveled the trails, took chances with his life, and rode like he wanted to die.

He did.

Want to die.

Sometimes.

Dappled sunlight forced its way through the treetops, but the glare of nature's spotlight made it harder to navigate the random roots and rocks bisecting the track. Seth squinted and adjusted his grip on the disc brakes. A chipmunk dashed across the trail and almost bit it on Seth's tire. The switchback barely slowed him today, so adept was Seth at making the bike go where he wanted it to go and nowhere else. How far he had come from when he fell off two trail bridges in one day and bent his cycling prosthesis. He bent it back. No harm, no foul.

The mountain biking was Seth, daring the Reading Man—or, God (might as well call him by name) to knock him off a cliff, to put a rock in the way of his tire and shoot Seth head over heels and handlebars into a ravine and into the great beyond, where they could read books together, and Seth could play cards with the Reading Man. Poker was a nice indoor alternative to fishing. God fished. Everyone knew that, but maybe God would be flexible for Seth and do something fun instead, like cards. Maybe God could be persuaded to turn water into bourbon instead of wine. And no more hangovers, please, God. No hangovers.

No hangovers and no fishing. Seth didn't enjoy hooking the worms, and he had no idea what he would do with a fish if he caught one. Instead, whenever he found himself near a fresh body of water, he sat beside it and asked the Reading Man to visit his dreams and reveal what had happened to Monroe. And whether Ivy was to blame.

Chapter 22

IT WAS EARLY. THE sun was not yet high in the sky. Seth's campsite, his orange dome tent and teal hammock, stood out against the evergreens and the fallen pine needles. A month had passed since the fire at Miles's home; the longest time Seth had remained at a campsite. Grief kept him from getting on his bicycle and pushing on to the next destination. To think about going anywhere but back to Huntsville felt like abandoning all hope of finding Monroe. Going to Huntsville in search of her was futile. So, he stayed put.

Plus, he had miles of double-diamond singletrack to ride, to play roulette with his life. The wind on his face, the focus required not to ride over a cliff, the constant motion of his pedals going, going, going, and still ending up back at the same trailhead—bingo. By day he careened along the trails, and at night he sauced himself to oblivion. Something held him in limbo in the Daniel Boone National Forest. Rather than wonder what held him down like cement blocks on his soul, he muttered snatches of "Love Me Dead" as he set up his camp stove and heated the water, the hiss of propane reminding him of snakes.

A squirrel sat on the bike panniers, nibbling graham crackers. A small tongue of flame kept the critter from coming too close to the fire ring.

"Hey, little guy."

The squirrel looked past Seth, dropped his meal, and scurried up a tree. Seth turned toward the packed-earth trail and spotted someone. The shock caused him to choke on his own saliva.

Ivy.

Forgetting he held his mug, he spilled hot coffee on his neck when he tried to rub away what he thought was a dream.

He would know that cocksure gait anywhere.

She stopped and turned on her heel, approached the campsite like she was just anybody normal out on a morning hike, asking for directions. Thirty feet of forest separated them. The closest they had been in seventeen years.

Oddly, Seth was neither drunk nor hungover—shocking—because every day since he heard about Miles's death, he woke hungover and, first thing, guzzled enough electrolyte water to rehydrate his raisin-y self, enough to give him energy to hop on his mountain bike and slalom the trail as hard as he could, taking greater and greater chances with his life and yet never managing to lose it.

Why was he not hungover this morning? Because, two nights ago, the Reading Man had told him in a dream to *knock off the sauce tomorrow.* His words—*trust me, just tomorrow,* he had said.

Seth trusted.

Last night and contrary to Seth's expectations, he fell asleep without having consumed a drop of alcohol. Because of the Reading Man's instructions, Seth had used his evening drinking time to bicycle into town, to Bach's where they served hamburgers, hot dogs, pierogies, cheesesteaks, and, most importantly, twenty-five flavors of soft-serve ice cream—including Seth's favorite, peanut butter. At Bach's, Seth dined at a picnic table, protected from the sun and rain by the corrugated fiberglass roof panels, once-clear, now green with algae and mold. A ceiling fan affixed to the two-by-fours kept the flies away. Almost paradise. Would have been, had Monroe been there. Or even Miles, the big lug of a man. Poor, dead Miles.

As it was, Seth had eaten his dinner alone, with only his memories for company—good and bad. The Reading Man advised Seth not to drink. And bingo. Seth listened. For once in his life, he listened.

Which was why he wasn't too fuzzy and bleary-eyed to make out that Ivy wore a red bandana in her hair, the thick curls spilling out. Her face, flushed with exertion, told him she'd been walking a while already, though it was early in the day. She wore high-top sneakers, not good for hiking. Silver hoop earrings the size of a baby's head brushed against the sides of her neck. Her eyeliner had smudged into what looked like soldier eye black. Cutoff shorts emphasized her long, grime-smudged legs.

Seth had kindled the hot coals into a small fire that morning. A thick tree trunk served as an ottoman to prop his stump, and the ultralight camp chair allowed him to recline. He almost fell out of it when he saw her approach. The burn of the coffee on his neck told him he was awake, but it didn't tell whether he had lost his ever-loving mind and was hallucinating.

He whispered her name.

Ivy stepped off the trail, ten paces from Seth.

Like she heard.

Seth let go of the mug, coffee forgotten. *Everything* forgotten. Ivy smiled her toothy, some-might-say glamorous smile.

"Not going to say hello?" She approached and dropped into Seth's hammock.

He said nothing. Was paralyzed or in shock.

In the hammock Ivy rocked, using her feet to push. "You're a disappearing act," she purred, "the whole you, not just your foot."

And just like that, Ivy shamed him into pulling on his cycling prosthesis because it was propped against the tree trunk beside him, and his walking one was beside her in the hammock.

Now that she was here, Seth felt a strange, mysterious acceptance. He wanted this over with. It had been a good run—the cycling, the friends, the food. He wanted to go home, and since there was no home, *going dead* might not be so bad. It was the idea of death pursuing him that exhausted Seth. In his imagination, the grim reaper was Ivy in a police cruiser with lights flashing, eternally chasing him down every highway and country road. Never allowing him to rest.

This must be what it felt like to be a final girl. Not the girl part, of course. The focus. The fight. Here was his Jason Voorhees. His Michael Myers. His Freddy Kruger. And she was stunning.

He had questions.

She lit a cigarette. "How about some coffee?"

"I don't have sugar," he said.

"You're all the sugar I need."

Seth rolled his eyes, glad for the distraction of making camp coffee. It was a little harder to walk with his cycling prosthesis, but he made do. Did she notice his hands tremble as he placed the mug on the camp stove? As he adjusted the gas canister to heat the water? His mind was resolute, but his body quivered like a bowstring. Questions, fears, and memories were a jumbled pile of ants in his brain. He pulled them into focus, into one Rocky Balboa knock-out imagining where he gloriously repented of his many flights of cowardice. All while the propane hissed and the water heated.

Ivy leaned out of the hammock and tossed pine needles into the fire, making it crackle and billow smoke.

The water boiled. Seth swirled the instant coffee with his spork and offered her the mug.

"You always were polite. I think that's what I liked about you. Wouldn't even choke me when I begged for it."

"Stop," Seth grimaced. "Please." He held out the mug until she took it from him. He had questions, but they weren't for her. This was a revelation: her answers would all be lies. He didn't need to hear anything she said.

She mimicked him saying, "Please," and laughed. "You can't help yourself, can you?"

"Did you do it—Miles's house?" Seth's question was a ruse to keep her attention elsewhere as he reached beside her, groping in the hammock for his walking prosthesis.

She narrowed her eyes.

"It's a yes or no question," Seth pressed.

Before she could respond, and because he already knew the answer and had only wanted to hear her admit it (but not enough to hesitate), Seth swung the prosthesis with all the fear and resentment of seventeen years, and with the clarity of rage. The foot end connected with her cheek, slashing it open and taking her down.

Coffee exploded. Ivy, ate dirt, her curly hair fanned out like she'd been zapped with voltage. He didn't wait to see whether she rose, but scrambled onto his bike and took off, going the wrong way on the trail, not caring because the steep downhill would take him away faster. He could not chance a look behind him in case she would be there, standing, like the unkillable monster he imagined she was. No one could run through the woods as fast as his bike could take him, even with the curves and switchbacks.

The trail, once terrifying, was now his freedom road.

As he careened helmetless down the winding singletrack, leaving his tent and phone and everything he owned behind him, something shifted. A sensation began in his chest and squeezed and squeezed until something caved in, like a submarine that finally dives too deep and the hull implodes.

Why was he running?

What was he saving?

His skin. Nothing more. Not even his walking prosthesis, not his gear. Ivy wasn't dead, and she would have his bank card and his everything. So he had given her one good hit and saved himself, so what? For what? To scrape by in hypervigilance for another day? An endless string of days? Running from Ivy had been his strategy, always looking over his shoulder, waiting for her to pounce. Sure, he had made the best of a life with no mailing address, had made friends: Monroe, Miles, Liberty, and others.

But Ivy had dealt blow after blow to anyone Seth cared about. If Seth kept on running, he'd be the same old scaredy-cat Seth. Looking for (and, of course, finding) threats everywhere. Ivy would never stop chasing him, never leave him alone. The Reading Man had given Seth a heads-up on Ivy. To waste it would be...*sacrilegious*. That was the word that came to mind, which was how Seth knew it wasn't from himself. He never used big words like that. Another thought. Gift horse. Don't look it in the mouth.

There.

Words Seth could understand.

Turn around, Seth.

He understood that phrase too. Like the Reading Man was in his head.

He squeezed the brakes so hard, he almost flipped over the handlebars.

Heart pounding, breath hitching, *alive* and able to *make a choice*, he turned his bike around, pushed against gravity, up the hill he had just sailed down. Sweating and gulping air, he did not allow himself to think about what he would do or say when he returned to his camp, what he would find.

Ivy glanced up as he approached, hearing his rasping breaths. Blood smeared one side of her face, painting her neck and coursing down the gulch between her breasts. Her smile looked more like the bared teeth of a predator. In each hand, she held a longish strip of orange fabric.

His tent.

Destroyed. Pieces of tent were everywhere. Bright orange strips hung from the tree limbs like garland. Seth's walking prosthesis had been repurposed as a mallet, judging by the dents in it.

"Oh, you're back," Ivy said, "I'm redecorating."

Seth dismounted his bike and walked as slowly as he dared. Now that he knew what he wanted to do to Ivy, she might realize it was a different Seth approaching her. She might run away, not allow him the opportunity.

She stood her ground (good old Ivy), hands on hips.

Seth closed in until his chest brushed the tips of her breasts. The expression he wore, he had carefully cultivated: Reverence. Desire. Fear.

Ivy's expression told him she sensed something wasn't right. She could always smell deceit, perhaps because she had mastered it so well. Elegantly, she stepped back and away from him, the strips of his destroyed tent flowing out behind her like flags. The fire smoldered beneath a pile of pine needles and Seth's clothing. She picked up his prosthesis and used it to move the logs and feed the fire. Flames leaped in response.

The moment Ivy took her eyes off Seth, he charged. Like his old football days, driving her into the ground. Her head made a dull but satisfying thump, and a blast of breathy surprise erupted from her. Instantly, she attempted to squirm away.

With a rock from the fire ring, Seth twice swiped at her head. She raised her hands to protect herself, and Seth took the opportunity to wrest the strip of tent from her and wrap it around her neck.

"There. Happy?" He flipped her so her face was in the dirt. It allowed him to stamp his cycling prosthesis into her spine, the small head more cutting than a human foot (or his walking prosthesis) would have done. He balanced on Ivy that way, pulling on the tent fabric like a rein, bowing her at the base of her back.

"Happy?" he repeated.

Her skin blued, what he could see of her cheek, anyway. It was hard to tell with the blood. She kicked and scratched at the dirt.

Why had he waited so long? He had it in him to kill her and would have killed her that night seventeen years ago, if only he had been given the chance.

And she insisted on pushing his buttons. Chasing him down. Hurting his friends. *Choke me*, she had said.

He yanked harder and kept a more forceful pull on the tent fabric, until her legs stilled. Blood pooled where his prosthesis sank into her flesh.

Could a person break in half?

Yes—a person could be broken in half.

He had seen it with his own eyes.

Chapter 23

SEVENTEEN YEARS AGO

For the first few minutes locked inside the chest freezer, Seth wasn't afraid. He clicked his lighter on and off and made silly faces at his buddy, Woods, who sat as frozen as a corpse with his eyes wide and hardly blinking. Woods rocked back and forth and hugged his knobby knees. Because of that, Seth could stretch out his own legs in the ancient Morely Freezer that was as rusty on the inside as on the outside. The flickering light warped the spray paint "art"—a bright blue devil, somebody's simple rendition of their school mascot. Seth was in high school, and being locked in a 1950s era chest freezer perched on the edge of a hundred-foot drop didn't bother him as much as it should have.

Woods continued hugging his knees and gnawing on his kneecaps right through the jeans, making him look deranged. "How long has it been, you think?" Woods asked. There was a dark spot stamped on the denim where Woods's tongue had been.

The freezer was old, yes, and the accordion material that was supposed to make a seal had cracked in places. Still, Seth could hear nothing outside. No scuffling feet, no sticks crackling in the fire, no taunts from Ivy or her banging on the side of the chest.

When Seth agreed to climb inside, he figured they would be able to push the lid open, even if Ivy sat or stood upon it. The locking mechanism was one of those metal plates with a hole in it, meant for a padlock. Any stick thin enough to fit inside the lock shackle could easily be broken by the boys, he had assumed. But when they pushed against the lid, Seth realized: she *did* have something with which to secure the lock. The steel hinges were sound.

She was smarter than he had given her credit for. More wicked, too.

Only a week ago, Seth had chucked Ivy's padlock over the ravine, recalling the small ping of it striking a rock in the creek bed far, far below. She had accused him of not trusting her, said it was a love dare for him to let her lock him inside the vintage freezer chest. It was like when people fell back and a bunch of friends caught them, she said. Prove he loved her, she said. She pressed and got all pouty, so he swallowed the little, smooth key, grabbed the padlock, and dramatically threw it as far as he could. Then he passionately kissed her. *That* was his proof he loved her: her key would be inside him, forever.

Truth was, the key went right on through, and Seth had been no worse for the wear.

Now, inside the freezer, Woods gave Seth's leg a nudge, reminding him he had not answered the question of how long the boys had been locked inside.

"Dunno. I use my phone for time."

"And thanks to her stupid game, we don't even have our phones," Woods said.

The phone stacking game, Ivy's idea, was to have the three of them put their phones on the large, flattish rock, and whoever touched their phone first had to provide the beer next time. If calls or notifications came, they had to ignore them or else lose the game. Woods almost always lost, even though he hardly ever got notifications. If his mom texted, and he didn't text back...bingo. Woods was in for it.

When they played Stack the Phones, Ivy's buzzed and buzzed. It was like she wanted to play so that Seth and Woods could be jealous of how much more buzzing her phone did than theirs. And she had no trouble not checking who was texting or calling. She did not care what notifications she received. Today, Seth had put his phone in airplane mode to make Woods feel better about not getting any notifications. It was the last act of kindness he would do for his friend, and it made no difference.

Being Seth's friend was what proved deadly to Woods.

In the dark, dank freezer that crushed like a coffin, Seth had a sickening epiphany. The phone game, the freezer dare, and Ivy's possession of something to secure the lock were not coincidental. She had thought this through. She had *planned* this. That realization quickened the seed of fear inside him, a seed that would bulge and sprout into terror.

Pints Peak, everyone called it, and by *everyone* Seth meant high school and college kids. It had been Pints Peak as long as Seth could remember. An amusement park located two hours away had almost the same name, Pines Peak.

Both destinations were for fun, but Pints Peak was not for the innocent kind. Off the beaten path, farther down the creek and only accessible by trekking along the side of the creek to another, hidden trail, Pints Peak was a boon for troublemakers. The secret trail markers kept outsiders out, especially young kids or parents. If they tried to follow the trail, they were thwarted when it ended at the creek. Those few, lucky, *bad* kids knew the trail picked up again downriver at the point in the shoreline where the dinosaur tree—a fallen, half-submerged tulip tree "pointed" the way through the forest—to a deteriorating covered bridge on a no-longer-used road. The creek walk was a half a mile or so but felt longer, especially when the water was high and Seth had to wade through it with a case of beer or a bag of ice on his shoulders.

That's what the chest freezer was for. Time and erosion had filed away the shale, bringing the edge closer, so that one corner of the freezer hung over the edge. No one knew who put the freezer there, but thoughts of awe and gratitude were sent to the teenage Sisyphus who carried it to the top of the vista. As hard as it was to carry cases of beer, Seth could not imagine how the enormous freezer made its way. Its exact origins were a mystery, and each spring before the first trek to Pints Peak, kids would make bets on whether the freezer had finally tumbled off the edge.

Because of the popularity of the party spot, an assortment of trash collected on Pints Peak, and sometimes after school, Seth came alone to pick it up. Why he didn't tell anyone about his nature maintenance, he couldn't say, except he felt he'd be mocked for it. By Ivy, if by no one else.

Ivy was forever tossing garbage over the cliff. She'd stand atop the chest freezer and lean over, watching as it fell, listening for the far away sound of impact. She would take it as a personal offense, Seth cleaning the area, like he wanted to steal her fun. All rocks of throwing size had been dispatched that way.

On the days he came clandestinely to pick up trash, Seth also threw away the smattering of metal items used to secure the freezer lid: screwdrivers, carabiners, paper clips, and large nails. With every metal implement he tossed into his trash bag, two thoughts were in his mind. One: the trash might find its way into the ravine, so to toss the junk was to be kind to the environment. And two: Seth felt better knowing his girlfriend didn't have sharp implements at her disposal. A third thought would sometimes come to him: who in his right mind kissed *that* girl?

Seth's mind had nothing to do with kissing Ivy.

Like all immortal seventeen-year-olds, he figured he could play with fire and not get burned.

Inside the freezer, if Seth was fighting the lung-squeezing sensation of claustrophobia and the sting of being out-strategized. Disposing of the freezer locks was a precaution against her throwing one at him in a fit of rage. Ivy gave strong crime-of-passion vibes. But he had never plumbed the scope and breadth of her wickedness. Maybe if he wasn't preoccupied with getting in her pants, he would have seen her for who she was.

Truth was, Seth wasn't much of a thinker when it came to girls. He liked to know how things worked—things that made sense. Girls' actions made zero sense. They were like the ball on a roulette wheel, bouncing and falling with no way to tell where. Red or black? Would she be in a good mood or be Medusa? Sweet or savage? With girls, and especially with Ivy, there was no set of givens that he could plug into a calculation and get an expected return.

Last year, the fire pit had been moved back in case a drunk teenager stepped around the fire and found themselves at the bottom of the hundred-foot drop-off. Most kids agreed the big tragedy would be if the freezer tumbled down the gully while stocked full of beer. Seth, Woods, and other boys had tried to pull it back, but it would not budge. The ground had swelled around it, and the freezer settled into the earth over many spongy springs. Moving the thing was more trouble than it was worth, and messing with it further might send the freezer and a good chunk of earth sliding over the cliff.

While the freezer remained, it was a gift. Revelers could spend all night at Pints Peak, and the freezer kept the beer cold and refreshing. Sometimes Seth and friends brought sandwiches and cupcakes with icing. Thanks to the freezer, everything stayed cold even on the hottest summer days.

It was said, but Seth wasn't sure he believed it, that people had screwed inside the appliance. But who would want to do it cramped in a smelly old box, when you could lay a sleeping bag out on the bluff and do it under the stars with no one around to see or hear?

The fact, that—right now—no one was around Pints Peak to see or hear turned Seth's blood cold.

"Ivy, open up!" Woods's hollering shook Seth from his ruminating.

For emphasis, Seth also punched the top of the chest freezer.

"What do you think she's doing out there?" Woods asked.

"How should I know?"

"She's *your* girlfriend."

Seth would hear Woods say those words hundreds of times in his mind in the years following that night. They accused him. Blamed him. They said he should have known.

The stench of mold and spoiled yeast could not compete with the smell of fear in the blacker-than-night freezer. Seth's own sweat began to choke him. He flicked the lighter on because the blackness got too black.

Woods didn't even have a lighter. "Why do you even like her, man?" he asked.

Good question.

"I know she's pretty, but screws are loose," Woods continued.

"Shhhh..." Seth said.

"I don't care if she hears me. HEY, IVY. YOU'RE A HEAD CASE." To Seth, he said, "This is it, man. I'm done with her. You will be too, if you know what's good for you."

"We were dumbasses for getting in the freezer," Seth admitted.

Woods kicked him, but not hard. "I only got inside because you did."

As the minutes turned into hours, the boys fell silent. Seth may have slept. Without a doubt, Ivy had either left or was asleep outside.

Something jolted Seth awake. Maybe. It was difficult to know for sure. Someone kicked him.

Woods.

Someone screamed.

Also Woods.

Oh, right. They were stuck in the freezer. Seth's aching shoulder and neck reminded him, and his flattened ass was never going to pop back into shape. Woods's legs were on top of his, and he was either having a nightmare or losing his mind. His sneakered feet went up and down on Seth's belly and—*oof!*—his balls like drum mallets.

"Woods. Knock it off, will ya? You're going to spill us over the side with all that rocking." Seth couldn't reach him without curling into a ball himself. The slaps of his hands were ineffectual. "WOODS. WAKE. UP."

He did. With a howl that popped the hair on Seth's neck.

"I can't breathe." Woods pressed against the sides of the chest, as if he could muscle a bigger space for them. He grunted with the effort.

"Easy, Woods."

"But don't you feel it? The air isn't as...I don't know. Good. My throat's sore from sucking in, and it doesn't feel like I'm getting enough oxygen."

Seth took a breath. The air was stale and gross. "I'm sure there's holes." He tried to sound confident, but the truth was he didn't know if they were suffocating. How long did it take for two people to use up the oxygen in a chest freezer? Maybe Woods was right, and they were going to drown together in this horrible box. He began more intentional, slower breaths. He began to plead with God that old freezers were not airtight.

Woods's breathing had become labored as if he were walking up a hill. He tore at the corners of the freezer, kicked his feet, and punched the sides. Seth's own sense of helplessness surged as Woods lost his mind. Panic was the killer. Every movie of all time said so.

Woods kicked the lid in earnest.

Then Woods puked.

Chapter 24

Funny how hell was whatever worst thing you had experienced. Hell was the dark. No, hell was suffocating. No, hell was the bit of corrupted air you sucked in that pulled your guts like greedy fingers and tried to push out the contents of your stomach. Hell was you, trying to pinch your nose and gulp with your mouth and push away from your buddy, Woods, but getting slick and chunky, viscous goop on your hands and slipping in it. Wiping it on your own jeans because the walls were too rusty. And hell was wanting like mad to lose your shit, too, and kick and bang like the orangutans at the zoo, but doing so would mean you were sure to die together in the airless box. This hell had requirements: Calm down. Show restraint. Discipline your lungs. Economize. Breathe shallowly. Squeeze your quads, flex your feet. Tell your friend Woods you're very, very sorry you got him into this, but you'll be damned if the two of you won't get out. "Just, be quiet, Woods, so I can think, okay?"

Yes, Seth had said that last bit out loud.

He must have, because Woods stopped screaming.

The lock jangled. *About fucking time.* Seth was ready to breathe air and stand and celebrate and kill Ivy. How many times had he imagined pushing her off the cliff while they languished in the freezer? Thinking he was free, Seth pushed at the lid. Woods joined him.

The lid opened a crack. A zip tie had been secured before the other tool had been removed, allowing the boys to see freedom but not grasp it. At least they could breathe cool, unpolluted air.

Ivy had to be nearby, but Seth could not see her through the crack.

"I'm going to kill her," Woods said.

"Not if I kill her first," Seth whispered.

Though the lid only opened an inch, he could see the tops of trees against the dawning sky. Feet scuffled nearby. Had she heard? No matter, he had to make her believe he wasn't mad, that if she let them out, everything would be okay.

"Hey Ivy, you got us. You got us good. Now let us out," Seth added, "I miss you, babe." He never called her *babe.* That screw-up betrayed his desperation.

"Ivy, what did I ever do to you?" Woods tried to reason with her. "C'mon, let us out. This isn't funny."

Understatement of the century.

"Let me try something," Seth whispered. "Make yourself small so I have room to lie on my back."

"Dude..."

"Trust me." (*Trust me.* How those words replayed in Seth's mind over the years.)

Seth managed to lie down, felt Woods's cold puke seep through his t-shirt, the slime of it on the small of his back. He tucked his legs to arrange the bottoms of his feet against the freezer lid. Each hand braced a side, and the rust helped his grip.

"Okay, when I count three, help with your hands. I'm going to kick."

"Wait!" Woods said.

"What?"

Woods got quiet. Through the crack and the feeble light of daybreak, Seth could see Woods had his eyes closed.

"Woods?"

"I'm trying to pray," Woods said through clenched teeth.

"Oh," was all Seth said all those years ago, but Woods's prayer and what happened immediately afterward had paved a dark road in Seth's soul that—until this moment—he had forgotten about.

Woods had prayed. Seth had not.

When Woods finished, he opened his eyes and flashed a hopeful smile (his last), giving Seth a quick nod.

"Here goes," Seth said, "One...two...three..."

And Seth gave that lid everything he had. Both boys did. The zip tie stood no chance against the adrenaline of two caged boys. The lid flew open so hard and fast, it bent the hinge and slammed the lid against the side of the freezer.

Woods, stiff and weak, pulled himself up with shaking arms, was nearly standing—

"Ivy, no—" Woods's eyes bulged.

Seth's world (the freezer) lurched and tilted violently, his body dragged toward Woods, his back sliding along the goopy mess. The freezer thrust forward, slamming Woods's face down toward Seth, who was struggling to pull his legs under him and stand himself. Woods's head hit the side of the freezer, and Seth felt a spritz of something on his face, tasted metal.

The freezer pitched forward, sliding over the cliff. Seth's head clunked against the side—now top—of the freezer that in a split second had changed orientation, yanked downward by gravity. Woods flailed, hands raised above him like a worshipper, his forehead split open, clawing to get back inside where Seth was. Both Woods and the freezer-with-Seth-inside fell at breakneck velocity. The boys locked gazes for those interminable seconds. Tree tops, tree trunks, and the segmented shale cliffs passed by while Seth braced his hands against the sides.

The freezer hit something solid, and Seth's hunched back slammed against one side. The silly image of a human pinball came to him then, and just as quickly left, as the box tumbled, did a somersault through the air. Branches and tree trunks made thwacks and thumps against the freezer and slowed or spun it. He had time (or did he imagine it?) to think that amusement park rides simulated this feeling. He had time to address God. In his mind. To think: God...is this it?

An excruciating burst of pain in the back of his head, his back, his everything, and bingo. Lights out for Seth.

Seth opened his eyes to gauzy white clouds and a cerulean sky. Gnarled green fingers reached for him from either side. After a few blinks, the fingers clarified into trees leaning into his peripheral vision, the branches swiveling in the breeze. A broken cottonwood branch had pierced his wrist, clean through. He swiveled his arm, inspecting it with a combination of awe and horror. The medallion-shaped leaves were still perfect on the side that didn't pass through his flesh. Water babbled and lapped against the freezer. Careful of the branch, he touched his chest and legs, patting and half-expecting to find pieces of himself missing. The back of his head was sticky, and his fingers came away bloody.

His legs, back, and butt radiated an intense and increasing agony, and the feel inside his skull was that a whole box of sparklers had ignited in there. He wished for unconsciousness to take him again.

It didn't.

The top of the cliff was far away...so far. Had he really been up there? And fallen? And lived. And—

Woods.

"WOODS!? WOODS, WHERE ARE YOU?" Speaking hurt so badly, Seth thought he would pass out again. The idea of moving an inch was unthinkable, let alone climbing out and searching for his friend. Seth wasn't sure his legs would obey him.

Seth thought he must be hallucinating. A figure stood at the top of the cliff, hands at her sides, leaning forward, scanning the valley. A shower of pebbles hit the sandstone and rained into the water. Something plunked into the creek.

A rock?

No, Seth saw the second item tumble down the side of the ravine before it was lost beneath the water: a phone.

Ivy had tossed their phones over the side.

Seth played dead until she was gone. Played dead, yes, but also a part of him died in that ravine. His girlfriend had either meant to kill him or didn't mind if it happened. Woods was collateral damage.

Chapter 25

SETH STOOD OVER HIS lifelong enemy and hesitated to kill her—to eliminate Ivy from the equation of his life. Destroying her was the highlight reel of his dreams. Ivy's death would bring him peace, if not true happiness. An eye for an eye. Life for life. Hers for Woods's. Seventeen long years overdue.

She had weakened. The hacking of her squeezed-off airway stopped.

He paused. Part of him didn't want to do it. The part that made him run?

No.

Seth had been running scared for years, but not from Ivy. He ran from the part of him that wanted to take her life, which, he might as well face it, made him no different than her.

It was a small prayer, almost wordless. Seth asked for God's interference, for a bending of Seth's will into whatever God thought best. In this one, murderous moment, if Seth were more of a Bible reader, he might have prayed: *Your will be done.*

Instantly, his memory turned on, hummed like a slide projector in crisp focus on the white wall of his rage. First slide: a long-ago conversation in a 1950s Morely chest freezer.

"This isn't about you. You shouldn't be here," Seth said.

"I feel so dumb, you know?" Woods's throat had tightened at the emotion his words brought up. "I thought she might be crazy enough to do something, but not with me around." Woods grunted, "Fucking Ivy."

"I admit, I never thought she'd take it out on you, Woods. Me, yeah. But not you."

"I'm gonna kill that bitch when we get outta here," Woods said.

"I'm gonna help you," Seth said.

Had he meant that, at the time? He didn't think he did. But it didn't matter. He had said it. Years ago, in the blackness without enough air and full of fear and loathing and the possibility that they would not get out of the freezer, ever, he said he would be Woods's accomplice in killing Ivy.

And she felt threatened, she said. *She* felt threatened. How rich.

Next slide.

Ivy showed up at the hospital smiling sweetly, tears streaming down her cheeks. She threw herself on his hospital bed and hugged him. "I can't believe you're alive! If you hadn't stopped him, I don't know what would have happened."

"Who? What?...what are you talking about? You—"

She planted a crushing kiss on his lips and whispered, "Be quiet." Knowing his parents and nurses were in earshot, Ivy began to weave the story that painted Seth as the hero and Woods as a predator. Woods had attempted to rape her, and Seth came to her rescue, she said. The boys tussled against the freezer, sending it over the side along with them.

Ivy was terrified and in shock. She should not have been drinking at Pints Peak with Woods. That was why she didn't tell anyone. The boys were obviously dead (obviously?) and she couldn't help them. Only in whispers, Ivy threatened that if she wanted to implicate Seth in Woods's murder, she could, at any time. She would say she had been afraid to come out with the fact that *both* boys assaulted her because she had feared retribution from Seth.

"I'm going to tell what you did to us," Seth whispered back.

"Who do you think they'll believe? You or me? Who's going to believe I'm strong enough to push you and Woods over the cliff? Look at me."

She was right. At all of a hundred pounds, Ivy didn't look like she could toss a child off a cliff, let alone a freezer.

"All you have to do is say the freezer went over while you were fighting," Ivy said.

"But why'd you have to say that bullshit about Woods? He's our friend."

"Sticks and stones are not going to hurt him anymore. And Woods was never *my* friend."

Seth asked, "Did you do it?"

"Do what?" (Like Seth was crazy for asking.)

"Push the freezer."

"You're psychotic."

"I felt it jostle."

"Jostle? What's that even mean? Are you accusing me of *intentionally* pushing you off the cliff?" Her voice stayed at a whisper volume. Her tone shamed Seth into silence.

Next slide.

When the detectives came to question Seth, he was doped up with pain medications. Unlike Ivy, he was not a skilled liar. He faltered in his version of the story.

The detective pounced.

Seth got his lies mixed up. He balked. Caved. Told the truth through tears to a hospital room full of dropped jaws.

Next slide was Woods's funeral. Seth lied to Ivy and said everything had gone fine in his police questioning. He didn't have the guts to tell her the truth. Even when she was arrested, Seth said he didn't know why, that he expected he'd be arrested too.

Last slide, months later.

Seth didn't have the luxury of lying. In a courtroom, Seth's testimony corroborated forensic evidence that the boys had been locked in the freezer, and that it had been shoved off the cliff. Ivy was able to do it with help from physics—Seth unknowingly kicking and Woods standing at the unluckiest time. Whether or not she possessed enough strength to push the freezer over the cliff was immaterial. She planned harm and executed it. Guilty as charged of murder and attempted murder.

She didn't cry, but the look she gave Seth across the courtroom. *How-could-you?* her face said. *How. Could. You. Betray. Me?*

When Ivy went to prison, Seth hoped he could leave the horror behind. He was guilty, too, guilty of getting his friend, Woods, killed. If Woods had not been Seth's friend, Woods would be alive today.

Seth's past was not a rocket thruster he could jettison as he pushed forward into his future. It was dead weight, he found, as year after year his thoughts were full of poison and bones. And memories. Memories that turned into nightmares and were only slightly buffered by alcohol. Seth found he could not hold on to a relationship. For every woman who got close to him, he found a reason to end things. Or he treated his lovers terribly until they had enough and dumped him. That was easier.

The closer Ivy's parole date came, the harder it had been for Seth to lead a "normal" life. Even having an address felt dangerous. Having routines. Getting his foot crushed changed everything. Meeting Miles. And Monroe.

Then Dazey showed up at Miles's home. When Ivy killed Lavender, Seth ran from his demons in earnest. Not only for himself this time, but for anyone he had feelings for. Monroe, especially her.

The memory show ended.

Seth noticed a silver chain in Ivy's hand. She had been trying to get his attention by shaking the hand that clutched it, which, in her prone and suffocating and impaled position, was more of a tremble. The only reason the necklace had gotten his attention was because of the slight tinkling sound it made when the chain scraped itself. And it glinted. Sunlight caught it exactly right, and for a moment, the sun reflecting off the silver blinded Seth, stopping him cold.

A cross.

One he recognized.

Horror filled his heart.

Yes, he had seen it before.

All thoughts of Ivy-torture forgotten, Seth dropped to his knees and yanked at the necklace in her hand. With all her strength, Ivy clutched the chain. Seth could swear he saw her lip turn up, so that—were she not in pain—she would be smiling.

"Let go," Seth demanded. He pulled the cross charm closer to inspect it and was immediately certain that God did not exist—could not exist if what his eyes told him meant what he thought it did.

M-O-N-R-O-E was etched into the silver cross.

Choked laughter issued from Ivy's clamped throat. The half of her face that wasn't in the dirt showed her to be sneering.

"What. Did. You. Do?"

Ivy coughed until she puked.

Seth grabbed a fistful of her hair and lifted her head, bashed it into the ground—into her own vomit—over and over. "Where. Did. You. Get. This?"

Even as tears ran down her cheek, Ivy cackled, "You *know* where I got it." A coughing fit rocked her. "What you really want to (cough) know is, where IS the (cough, cough) fabulous (cough) Marilyn Monroe? Right? That's the question. I *was* going to show you. (cough) Why do you think I'm here? But after what you did to me..." Here she grimaced, coughed, and rubbed the puke from her forehead. "I don't think I will show you, after all."

Seth pounced on her again, hating that she laughed, that she showed no fear. Even more than that, he hated that she *had* no fear. Nothing Seth did to Ivy mattered. If he killed her, she would laugh her way to hell. If he walked away, she would follow. She'd be on him like white on rice until he was dead or insane. And everyone he cared about would be dead, too.

Ivy tried to crawl away, but in her weakened state, Seth easily had the upper hand. He straddled her and tried to get hold of her neck, to choke her with his bare hands.

Ivy screamed.

Bingo.

After all the years of Woods screaming in Seth's memory, he now had another scream to balance the scales. Rather than choke her, he grabbed a fistful of that thick hair of hers and slammed her head into the ground as he demanded, "Where is she?"

Chapter 26

IVY STOPPED WALKING TO inspect a spider's web in the brush beside the singletrack trail, to watch it devour a moth. It took all Seth's willpower to resist the urge to push Ivy to walk faster. Provoking him was her objective, he knew. The more impatience he showed, the more Ivy would milk it, so he stopped himself from stabbing his finger into her back to prod her. Monroe was close by and alive, but not for long.

Seth pointed to the spider and said with forced blitheness, "Reminds me of you, dear."

For that, she kissed him.

He pursed his lips and turned his cheek. Her disgusting, tobacco-flavored tongue wormed into his mouth, and he didn't bite it off because she promised to take him to Monroe. He could not risk harm to Monroe.

Every so often, Ivy's steps halted, and she put a hand to her back where Seth had pushed his prosthesis into her flesh. Blood had glued her t-shirt to her skin, and the red blotch showed through the underside of the fabric. Around her head wound, she had wrapped a piece of Seth's tent. The orange fabric gave her the appearance of a fortune teller, especially with her enormous earrings. Only the smudges of blood, not altogether wiped away, showed that Seth had owned the upper hand at one point in the day.

Seth's shoe scuffed the back of hers because he walked too close behind, willing her with his mind to walk faster.

Ivy stopped, hands on hips. "Don't you want to know how I found her?"

How she loved to taunt.

"Your mother," Seth answered, recalling Dazey's visit and later, Lavender in the mailbox.

"Sure, Mom put her on the radar, but it wasn't till I saw her combing through what was left of your buddy's house that I knew you guys had a thing for each other."

A *thing*? Seth couldn't stop thinking about Monroe, but he was sure any thingness was one-sided. Ivy might be doing her usual: lying.

"Walk...please." Once Seth knew Monroe was unharmed, Ivy could wax glorious on her detective skills.

"Not moving another inch until I tell my story."

Seth sighed. Anything he wanted, she would do the opposite. Infuriating.

"I told little Marilyn that I worked at Green Spirit and knew you before you lost your foot. *Poor thing*, I said, and she bought it that I felt sorry for you—of course she did—and she asked if I knew where you would have gone. She missed you. YOU. Not that sugar daddy of a mortician who took in her stupid cats. Which I find suss as fuck. Why would she like you when she could have the Black Hulk?"

"You chose me, too...once upon a time," Seth growled.

She grabbed his crotch and squeezed his testicles till he thrust her hand away. "Only because the Black Hulk wasn't an option." She gave his balls a hearty (painful) smack. "At the funeral, little Marilyn and I became besties, and I knew she wanted to see you as much as I did."

Seth could not bear the idea that Monroe had feelings for him. He did not feel worthy of them. He remembered Monroe's tears when Seth left, but he thought she was angry at him for leaving Miles, not for leaving her.

Ivy began walking again and soon veered off the regular trail onto what may have been a deer trail. It was narrow and hedged with thorny bushes that Ivy pulled out of her way and let snap back into Seth's face. One caught his lip. As blood ran into his mouth and down his chin, he fought the urge to wipe his face on the back of her T-shirt.

Try as he might, Seth could not see the path ahead. The bushes were thick around them, and she blocked his view until the terrain gradually took more of a downhill slope. Cattails and the increasingly spongy, foot-sucking ground told him they headed toward stagnant water, where the smell of rotting vegetation cloyed at their noses, and the guttural buzzing of dragonflies zigzagged around their heads.

Finally, Seth glimpsed a clearing with a small pond carpeted in thick, green algae. Rocks studded the surface, as well as a couple of downed trees, long ago shorn of bark and branches. Fifty feet away on the opposite side of the bog, a rusty, decades-old pickup truck had been backed up to the water's edge, tailgate down.

In the flatbed was a chest freezer.

Chapter 27

At the sight of the freezer, Seth's breath caught.

Ivy stopped walking, and Seth plowed into her back, printing his bloodied face on her shirt.

"Ivy...Ivy, why?" was all he managed.

She giggled as he pushed past her toward the truck. With its rusted-out wheel wells and duct-taped door panel, the freezer was new and clean in comparison. Seth trudged around the pond, hobbled by the glue-like muck. As he reached the halfway mark, the ground got wetter and less firm. About twenty feet from the truck, it became almost impossible to pull his foot out of the last step. In one syrupy puddle his prosthesis stuck fast. He fell on his side and got a mouthful of mud.

He smacked his head with his palm, realizing Ivy wanted him here. Stuck. She tricked him again. While he was struggling in the muck, she had rounded the pond on the other side and made far better progress. Although her steps were labored, she didn't sink as Seth had. On her feet were what looked like boxes.

"Mudders," she called out, her teeth flashing. "I wasn't sure they'd work, but I'll tell you what—they do. What's that dumb word you say, Seth? ...Bingo? BINGO. These suckers work like a charm." She leaned into the truck bed and used her fist to knock on the freezer. It trembled in response, and Seth heard smothered, indecipherable words.

Monroe.

With renewed panic, Seth tried to stand. His prosthesis was lost, deep beneath him in mud that threatened to pin his arms, sucking them into the mud each time he tried to push himself out.

"Monroe!" he called out. "I'm here!"

"Marilyn, the cavalry's here," Ivy taunted. "Told you he'd come. Sorry we're late, but he ran away like he always does. You know how he is. Good thing I gave you air holes." Here, she held up a cordless drill and made it whirl loudly. "See? This is proof. I knew you couldn't bring yourself to kill me. I wouldn't have gone to all this trouble if I wasn't absol-fuckin-lutely sure you didn't have the guts to kill me."

From the freezer, Monroe pleaded for help. It was hard to understand her words, but the terror, Seth understood that all too well. He reached for a branch from a downed tree. It held as he pulled himself out of the mud, belly down. Against the mud he used his hands like paddles to propel himself forward, resisting the muck that wanted to swallow him. Never in his life had he felt so helpless as he did now, on his belly in the mud.

Ivy sat on the downed tailgate swinging her feet breezily. She reached back and slapped the freezer. "This makes us square, Seth. Her life for mine. I mean, she's what? Twenty something? I'd been in prison for years by the time I was her age."

"I'm sorry, Ivy. Is that what you want to hear?"

"Um, yeah. I like how it sounds when you say it. Say it again, Seth."

"I'm sorry."

"For what, Seth? Why are you sorry?"

He resumed his serpentine mud crawl. "I'm...sorry...I...I..." He slammed his hands in the mud. "Jesus, Ivy, I don't know what I'm supposed to be sorry for. Telling the truth?! Don't hurt Monroe. She didn't do anything to you."

Like Woods. That, he did not say.

Ivy pushed her lips into a duck shape. "Do you know what they do to you in prison? Everybody talks about the men—what happens to them in prison. But I'll tell you..." She bit her lip and blinked away whatever emotion threatened to overtake her. "At least with men it's this." Ivy spread her pointer finger and thumb apart to show the usual size of a penis.

Seth had no idea what she was getting at, and he didn't care. What he did want to do was keep her talking until he could get to the truck.

"I'm sorry you had to...endure prison, that it was...bad there," he said.

Ivy pulled her t-shirt away and lifted her bra, revealing a breast that had been mauled.

Seth winced without meaning to. "Ouch," he said for her benefit, but kept moving.

"That's nothing. I've got worse." Ivy shook her fist, making a muscle. "Assault by penetration. Bitch put her arm in me. I didn't die, but I could have. You would have liked that, wouldn't you?"

Seth almost reflexively shouted that, yes, he would be delighted to hear of her demise. Instead he managed an anemic, "No."

Ivy put her face to an air hole and whispered something to Monroe.

"I didn't mean what I said all those years ago," Seth said, trying to keep Ivy talking to him. "In the freezer, when I was with Woods. I know I hurt you." Did he sound sincere? Was he sorry for that part of the past? Right now, he would say anything, *do* anything to save Monroe. He'd kill Ivy to save her. Wouldn't bat an eyelash over it.

How rich that now, when he would not hesitate to finish Ivy, he no longer had his hands around her neck.

Ivy hopped to a stand on the truck bed. She bent over and spoke into what Seth assumed was an air hole. At thirty feet away, he couldn't be sure, but the chest wobbled in response. She stood and gave the top of the freezer a pat.

Seth used every ounce of strength to pull his body through the mud as he spoke.

"How long?" He called out.

"You want to know if your girl's had the full Woods and Seth freezer treatment? Has she been in there all night? Has she pissed and shit herself? Or puked, like Woods? When I thought you were going to kill me at the campsite, I laughed. You know why? Because how stupid can you be to think I wouldn't have the perfect revenge, with sixteen years of hell to plan it, as if I didn't have time to think of *everything*."

Dread twisted Seth's insides.

"Why'd you kick the freezer off Pints Peak? I don't get it, Ivy. Putting us in there, sure, that was the sort of thing you did. But I gotta tell you, the thing that's never made sense to me is—what were you thinking when you kicked that freezer?"

He couldn't be sure, but he thought her eyes welled with tears because she wiped at them. "Maybe if you read my letters, you'd know." She jumped out of the truck bed.

Seth breathed a sigh of relief.

Until she got into the truck cab, and the engine turned over. Was she going to leave him there? Take Monroe and let him wonder about her fate?

The white back-up lights indicated the transmission was in reverse.

Oh God.

Oh no.

No.

No.

"NOOOOOOO!" Seth shouted.

The truck backed up; tires sinking into the mud, deeper and deeper as they rolled. The tailgate reached the waterline, slid into the water, yanking the cab off the ground, pulling the freezer down the ever-sloping truck bed like a slide. The front tires spun in the air, throwing mud globs like paint, even as Ivy jumped from the moving cab and struggled to where her oddly shaped boots lay.

Seth's frenetic efforts to pull himself to the sinking truck were futile. He opted to try for the water. To get closer to the truck that way, though he knew it was pointless. The fifteen feet between him and the truck might as well have been fifty. Not even Sisyphus could pull a chest freezer out of a bog.

If Seth could get to her, maybe he could pry open the lid.

"Monroe!" He called her name, willing the scene before him not to be true.

"Monroe, I'm here." He wanted her to know he saw her. More than that, he wanted her to know it was him, Seth, and not a stranger.

Her screams became stifled as the freezer sank into the water; the bright green algae lapped the sides. Large air bubbles broke at the water's surface, as the freezer and truck were swallowed.

Seth roared a string of curses at the picture-perfect sky.

Beneath the water, he could still hear her punching the freezer as he desperately tried to maneuver from the bog into the water. The same air holes that kept Monroe alive until Seth arrived would hasten her death now that he was here. Unless he figured out how to open the lid, the freezer would fill with water and drown an innocent woman whose only mistake was to be Seth's friend. Like Woods.

Seth managed to wade into the water, but the bottom sludge still ensnared him like quicksand. Thrashing only sunk him deeper.

"You deserve each other." Ivy shouted as she disappeared into the reeds.

Seth called out after her, but it was no use. Every second that passed, Seth knew the freezer filled with life-killing water. With strength he did not know he possessed, he pulled his legs out of the mire and swam until he could take hold of the truck's side mirror. The mirror was the only thing above the water that offered him purchase. He swung around slowly, so fucking slothishly, and felt with his foot in the water beneath him for the freezer top. He could feel the sides of the truck bed, and he guided his foot down and swished it around, searching, wishing that he would feel a hand grab his foot, that somehow Monroe found a way to open the freezer and only needed a hand up to the surface.

Even as he imagined this, he knew it was not possible.

He cursed God and Ivy and the world that had conspired against him. Still, for many minutes, he tried. With one hand holding the mirror, he put his head in the murky water, hoping he'd be able to see something.

Nothing.

Nothing.

He could barely make out his hand, inches from his face.

Did she still live? How long would it take before the water filled the freezer? Knowing the innocent Monroe suffered this fate while Seth remained alive was too much to bear. At least Seth had Woods with him.

Monroe had no one.

More, smaller bubbles cracked open on the surface as the gentle Monroe struggled. Seth wanted it to end. Was it too much to ask for a quick and painless death for Monroe? What sort of God wanted Seth to listen as Monroe agonized her way into Heaven—surely she would go to

Heaven and be free of suffering? She and Miles were of one mind about Heaven.

Not Seth.

Look what all that faith had done for them.

Time passed. The sun set, which was infuriating. There were not adequate obscenities to communicate the injustice that the world continued spinning and time kept passing after Monroe's death.

After all his tears were shed, a steely resolution set in, and Seth—possessed with free-fucking-will—crawled out of the marsh and hop-crawled back to his campsite. With some duct tape and a four millimeter Allen wrench, he managed to fix his remaining, broken prosthesis. Other than his wallet and clothes, he didn't bother to pack up his belongings. He had a destination, and this time he would not be diverted, distracted, or thwarted. *So help him God* almost went through his mind, but he squashed that thought.

In this endeavor, God would be of no help.

Chapter 28

Twenty-four hours later, Seth arrived at his destination, looked around, and shook his fist at God. He swore. He stomped his feet, a shock of pain traveling up his leg as his stump hit the prosthesis. Here he was—a grown man throwing a fit as cars whizzed by him on the Aurora Bridge.

"Can't give me a break, can you?" Seth grabbed onto the suicide prevention bars and shook them like a crazed jailbird. Terrible luck. Terrible fucking luck. All he wanted was to go out flying. Was that so much to ask? To follow Miles and Monroe into death.

Not like Seth hadn't done his homework. Google said (okay, Seth inferred) that the Aurora Bridge in Seattle was perfect for jumping to one's death, number two in the country, in fact, right behind the Golden Gate Bridge. Of the two flights out of Lexington, Kentucky, the one to Seattle was direct. That was how Seth had decided which bridge to commit suicide from, all else being equal.

But no. Not equal.

That was Seth's luck: thinking number two was good enough.

As he walked the bridge's narrow sidewalk, he Googled: *suicide prevention barriers aurora bridge* and found out the construction on the metal fence and nets had been completed only months before. Had he not dicked around by bicycling around the country, he would have been in time. The barrier would have been unfinished.

On his warped and chafing prosthesis, Seth limped farther along the sidewalk to figure out if there were places the barrier could be scaled. Cars and trucks created a hot and stinky breeze of exhaust. The noise of them made it so Seth could hardly think.

As he got closer to the Queen Ann side, someone appeared from the pedestrian underpass: a kid, mostly grown, wearing jeans and a hoodie and holding an open computer. Seth stopped about ten feet from the kid, who was searching the water or the bank below. When he saw Seth, his face scrunched up, like the kid knew Seth was up to no good. How could he know that?

Seth decided to play it cool. "What's the computer about?" Seth shouted to be heard above the traffic.

The kid shouted back. "This is a laptop."

"Oh...right. So, what's it for?"

"I'm testing a program I wrote." They were close enough that the kid no longer needed to shout.

Seth relaxed. "I was just looking...at the water."

"The view is nice," the kid agreed but gave Seth a sidelong glance.

Seth quickly looked away. "Why'd they put these stupid things up?" He referred to the barriers. "Ruins the view."

The kid raised his eyebrows and continued working. He alternately typed and swiveled the laptop camera through the bars as far over the side of the bridge as he could reach, panning it back and forth.

"Aren't you worried you'll drop your computer?" Seth asked.

"Nope."

"It's a long way down."

"Yep."

"You taking video with that thing?"

"Yep."

Seth gave an exasperated sigh. "You got me. I don't want to be rude, but what are you doing?"

"This *laptop* has a program I wrote for school. It's a duck finder. I want to see how far away I can be and still have it recognize a duck."

"Why would you want to do that—recognize ducks down there?"

"The duck is what I'm using to test the program," he said. "I picked something random that I might see. Once I get the program right, I can use it to find anything I tell it to scan for. Like glasses or phones...or *anything else* that happens to go over the side."

Seth got the kid's drift.

People.

The kid could use his program to help search for jumpers.

"What good is it, now that this is here?" Seth grabbed one of the metal fence poles of the suicide barrier.

The kid shrugged. "People find a way."

Seth snorted.

The computer geek was originally from Ohio but currently lived in Seattle, interning for the summer. They had a conversation about backpacking and cycling, and the kid never brought up Seth's prosthesis. Seth wasn't sure he even noticed it until Seth asked whether the kid had been to the Golden Gate Bridge.

At that, the kid scanned Seth up and down, looking for tells, maybe.

"No, but I read that they're putting in nets there, too," he said.

"But they haven't, not yet?" Seth tried to keep the hope out of his voice.

"Want to see something?"

Seth wasn't sure he did want to see something, except for the water, smashing through his face at high speed. "Sure," he said.

The kid pulled up a picture of Earth from outer space. Then he pulled up a picture of the bridge, of people just like them on the Aurora Bridge. Then he pulled up a picture he had taken of the shoreline, more than a hundred feet below where they stood.

Ducks.

There were ducks in the water, invisible from this height. They spun and bobbed and used their beaks to draw water for their backs, working it into their feathers. Light hit the beads of water on their sleek backs, bedazzling them.

This gave Seth pause, how the kid's computer program could pick up something feathery in the water below, too far for his naked eye to see but there, nonetheless. What Seth had in his imagination was a faraway, indistinguishable, and long lost, never-to-be-seen body, smoothed by distance, the way the earth looked when you viewed it from an airplane. Or from outer space. The farther away you got, the prettier the world became. This kid's program brought the far, near. It would bring the details of his broken body close, were he to jump.

"There's always tomorrow," the kid blurted. "The bridge isn't going anywhere."

It was Seth's turn to give him the side eye.

"Most people who try it live," the kid continued. "When a body hits the water from a hundred sixty-seven feet—that's the distance from the middle of the bridge—it's like what happens when a body hits concrete. You have widespread, multi-organ trauma, a compressed spine, bone fractures..." The kid described, in scientific minutia, the possibilities for the human body when subjected to distance and gravity.

"Okay, Bruh. I get it." Seth held up his hand, "Enough."

"Sometimes your eyeballs pop right out of your head," he added.

"Bullshit."

"Yeah, I'm joking," he gave a faltering smile. "Only about that. The rest is true."

Seth laughed. Instantly, he felt guilty for forgetting Monroe enough to laugh. Dead in a freezer beneath a carpet of algae, Monroe would never laugh again. How could he be so selfish to up and kill himself without telling anyone what had happened to her? She had family and loved ones who deserved closure. How could Seth leave her in a freezer in Kentucky?

Seth must have mumbled some bit of the chaos in his mind because the kid said, "Kentucky has some great vistas—better views than this." As in: *Don't do it.*

"You're right, I should go back. Thanks...and good luck with the duck finding." Seth called out over his shoulder as he hustled back across the bridge to where he had left his wallet and a hasty Last Will and Testament, a scribbled note directing whoever found him to give all his settlement money to a no-kill animal shelter. He crumpled it up and put it in his pocket. He had all the time in the world to kill himself.

First, Monroe.

Seth looked back across the bridge to wave goodbye, but the kid was gone.

Chapter 29

The flight from Seattle back to Kentucky included a layover. At a bar in Atlanta's Concourse D, Seth settled in to get hammered. The bartender was acting flirty. She charged Seth for single pours but poured him doubles of Buffalo Trace (bless her). Bartending helped her pay for college tuition. "Criminal justice," she said. "I love a good mystery."

Said with emphasis and a coy eyebrow arch.

Once he had oiled with three generous drinks, Seth shared a convoluted and increasingly slurred description of his journey up to that point. He felt himself choke up as he asked whether he should show up unannounced at a Kentucky police station and invite them to follow him to a swamp where a body was decomposing in a chest freezer? Or should he call ahead? What would she do?

She suggested he call the police straightaway. "Or...I can call for you?" She grimaced as she pulled out her cell phone. She'd been hanging on his every word until the part about Monroe and the freezer.

Seth blurted, "It wasn't me who put her in there."

The bartender backed away, stood on the other side of the bar, and glowered at him.

Two airport police officers arrived, and each one took an arm, guiding Seth into a private room near the TSA lines. They questioned him as to the story he told the bartender, who, they said, he had "shaken up."

"I'm litterly on m' way t' the p'lice," Seth slurred.

"You're with the police."

"The Kentucky p'lice," he countered.

As he surrendered details about Monroe, one officer asked why he hadn't reported the murder right away to the Kentucky police. "And why did you leave the scene?"

"Well, that's a long story," Seth hiccupped.

Like they had any right to Seth's plan to end his life or his change of mind. Other than public drunkenness, they didn't have any reason to hold Seth overnight, but they were going to call the Lexington Police Department and let them know to expect a visit from Seth. What was his flight number? They pushed coffee into him mercilessly and did one of those eyeball checks where they passed a finger back and forth in front of him before they allowed him to return to the concourse for his flight. They watched when he used the restroom, and they watched him board the plane.

The flight attendants denied having any booze for sale, even though other people had drinks. When Seth pointed to the lovely single serving of Bacardi on the tray in the row in front of his, the attendant stonily said they had run out. Of everything.

In Kentucky, two police officers greeted Seth as he stepped off the plane. They gave him a "free" lift to the police station where a detective took his statement and asked a ton of questions. Sober, it was easier to answer.

But even sober, he had trouble convincing the detective and his officers to believe a chest freezer filled with a dead woman was submerged in a swampy area in the Daniel Boone National Forest.

"Atlanta airport police contacted us after your stunt at the bar. We had the park rangers check it out. They said the area was clear."

"They searched the entire national forest?"

The detective waved a dismissive, frustrated hand. "And you didn't do it?"

"Do you think I'd be here telling you about it, if I did?" Seth retorted.

"Why didn't you come forward when it happened?"

"What does it matter? I'm coming forward now."

"There still might be tracks from three days ago," one officer chimed in.

They decided Seth should guide them to the spot. He had a feeling they'd want him to do that. He shuddered.

Things unraveled fast once he showed them the tire tracks and the footsteps. A park ranger arrived at the site with a set of rubber waders. After about ten steps into the pond, he stumbled into the grill of Ivy's truck. It took less than one hour for another park ranger, a forensic scuba diver, to join them. She confirmed a freezer was submerged, and it had holes drilled into the sides. Something was inside. Hard to see in the muck.

The medical examiner's team pulled a stretcher from their van. A tow truck's back-up alarm beeped as it pulled into position.

The diver chained the freezer and handed the chain off to a police officer who attached it to the hydraulic wheel lift of the tow truck. Gears whined, and the freezer broke the surface, spilling water out the drilled holes like a grotesque, spinning fountain. Seth turned away and leaned against a tree to catch his breath.

More cops and firemen came. And the coroner. A stretcher waited beside the murky pond.

Two firemen set about removing the lock with vice grips and a rotary saw.

Time for Seth to walk away.

Two patrolmen followed. Someone admonished, "Hey, don't let him go too far."

Seth found a patch of grass firm enough to drop onto his back and throw his arms over his face. He had not thought this part through. Even from twenty feet away with a dense hedge between him and the pond, Seth could smell rotting flesh. They had opened the freezer, then.

Seth wiped away the tears that blurred his view of the clouds. At least Monroe would have a burial, and whoever loved her (and who could not love her?) would have closure. The right thing to do was often the hard thing to do.

A shadow blotted out the sun, and Seth found himself looking at a frowning detective.

"I know this is hard, Mr. Olivern, but I need to clarify something with you, okay?"

"Okay..." Seth said.

"You're not on any mind-altering substances right now?"

"Unfortunately, no."

"You gave this description of the female to the officers, right?" He held out his phone, showing Seth a picture of the detective's note, his hand-written description of Monroe, as described by Seth.

"That's right," Seth sniffled.

"Would you mind coming with me, please," he said. It was a directive, not a request.

"NO! ...I mean, yes. I mind."

"Mr. Olivern, you need to come with me."

Worms thrashed in Seth's guts as the man led him to the overturned freezer. Two more medics stood at each end of a stretcher with an empty black bag. Another detective took photographs of the inside of the freezer. One motioned with his hand for Seth to come closer. The reek was overpowering. How could they stand it? Seth's legs would not move.

He cupped his hand over his mouth. He shook his head and planted himself. They could not make him look at Monroe like this. He had an image of her sitting in the sunlight at Miles's place, a cat in her lap, holding her braid as a toy, hair wisps framing her face. The smallness of her hands, the—

Seth was grabbed on either side and hefted against his will. He shut his eyes against the sight, could not believe this was happening. How could the computer kid be so wrong? Coming here helped nothing. Seeing Monroe like this would bring nightmares beyond belief.

There's always tomorrow. The kid's words came back to him. Tomorrow, he could die.

Fine.

Whatever horror God wanted him to see, he would not turn away.

He opened his eyes.

Chapter 30

The woman lying in the fetal position inside the freezer had curly red hair pulled into a braid at the top and buzzed everywhere else. She was muscular and freckled. Her front teeth were gold caps. Scars corrupted most of her exposed skin, intentional shapes cut deep enough to warp and bubble. She wore black lace-up military boots, holey jeans, and a leather jacket with no sleeves. Zip ties secured her arms behind her back. Huge, thick fingers ended in unpainted, bitten nails.

Not Monroe.

NOT

MONROE.

And bingo. Seth found himself looking at the sky. He must have fallen over. The detective leaned into his face and wore a puckered expression.

Seth didn't care.

Monroe had not been the one calling for help, banging on the freezer. Monroe might be somewhere safe right now, playing with a cat, smiling.

This woman before him—Seth didn't want her to be dead, but he thanked God she was not Monroe.

"Want to explain why you described the deceased as 5'2", a hundred ten pounds, long brown hair? Cause this ain't that, my friend."

Now what?

The truth. Seth heard a voice in his head. That of the Reading Man. Seth tried not to hear him. Tried to focus on an answer that would not involve—

The truth will set you free.

He took a deep breath, remembering a promise he had made if God would save Monroe. This wasn't what he had in mind.

"You know this lady?" the detective asked.

"No, sir. I've never seen her before."

The detective popped a stick of gum into his mouth and chewed it, glanced from Seth to the body and back several times. "Right. Doesn't look like your type, exactly. Need you to come back to the station, if you don't mind."

Like it mattered whether Seth minded. The detective made small talk that didn't feel small on the ride back to the station, but he allowed Seth to sit in the passenger seat.

"Should I get a lawyer?" Seth asked.

"I don't know. Did you do anything wrong? Do you have something to hide?"

Everyone has done something wrong. Everyone has something to hide.

"No," Seth said, "I don't."

At the station, Seth told all to a room full of spellbound detectives and beat cops. At the end of his tale, one of them asked, "This Monroe, do you know her full name?"

Seth shook his head. "Ann didn't know it, either. They worked together at the shelter, though."

"We'll need you to stick around town for a couple of days, and even after that, I'll need you to be available. Once we find out who our Jane Doe is, we may need to talk again. My guess is, she's a friend of your ex."

"How do you know?"

"The scars. I'm thinking she had an allergy to tattoos, but in prison you got to choose a gang, and you got to wear it. Hers is tattooed on her neck and hands, see? Likely those two knew each other. You said Ivy mentioned a sexual assault in prison. Did you look at the victim? Even dead, she looks like she could take on Joe Rogan in a fight."

"But Ivy had Monroe's cross necklace."

"She had a necklace with the name *Monroe* on it. I can get one, too—next day delivery from Amazon."

Fucking Ivy. He hit his head with the fleshy part of his hand.

Ivy enjoyed hurting Seth, whether with the truth or with lies—it didn't matter. And, he recalled, she had addressed the woman inside the freezer at one point, Seth was almost positive about that. He figured she was speaking to Monroe. Why? Because she said it was Monroe in there.

Ivy killed Woods, and Ivy got prison, and Ivy got molested almost to death (Hurrah—sorry, God). Then Ivy, not to be outdone, not *ever* to be outdone, hunted down her attacker and used her to get revenge on Seth. Killed two birds with one stone.

Ivy was still out there.

Fucking Ivy.

Chapter 31

IN KEEPING HIS PROMISE to the detective to "stay close," Seth spent a week at the Lake Cumberland Resort in Burnside, a town less than ten miles from the Daniel Boone National Forest. It had a lake and a pool but no bathtub in his room. Getting around on crutches was a pain in the ass, so Seth did little more than lounge by the pool and read. No amount of duct tape or Bondo was going to make his jury-rigged prosthesis comfortable enough for walking.

Ivy had destroyed three, count them, three, prostheses.

When the detective called, Seth was nursing a sparkling water and sucking on Andes Creme De Menthe chocolates. A pile of balled-up green wrappers grew in proportion to the amount disappearing from the box as Seth mindlessly popped them while re-reading *Watchers*. He had been cleared of all charges relating to the murder of Sandra Nance, the detective said. "Poor" Sandra had been an ex-inmate known to have "a relationship of some sort" with Ivy. That's what a fellow inmate confessed in an interview, no doubt leaving out the violent details of the "relationship" for the inmate's own safety.

"And Ivy?" Seth asked. "Have you found her?"

The detective scoffed. "She's wanted for questioning and is a person of interest. Breaking parole is reason enough to make an arrest, but we'd have to find her. Unfortunately, we didn't find any DNA at the scene, other than yours. I wouldn't hold my breath."

Seth had been holding his breath about Ivy for seventeen years. It was high time he stopped.

"You're free to leave," the detective shook Seth's hand.

Free.

To leave. To stay. To drink. To grieve. To make amends? To search for Monroe?

Free to *not* jump off a bridge. Good thing he met the computer kid.

Straight from the airport, Seth took an Uber to the Doe Pond Library. Everything was as he remembered, the fountain, the geese, the kayakers. There were the same sounds of splashing and screechy swimmers, and a lifeguard telling them to stay off the rope.

Seth felt—no other way to describe it—*called* to return to Huntsville.

It was a given that he would begin his quest at the library. Libraries were solid, stable places, unaffected by the passage of time. Seth wasn't surprised to see the familiar, kind face at the circulation desk. And the clerk remembered Seth.

"Been a long time," was his cheerful greeting.

"A year," Seth agreed. "I'm afraid I lost my library card."

"No worries..." And he set about getting Seth a new card.

While the clerk typed, Seth asked if he had seen the young man, Noldy, lately.

The librarian stopped typing, and thought for a second, trying to make a connection.

"The kid with the acorn bracelet?" Seth offered.

"Never met a Noldy," he shook his head. "And I've been here a while."

"How about Arnold?" Seth asked. "He said he went by 'Noldy,' though. He helped me out, and I want to thank him. Better late than never, right?" Seth described Noldy to the clerk, and the clerk's face scrunched up as he searched his memory.

"That sounds like Michael..."

Seth brightened.

The clerk did not. After a thoughtful pause, he said, "I'm sorry, but Michael passed away."

"When? How?"

"There was an accident." He typed, obviously searching the internet. "Sorry, I forget exactly. It's been a while..." He scanned something on his screen and his face saddened. "Yes, a tree fell in the woods back there." He pointed in a direction outside the library, as if Seth would understand. The clerk continued reading. "...Michael Arnold died tragically on July..."

Whew. Seth saw Noldy in August.

"...while climbing a tree, trying to retrieve his drone."

"His what?"

"His drone."

"Is there a picture?" Seth's skin crawled.

"Sure, but I can't spin the monitor, so I'll print the article for you."

While Seth waited for the print, he had a one-sided conversation inside his head with the Reading Man.

This is f-ed up, man. Don't tell me the kid wasn't real. Was Monroe a phantom, too? Miles? Am I crazy? No. I'm not crazy. I drink too much, is all.

The librarian handed over the copy of the news article, which Seth folded and didn't dare glance at, yet.

"Let me finish setting up your new card…"

Seth squeezed the folded paper to keep from walking out and to keep himself from looking at it. He thanked the clerk for his new card and raced back outside, sat with his folded paper on a bench, the same bench he had sat on forever ago when he had a fresh amputation and his plastic bins containing all his possessions. He recalled something the super had said when he dropped the bins off. *You can't camp forever, Seth.*

But he had camped for a year, and there were moments he wouldn't trade.

Seth gripped the folded paper hard enough to crinkle the page. He looked up at the blue sky with its cottony clouds—a nice, normal-day sky, but Seth knew this wasn't a normal day, not for him.

Knew.

He unfolded the paper.

There the kid was. Noldy. Smiling. Holding his drone. Wearing his acorn bracelet.

Tragic Accident Takes the Life of Local Youth

The article described fifteen-year-old Michael Arnold, who loved rockets and airplanes (and don't forget, marijuana) and, according to his father, had been excited to receive a drone for his fifteenth birthday. Michael went missing on July 30th and was found on August 11th by a jogger. He had climbed the tree to retrieve his drone. Strained by Michael's weight, the rotted limb broke off and fell, pinning him beneath the creek water.

Seth checked his texting history with the super, checked the day he had brought the bins full of Seth's possessions to the library.

July 30th.

The day that Noldy died and was pinned beneath a tree limb.

But the kid had visited him at the hospital. The super and Miles were in the room. Seth tried to recall: had anyone spoken to Noldy? Or answered a question from him? They hadn't laughed at Noldy's jokes. That, Seth remembered.

Noldy wasn't there, not for the others. Only for Seth.

Somewhere along his journey, Seth had decided that the Reading Man from his dreams was, in fact, God. He knew it would sound foolish to anyone if he tried to explain.

"Why the name, Noldy?" Seth asked aloud, but it was meant for the Reading Man.

Why not?

Had he heard that? Was that himself answering back? Or the Reading Man, in his mind.

"Noldy's so..." Seth began.

...short for Arnold, like the kid said.

"He smelled like pot."

And I made wine. What's it to you?

Seth's internal (possibly schizophrenic) conversation was interrupted by the buzz of his phone, a text from Liberty.

gabe kissed me!

There were more emojis than Seth could count. Hearts and smiles and prayers and exploding fireworks. How great that Liberty was happy. Seth smiled at the vision of Liberty and Gabe together.

omg

best day evr

And he smiled at her text coming right then, right when he wondered what the point of life was.

The point of life: Gabe kissed me. Best day ever.

A moment of joy, not to be forgotten or passed thoughtlessly over, but to be savored. Like a shaft of sunlight after a cloudy time. The point was to hold life loosely with a thank-you and a nod to mystery. Was Noldy a figment of Seth's imagination? Was his phone record somehow off—like a computer glitch?

No, Seth decided. Noldy was a gift sent when he needed it, in a package he could accept.

On the bench in front of the library, Seth determined to live differently. He would no longer search for Ivy around every corner. For seventeen years, Seth had run from his fear, until a switchback turned him around to meet it head on. *Almost*-killing Ivy was the only outcome that could bring justice for Woods. Killing her, while still an attractive idea (Seth was a work in progress, after all), would make him into the monster he believed *her* to be.

That memoir Seth had "accidentally" read months ago (there were no accidents)—came to mind: *Maybe You Should Talk to Someone*. Yes, Seth should talk to someone. To God. Start there. Seth would bring his fear and guilt and indecision to the great Counselor. And it wouldn't hurt to talk to a small-c counselor as well. Hit that shit from every angle.

Bingo.

Chapter 32

Although Seth could afford a nicer hotel, he stayed in the Eastbridge Inn for old times' sake, hoping to see Cheryl and thank her for suggesting he visit the Royal Gorge Bridge. Nothing about the lobby had changed. Seth noted the same sturdy, uncomfortable accent chairs, the same brass flower centerpiece, and the same abstract artwork that looked to be the fingerpaintings of a giant child.

Cheryl wasn't at the lobby desk.

"I'd like a room close to the pool, please." Seth leaned his crutches against the counter so he could hand his credit card over. "Is Cheryl working today?"

"Cheryl? She no longer works here." The twenty-something bouquet-of-a-girl took note of Seth's crutches. "Would you like extra pillows for your leg?"

"Nah. It's not an injury. I lost my foot in a work accident. Best thing that ever happened to me."

She pushed her lips out like a duck. "If you say so...here's your key card." And she explained all the amenities of the Eastbridge Inn that Seth already knew.

As Seth settled into his room, he considered marching over to Mr. Limb Fairy's office and demanding—no—asking politely if he could be seen before his scheduled appointment. He had called the office while awaiting his flight. The receptionist coldly (and, he was pretty sure, gleefully) informed him that the first available appointment was three weeks out.

Did he want Monroe to see him without a working, walking foot? Yes, he decided. He did. The prosthesis didn't make him whole. It was a tool. A damn fine tool that Seth really, really, really wanted, especially if he were to see Monroe. But he wanted to see Monroe more than he wanted to walk. He wanted to see her more than anything, really.

Patience, Seth.

The internet was useless. With only a first name, Seth could not find her. His last hope was that his appointment with the limb fairy would yield both a new foot and information on Monroe. If Miles was friends with the limb fairy, and Monroe had been friends with Miles, well...at the very least Seth hoped to learn her last name.

But the limb fairy had lost touch with Monroe.

"I saw her at the funeral," he said. "She took it hard, especially because of how he died."

"Trying to save the cats." Seth said.

"Yeah."

"So, you don't know where she is?"

"I don't."

When it became clear the search for Monroe was futile, Seth consoled himself that at least she lived somewhere. He prayed—yes, prayed—she was happy, wherever she was. What choice did he have but to turn his attention back to the pressing, sometimes blissfully mundane tasks of life? He found a therapist, a yoga studio, a coffee shop. He purchased two bikes, one for the singletrack and one for the road, although he did not buy panniers because his long-distance days were behind him.

He searched the homes for sale.

Bingo.

Seth cashed out his settlement to purchase property in a village thirty minutes from Huntsville. One tiny structure sat on a three-acre property of woods and grassy fields. The realtor explained the mother-in-law suite was all that remained after a tornado obliterated the main house and many of the trees in the forested lot. Worse, the father, mother, two kids, and the family dog were all crushed to death while sheltering in the family's basement. The mother-in-law had died months before. Her empty suite survived completely intact.

Mysterious, cosmic fuckery of this sort prompted Seth to offer the full asking price in cash.

While he waited for the title work to go through, he drove to Michigan to visit Liberty before she went to college. Would it be awkward seeing her in person? Seth felt more comfortable sharing his thoughts via texts. One look at her, and his worries evaporated. Liberty's friendly peck on his cheek set the tone, and the two unlikely friends picked up the thread of conversation easily. He took her to the Potter Park Zoo. They enjoyed ice cream and laughed at the rhino's endless fountain of urine.

Liberty wasn't one for small talk, so Seth wasn't surprised when she brought up Ivy.

"You patch things up?" she asked. All Liberty knew was that one of Seth's exes "gave Fatal Attraction vibes." She had to look the movie up, said it was cheesy.

Seth scoffed. "One doesn't patch things up with Ivy. But we did have a knock-down-drag-out fight—long overdue—and I don't think I'll be seeing any more of her."

"If she's so bad, why'd you like her in the first place?"

This time he winced. "I was a stupid kid."

Liberty looked thoughtful. "Girlfriend buffet."

"I don't get it."

"You thought you could take what you wanted and leave the rest."

"Not all kids are stupid," Seth admitted. After an amicable silence, he decided to share something that made him happy. "It's been twenty-seven days since I've had a drink."

"Your face looks better. Less puffy."

He grinned. "You don't have any filter, do you?"

"Nope."

As the day waned, Liberty suggested Seth grab a pizza and a movie with her and Gabe, but Seth still had three hours to drive to Traverse City, where he wanted to spend the night. Nice guy that Gabe was, he might not appreciate a third wheel.

Seth had decided to revisit his favorite things. Like Liberty. Like Sleeping Bear Dunes. He kissed Liberty on the cheek and caught the scent of her vanilla perfume. It reminded him of Monroe.

"Who's Monroe?" Liberty asked.

"What?"

"Your necklace." She pointed. Seth always wore the cross with her name on it as a reminder of where he had come from and of the people who had done him so very right and kind.

"A friend—"

Liberty began a happy bounce.

"Not like that." Seth stayed her. "An old friend I used to know."

"I'm glad we're friends," Liberty said as she wrapped her arms around him.

It was late September, but the locusts were still making their squeaky wing music when Seth closed on the house. No more living like prey. The evasive lifestyle Seth styled as an "adventure" had come to an end. Contrary to his assurance to Liberty, there was no guarantee Ivy wouldn't show up one day and throw open his door, as Dazey had.

He would face that day if it came.

If it came, Seth would be like Miles. Strong. Resolute. *This is my house*, he imagined himself telling Ivy. Or Dazey. Or anybody who meant to do him dirty. Could Ivy burn his house down, as she had done with Miles? Sure, she could. Anybody was free to do anything their free will could think of, but should Seth live in fear? No. Not anymore.

To get a comfortable prosthesis, it took a slew of appointments and re-fittings with the limb fairy because, as it turned out, Seth's first two prostheses were "miraculous" in their fit—Mr. Limb Fairy's word. Most amputees struggled to get a good-fitting prosthesis, one that didn't cause significant chafing and swelling. Some people ended up needing a second amputation above the knee because they didn't take care of the stump.

Or just because of dumb, bad luck. But not Seth, who had seriously mistreated his stump for a year while cycling across the country.

Luck was something Seth had stopped believing in.

No question about it. Seth had not taken care of his stump properly. And yet, here he was, no infection. No second amputation needed.

"You might thank God for that," the limb fairy suggested.

For the prosthesis, the doctor would not accept payment.

"I'll tell you what, Seth, if you want to donate what you would have paid for your prosthesis to a charity, that will suit me fine."

"If I pay you, you can turn around and donate it." Seth countered.

"This way you have the choice," he said. "My church is raising funds to help rebuild an orphanage damaged by flooding." The limb fairy showed pictures of the kids living in makeshift tents and old shipping containers. "If you want to help, that's up to you. A yes only matters if you have the option to say no."

Seth donated.

And volunteered, whenever the limb fairy invited him. Together, they delivered Meals-on-Wheels, donated blood, and rode a bicycle race for charity.

One Saturday while Seth and the limb fairy were shoulder to shoulder working in the community soup kitchen, the limb fairy—Mike—pulled Seth aside. "How are you, Seth?"

He asked that every time, but this time, the question felt weightier, more profound.

"I'm...okay?"

"Just okay? I think you're about to be better than okay, because my friend Bob—your old supervisor from Green Spirit—he adopted a cat."

"Okay..." A steaming dollop of macaroni and cheese dropped onto Seth's shoe from the serving spoon he absently held.

"Bob's wife wanted a particular breed none of the local shelters had, so he ended up getting it from a no-kill shelter in Slatersville."

"That's good. Rescuing is—"

"From *this* shelter." Mike pulled out his phone, showed the screen. "Here..."

Seth's jaw dropped open as Mike enlarged the screen to show the familiar woman holding two cats in front of a building, what was once a mechanic's shop and now painted with bold and bright colors.

"Those are Russian Blues she's holding," Mike said, like that was what they were talking about. "Did you know they're the friendliest—"

"Did you know where she was, all along?" Seth's heart hammered.

Mike, the limb-fairy-turned-friend, laughed. "No, Seth."

Seth bear-hugged him.

Epilogue

SETH STOOD ON THE bridge and gazed at the rocks and the serpentine river, far, far below. Wind whipped the strands of hair that had come loose from his ponytail over the five-mile hike along the east fork of the San Gabriel River. With his prosthesis, the trek was challenging, especially at the creek crossings and boulder-riddled sections. He had started out early, when the ashen sky began to purple in the east, and now a sliver of sun splashed gold upon the Sheep Mountain Wilderness. Seth's destination: The Bridge to Nowhere.

Fitting name.

Built in 1936 and never used, the bridge project had been abandoned because of flooding. Forgotten relics of the construction remained: blocks of concrete with steel rebars sticking out like needles in pincushions, concrete mixers half-digested by yucca trees, and a rusted cable used for carrying buckets. The bridge could have described Seth's life: unfinished. Going nowhere. Broken.

But someone had a vision of how a Bridge to Nowhere could be useful.

With no suicide barriers, no nets between him and the gulch far below, Seth stood on the bridge contemplating all that had transpired to bring him to this place. A running-man existence had been his strategy for seventeen long years. From his guilt over Woods, he ran, unconscious of the forces that spurred him on. Back then, he could not have articulated his motivation, but now he understood that running had been his way to avoid Ivy and his all-consuming desire to kill her back, for Woods. When he lost his foot (and—by extension—his self-determination), death by drink was an outcome he could control.

But then...Miles. And Monroe. And all the other people he had met on the road who treated Seth as a whole man even though he didn't see himself that way. It took Seth losing his foot for him to experience the kindness of strangers. And angels, or whatever Noldy was. How funny that Seth did his best running when he was down a foot. In those dark days, he had told himself he was having a grand adventure, but secretly he still searched for the perfect bridge to fling himself from. His plan: guzzle a load of bourbon (the absolute best) and sit on the ledge with a bottle. Set the empty on the ground beside the ledge, and bingo—people would think how sad that the drunk *accidentally* fell off the bridge to his death. (But—they'd tell each other—he didn't suffer. All that bourbon, the man laughed all the way down.)

Seth had wanted a bridge because he felt he owed that much to Woods. And he had wanted the bourbon because he wanted to have the last laugh. Take that, Ivy.

As Seth leaned over the brink searching himself for second thoughts, a bighorn bounded like a dancer over the rocks and continued down the ravine.

The bighorn was a sign.

Seth should follow.

Down to the river.

Over the narrows, Seth poised and composed himself, readied his body to fall one hundred twenty feet into the river gorge. One last gaze at the sky and a silently mouthed *thank you*. Thank you for this wonderful, tall, unused, and abandoned bridge.

Seth jumped.

Fell.

Flew.

Felt the jolt of his beating, banging, hammering heart and the burst of joy in his soul as gravity yanked him faster and faster and faster, and the ground rose to meet him, to kiss him.

A sound escaped his throat, half scream, half laugh.

The silver cross necklace with M-O-N-R-O-E etched into it tickled his ear as the rush of wind yanked on it. Seth's hair came loose from the rubber band.

The bungee cord caught, and Seth swung in a great arch over the river where—the day before—he had splashed and cavorted with Monroe.

Yesterday, he held Monroe's hand aloft as rushing water whisked them down a mossy rock as fast as any sliding board. There was no picture of that moment, except in Seth's mind. The picture he sent to Liberty was the one Monroe took of him leaning off the Bridge to Nowhere, about to experience his first bungee jump.

kissed monroe, he texted. **best day evr**

Liberty replied with smiley faces, hearts, and a thumbs up.

The point of life? Seth didn't have all the answers. He still couldn't fathom why a whole family had died tragically on the land he purchased, why the mother-in-law suite he lived in had survived intact. He utterly rejected the idea that tragedy was punishment. Just take Woods, for instance. Take Miles. Bad things happened to good people. And good things happened to men like Seth. He settled on the idea that he had two options: one, live in cynicism and fear that he, too, would be surreptitiously yanked from this life by fire, flood, or Ivy. Or two, trust he would leave this life when it was his time and until then enjoy the fuck out of it.

For Seth, Ivy had become a slight noise in the background of his life, more of a ticking clock than a ticking bomb.

Becoming quieter by the day.

Seth could never be positive with the likes of Ivy, but he sensed in his gut—no, in his spirit—that she was finished with him. She had done what she came to do, killed who she wished to kill. Seth wasn't on that list. So long as Seth didn't put himself on her radar, he didn't think he would ever see her again. They had traded lives: Seth settled down, and Ivy set off.

Over tearful conversations, Seth and Monroe were able to figure out how Ivy had managed to fool Seth into thinking it was Monroe in the freezer.

On the morning of the fire, Monroe had come to take care of the cats, as usual. A fireman broke the news that Miles had been found with Charcoal, dead in his arms. Other firemen helped her gather the cats and provided carriers and transportation. It was up to Monroe to make sure they were taken to no-kill shelters, rather than the county facility. So preoccupied with grief and the overwhelming job of finding homes for the cats, Monroe almost didn't recognize the younger version of Dazey Wotterich.

"I like your necklace," was Ivy's insincere greeting.

Monroe was instantly wary. The two women had a short, tense conversation about Seth's whereabouts. Monroe didn't give any information because she didn't have any.

But a few minutes later when she tried to call a shelter, Monroe realized Ivy had stolen her phone. When they couldn't locate Ivy or the phone, the police advised Monroe to do a remote wipe. This protected her data but disrupted cell service. It didn't matter. The phone was the last thing on her mind.

After the funeral, Monroe packed her car and drove the four hours to her parents' home to grieve. She ended up staying. Huntsville had too many painful memories. When Seth showed up at the shelter, Monroe was *not* entirely happy to see him. In time, that changed.

It was Mike the limb fairy who designed a cuff for Seth's good leg and a secondary suspension around his waist. Seth had to sign a special indemnification contract, holding the bungee company harmless in the unlikely event his contraption malfunctioned.

Next to do the jump would be Monroe, who had come up with the idea for Seth to finally fly. Not to his death, but to fly and fly and fly every day. On to the next adventure. The jump was part of a getaway trip to celebrate the grand opening of the Miles-to-Go Animal Shelter, in honor of their friend. The pets would be trained and paired with volunteers who took them to local nursing homes and rehabilitation centers, hospitals, and homeless shelters to bring a smile where they could. Petting a purring cat or getting a sloppy dog kiss could be the difference between despair and hope. It wouldn't cure the evils of the whole world, but it made Seth's world brighter.

Ivy was still out there, somewhere. Nothing had changed. Everything had changed.

A Note From the Author

Is life—especially one of regrets—worth living, and is God worth following? These are the questions I try to answer through Seth.

Seth and I share a love of the outdoors, mountain biking, bourbon, and ice cream. My original idea for the story was: A man decides to commit suicide, but before he follows through, he has an epiphany: Why not do all the things he was too afraid to do when life had no expiration date? He'll be dead soon, so...

Messy, I know. But it makes dark sense.

For this horror-inclined author, it's not enough to have the monster be oneself. Enter: Ivy, the embodiment of Seth's regret. She is the past from which we run, the shadow we can't lose. *Switchback* became a book about facing fear and finding something (let's call it faith) to give life meaning. Seth doesn't impose religious doctrine on his ordeals and decisions; his lived experience prompts him to put his faith in God. *Switchback* began as a simple voyage & return plot and morphed into a bildungsroman story. I'm convinced we are all on a faith journey of some sort. We're all sweeping our gaze around this world, trying to decide where to place our trust, who to lean on, what convictions to lean into, what to do with our few and precious years.

May Seth's brazen and irreverent questions provoke and challenge you to figure out what you believe. Not everyone enjoys wrestling with this question. I ask your forgiveness if you were miffed at the side dish of philosophy with this fiction. I can't help myself (just ask anyone who knows me). Whatever your tastes, it's my hope that you enjoyed the story on its face and are inclined to ask: What if, instead of running and numbing, Seth had confronted Ivy? Maybe in prison? Or when she was released? What if he had talked with a trusted advisor or friend about his guilt over Woods at any time in his sixteen years of denial?

Switchback is precious to me for two reasons. One, I articulate my deeper faith convictions and struggles, something I have been hesitant to do in the past. Before I could write about it, I had my own bildungsroman to live out. I'm still at it and will be until the day I die.

And two, I have hidden some special people within the pages of this book. No, I'm not contradicting the copyright page. This is a work of fiction; however, some of Seth's lifesavers are based on my life-givers. You know who you are. xoxo

Acknowledgements

I'm grateful to author Neil Sater, who read the first, most raggedy and disheveled version of *Switchback* and offered thoughtful and detailed suggestions for readability, believability, and chronology. I'm certain his feedback gave the second tier beta readers a more enjoyable experience. The chapter where Monroe and Seth grow closer was added thanks to his suggestion.

The keen and astute eyes of authors Ann Heyward and Sean Seebach helped me produce a cleaner, more logical story. I am especially indebted to Sean for Liberty's age. She was originally younger, based on the crowd with whom I ran in my high school days. Between Sean's sound argument and his use of the word *cringe* to describe the friendship, as well as Neil bringing Mark Twain's comments to bear, I acquiesced. Here is what Twain said: "Truth is stranger than fiction, but it is because fiction is obliged to stick to possibilities; truth isn't."

Cindy Carlo is a sharply perceptive reader (and friend!) whose feedback gave me direction and elevated my spirit.

My husband helped me with some of the manufacturing lingo and is my most beloved beta reader. One of my favorite things in this world is that after he reads my work, we talk about the characters as if they're real. Many authors acknowledge self-determination in their characters, and I agree. Characters do what they want, often surprising me, their creator.

That is how the best twists and turns develop in a story: the author is just as surprised as the reader.

Also by KL Griffiths

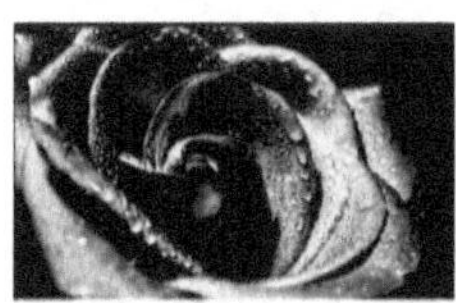

KL Griffiths lives in her imagination and works as a librarian in Northeast Ohio. She has published three off-recipe thrillers, *Spiked*, *Bookworm*, and *Switchback*, as well as award-winning horror and sci-fi short stories. Long before thriller was a genre, it was Kelly's modus operandi. Known to jump off cliffs and throw cartwheels in fancy places, her happiest moments are spent wandering the local trails with her husband, practicing yoga, and eating ice cream.

Join her conversation on everything deep, dark, and droll at klgriffiths.com.

www.ingramcontent.com/pod-product-compliance
Lightning Source LLC
Chambersburg PA
CBHW030426160726
47991CB00005B/1602